KAYLA BLAZE

A Tale of the New Southwest-or,
The Will to Resist

MARK GOODING

Copyright © 2024 by Mark Gooding.

All rights reserved. No part of this book may be reproduced, stored, or transmitted by any means—whether auditory, graphic, mechanical, or electronic—without written permission of both publisher and author, except in the case of brief excerpts used in critical articles and reviews. Unauthorized reproduction of any part of this work is illegal and is punishable by law.

This is a work of fiction, and any resemblances in the characters or settings in the story to persons, places, or institutions in the real world is entirely coincidental.

ISBN: 979-8-89419-013-6 (sc)
ISBN: 979-8-89419-014-3 (hc)
ISBN: 979-8-89419-015-0 (e)

Because of the dynamic nature of the Internet, any web addresses or links contained in this book may have changed since publication and may no longer be valid. The views expressed in this work are solely those of the author and do not necessarily reflect the views of the publisher, and the publisher hereby disclaims any responsibility for them.

One Galleria Blvd., Suite 1900, Metairie, LA 70001
(504) 702-6708

"So that one class *par excellence* may appear as the class of liberation, another class must inversely be the manifest class of oppression."

—Karl Marx

"[I]n the view of Infinite Purity, we are sinners all alike."

—Nathaniel Hawthorne

"When the right of every citizen to participate in the government of society is acknowledged, every citizen must be presumed to possess the power of discriminating between the different opinions of his contemporaries, and of appreciating the different facts from which inferences may be drawn. The sovereignty of the people and the liberty of the press may therefore be looked upon as correlative institutions, just as the censorship of the press and universal suffrage are two things which are irreconcilably opposed, and which cannot long be retained among the institutions of the same people."

•••

"If ever the free institutions of America are destroyed, that event may be attributed to the unlimited authority of the majority, which may at some future time urge the minorities to desperation, and oblige them to have recourse to physical force. Anarchy will then be the result, but it will have been brought about by despotism."

—Alexis de Tocqueville

ONE

Primordial Slime—or, A Confederacy of Dung Beetles*

*Dung beetles are ugly little bugs that eat shit. As I understand it, they tend to prefer vegetarian shit to carnivore shit, which might indicate some kind of moral judgment on their part. Perhaps, like good moral humans who choose vegetarianism for moral reasons, the little bugs disdain eating the shit of other sentient creatures out of sincere moral regard for those creatures—or at least for those creatures' shit. However, it seems highly unlikely that moral regard has anything to do with the little bugs' dietary habits, no matter how much our wishful thinking prompts us to err on the side of fanciful interpretation. A case in point: It was once believed that dung beetles were cooperative little helpers who would come to each other's aid when one of them was in trouble. But this misimpression has since been corrected, and it is now known that they eagerly steal from their fellows when they are in trouble. They are, however, still dedicated little shit eaters. That observation of them remains as valid as it ever was.

She was barely eighteen when we met that Saturday night at a party at the home of Dr. and Mrs. Roland McDowell.

Dr. McDowell, Roland, Roly—to those of us who felt comfortable calling him that—was no medical doctor. He was chair of the English department at the burgeoning Southwestern community college where

I was a probationary faculty member for five years, a tenured faculty member for three. A trim, sun-leathered man in his late fifties, with steel gray eyes, fading fine blond hair, and a sanguine complexion burned redder by the desert sun, he looked more like an ex-boxer, which in fact he was (Gold Gloves, 1965) than a Renaissance scholar of negligible repute, which he also was (I once came across a reference to his *Christian Iconography in English Literature of the Renaissance: A New Critical Approach* in an undergraduate seminar on Dryden, Swift, and Pope). When I first hired on at the college, he had been department chair for five years, nearly two full terms, and was angling for re-election in the coming spring. He would win that bid for re-election by a decisive margin (though technically we were not privy to the margin of victory in department elections, we had ways of finding out). I naively believed that he was a popular chair, well liked by all my new colleagues, and a shoo-in for re-election yet again the next time he ran. Even after witnessing the savage politics in a university English department as a graduate student, I somehow thought that a community college would be different, a more benign and cooperative environment. I was wrong.

Nobody seems to know who should get credit for the observation that the fighting in academia is so vicious because the stakes are so low, but whoever it was clearly had either extensive firsthand exposure or intimate knowledge as an outsider because, in my experience, no truism holds truer. If you believe in the Darwinian explanation for the behavior of organisms, human and other, as I do, then a college or university—pick one—will make you an excellent petri dish for conducting long-term research. There you will find wonderful examples of the struggle for survival and self-promotion, up to and including professional "murder" when required. The phrase "survival of the fittest," not coined by Darwin himself, is poorly understood and frequently criticized for connoting an inaccurate portrayal of the Darwinian environment—it implies that the most physically fit will always triumph over those less physically fit, and that perception, according to Darwin's apologists, not to mention Darwin himself, simply isn't true. And yet with slight adaptation, semantic adaptation, the phrase perfectly describes the struggle for dominance I have discovered in every human ecosystem I have ever observed. It should be revised to "survival of the most adaptable," or perhaps "survival of the best self-promoter," since it is not necessarily the most physically fit but the most adept manipulators who thrive in any organic environment. But it should absolutely retain the sense that selfish interests dictate human behavior.

The so-called "neo-Darwinians" I've read and read about, most of them good, wholesome "liberals" who worry about the moral implications of a theory of life that trumpets self-interest as its central premise, stumble all over themselves to assure us that "altruism" not only survives but thrives in Darwinism—hoping, I suppose, that permitting altruism to survive will make the theory more palatable to other good liberals among us, and perhaps stave off the aspiring eugenicists (historically good, wholesome liberals themselves) at the same time. But if they're honest (and they are not always honest), they must admit that the Darwinian version of "altruism" amounts to nothing more than one hand washing the other. In other words, I'll serve your interests now if I can reasonably assume that you'll serve my interests later, when I need your help, or if, by serving your interests, I can satisfy my own urge for power and control or assuage my own sense of guilt.

This selfish view of "selflessness" matches up perfectly with my own experience of the world, but it often grates on the delicate genteel moral sensibilities of the educated class, particularly the academics themselves. They'd like to think more highly of themselves. They'd like to think they're above the routine rutting and cloying and back-scratching and finagling and eye-gouging and hair-pulling of human interaction that keeps the human world going round. They are not. In fact, as the widely known and oft-repeated barb I referred to in the previous paragraph suggests, they may well be among its most rabid exemplars. What I'm not sure of is whether it's the low stakes of the struggle or the self-righteousness of the participants in it that makes them so voracious and determined, so dead-certain that whatever cause they're fighting for is not only just but momentously consequential, in fact essential. I do know that just about the only place I've seen an equal sense of commitment is in the religious zealots of, well—pick a religion, any religion.

Nonetheless, I first naively believed that things would be different at the community college. Probably, I was guilty of some presumptuous thinking myself. I had no experience with community colleges prior to my being hired as an instructor at one, and I think I believed that because community colleges are devoted primarily to teaching rather than to "scholarship" and research, the "publish or perish" mentality in universities that drives the institutions to promote (or not promote) faculty members on the basis of their scholarly output and not on the basis of their teaching ability, the community college would somehow be a more "pristine" environment. In fact, that was why I sought it out, deliberately avoiding the corrupt roil and hubbub of the university because I believed there was something "nobler" about teaching at a community college. And I was not entirely wrong; let me make that clear. Many dedicated teachers peopled my department and others; many students would be the first to tell you that. It was even said of yours truly, and not without some justification I immodestly admit, that *I* was such a dedicated professional myself. I confess without pride (for dedication is not always an admirable trait) that there is some truth in the assessment.

But self-interest? Inflated egos and chauvinistic self-promotion? Manipulation, subtle and otherwise? Along with petty squabbling in the guise of serious, consequential dialogue, a grossly exaggerated sense of self-importance and of the importance of our place in the world, and an accompanying (and sometimes frightening) sense that our objective was not to educate but to mend our broken students, to repair the damage done to them by prolonged exposure to parents, misbegotten religious training, and popular culture—these hallmarks of the community-college environment were certainly as prevalent as committed teaching, and they certainly did nothing to mitigate or contradict the famous cynical observation about vicious infighting in the hallowed halls of higher education. I'm a cynic myself and would never pretend otherwise, but in academia, where the living is just so damn easy, I found it particularly difficult to see what all the fuss was about or why anybody would expend energy ranting and raving about it. I fairly quickly relegated myself to that group of self-elected outsiders who shut themselves up in their offices, attend as few meetings as possible, try to establish and maintain relationships only with students, and make themselves all but invisible to their colleagues. I once heard a fellow outsider, an instructor in the college's business department, say that when he retired, he wanted his colleagues and other fellow employees to say, "Who? I didn't even know somebody by that name worked here." I decided I wanted to enjoy that same anonymity myself.

In such an environment—which is to say, I suppose, in any human environment, to a greater or lesser extent—being the person in charge, whether you're elected or appointed, can never invite unanimous support or consensus. So even though I considered Roly McDowell a decent, well-meaning man and a good chair, I should not have been surprised that he had detractors, a few of them passionate detractors. I found Roly pleasant, if reserved, modest, a good listener, serious about his work but with an engaging sense of humor, a sophisticated and urbane man who came from a markedly unsophisticated, uncultured upbringing. He was no elitist—at least he was no elitist in *that* crowd, where elitism is so pervasive—and yet he gave the impression, without ever stating it openly, at least to me, that he saw it in some way as part of our mission to render pearls from swine. Something in his own background may have brought about this attitude in him, I thought. He came from Arkansas—I knew that, but I didn't know where—and I imagined backwoods, barefoot children and hog lots, a boy in suspenders who escaped the squalor of a hillbilly barnyard and cast himself in a new image, with a doctorate in literature, a number of articles and at least two books published, and a taste for foreign films and the literature of the ancient Western canon. I was guessing about the hillbilly barnyard part. But I saw the rest of it for myself, and I saw little in it to disparage.

Roly was a liberal in the old-time sense. He saw it as our mission to educate, not to advocate. He believed in the virtue of a "liberal education," believed in at as a responsibility of educators in a free society, and he believed that there was something sacred in our public-funded, public-approved enterprise of making discerning citizens of our students, of providing them with at least a modest education in the history and traditions that had prefigured their own place in history—as Christopher Lasch put it, "their knowledge about the cultural traditions they are supposed to inherit." Perhaps I would have shared his enthusiasm for the profession, held it in the same high regard that Roly did—if, in fact, a liberal education were what students in today's colleges and universities were receiving. For the most part, it's not.

Never did I see Roly try to foist his own worldview, including his view of education, on his colleagues. Not once did I observe him take the role of preacher, pedant, or proselytizer. As a matter of fact, he was downright gullible, if you ask me, when it came to respecting the views of his colleagues about what higher education should try to accomplish and how it should go about accomplishing it. He seemed to feel that there was room in a liberal education even for very illiberal tenets of thought. Perhaps he had decided that what *he* would promote was a liberal education. What the rest of us promoted was up to us. We could, if we chose, entirely ignore Western thought, or even devote ourselves to bashing it to pieces, pretending (as some of us liked to do) that it was responsible for all the world's evils—an extremely shortsighted, parochial view of the world, especially for people who are supposed to be "educated" themselves, and who purport to educate others, but a remarkably common view among American academics at the close of the twentieth century. Roly didn't seem to care about that. We could take as broad a view of the world as we chose to take, or as narrow a view. It was "our" department, he repeatedly reminded us, and he would respect our intellectual freedom. I don't even know that he ever challenged anybody privately, out of our colleagues' sight and hearing. He certainly never challenged me, though I guess that as a fellow believer in liberal education, I never gave him anything to challenge. But I never heard even a whisper that he was challenging anybody else either—and academics, when their own pedagogy or ideology is challenged, are prone to scream bloody murder (they may not scream it to the challenger's face, but they will certainly scream it behind his or her back). So either Roly was ignorant of what was going on around him, in his own discipline and others—and knowing him as I did, I find that very hard to believe—or he was simply manipulating the system, using "academic freedom," his colleagues' academic freedom, as a handy excuse to refrain from challenging them about their doctrinaire pedagogies and thereby refrain from antagonizing them. A department chair election *is*, after all, in great measure a popularity contest.

Moreover, from what I could tell, Roly treated his colleagues in the department equitably and with collegial respect beyond respect for their ideas (however flaky either they or their ideas might be). He made every reasonable attempt to accommodate an instructor's request for a particular teaching load, schedule, or classroom. He stood firmly behind us in disputes with students, never openly siding with a student against one of us and only standing up for the student privately if he felt the instructor's professional ethics were in question. He represented us well in the world outside our department—by which I mean he represented us well to the administration and other departments. That's no easy feat. To return to our Darwinian metaphor: If you imagine an academic department as a nice little ecosystem, then maybe you can think of the college or university of which it is a part as an ecozone, a biogeographic region in which various ecosystems both share and compete for resources. Everybody's feeding at the same trough, and there's only so much food to go around. Part of what department chairs do is "get" for their own departments, and part of what they do is "get along" with other departments. Roly had a reputation at the school for both "getting" and "getting along" with admirable facility. He was able to get things—money, for example—for our department, sometimes at the expense of other departments, and still maintain a reasonably amiable relationship with those departments. His diplomatic skill went unappreciated by many of our colleagues in the English department, who only concerned themselves with life in our own little pond. But it was noticed and appreciated not only by other faculty members and department chairs but by administrators who profited from diplomacy and tact in the faculty leadership.

And finally, Roly had a good relationship with the office staff who worked under him. This I got on authority from an authoritative source, but we'll get to her later. For now, suffice it to say that Roly McDowell treated the "help" with respect, and that's more than you can say for some other department chairs and for some faculty members, who seemed to consider themselves and their glorious mission a little too important to regard the non-academic support staff as equals. This may not say much, if anything, about Roly's abilities as a department chair, but it meant something to the staff, and frankly, it meant something to me as well.

So it seemed to me that Roly McDowell was more than just a capable department chair; it seemed to me he was a damn good one. He could count on my vote for re-election as long as he kept running—at least he could count on it as long as he didn't abruptly change his ways. But he had his enemies, and some of them were downright vehement in their contempt for him and his minimal power over us. Some were openly hostile, I discovered, while others kept their feelings to themselves—but all of them had in common the desire to see Roly McDowell ousted in the next election.

Some were natural enemies, like Linda Ham, who apparently hated Roly for a fairly straightforward biological reason, at least if her emails to the department were any indication. In prim, articulate, well-organized little diatribes to her colleagues in which she always maintained a courteous and professional tone, whatever passions may have been churning beneath the composed surface of her prose, she complained about the perpetuation of "the patriarchy" in our continual re-election of a "white male" to the chair position. Apparently, it didn't matter all that much to Linda *which* white male we elected. Any of us would have been guilty of the same crime. When Roly's staunchest supporter in the department, and his personal friend, Gillian Greenback, pointed out to Linda, also in an email on which the whole department was copied, that white males were significantly in the minority in our department, and that if Linda was worried about Roly or any other white guy getting elected to the chair position, all she had to do was rally all the non-white guys in the department against his election, Linda responded with a solicitous lecture on "the power of incumbency," citing several scholarly sources and lamenting that it was the selfsame power of incumbency that kept white males in power virtually throughout the Western world. Presumably, overcoming the dreaded power of incumbency would lead us fairly directly to a world in which people live in joyous and perpetual peace and prosperity.

Others among Roly's antagonists were enemies he'd created for himself. His most controversial decision as a department chair, at least within the department, was to propose the notorious "three/two rule," as it was termed. The three/two rule was Roly's proposed method of getting us tenured faculty members to teach more composition classes. The bread and butter of a community-college English department is the hugely unpopular but almost universally required courses in composition—non-fiction prose writing—that students must complete as part of their general-studies requirement. Most students hate taking the classes—they fall into the same category of detested but inescapable coursework as, say, college algebra—and many instructors hate teaching them. The instructors, having matriculated as English majors, generally love literature and film, and they love having students who also love literature and film, and so discussing basic writing with students who do not want to be in the classes in the first place is not their idea of a fulfilling assignment. In the elementary and secondary schools, the way around an unappealing teaching assignment is to work your way into administration as quickly as possible. In a community-college English department, one way around it is to build a little seniority and latch on to some other course—in the humanities, perhaps—that might be a general-studies elective (so that students are still likely to enroll in it) but that will permit you the luxury of discussing something you personally enjoy. In our English department, as in other community-college English departments, a small klatch of instructors was particularly adept at cornering and hoarding the choicest of the so-called "plum" classes, and word around the department had it that at least one of my colleagues was teaching not a single composition class as part of his five-class-per-semester load, having garnered a general-studies course, Introduction to Film Studies, that was particularly popular as an elective, attracting enough students every semester to fill five sections of the course. My colleague, in other words, had established a nice niche for himself showing and discussing films all semester. As a result of the tenured faculty members' avoiding the teaching of composition, the scads of composition sections, readily filling every semester simply because the hated classes were required for all degrees, had to be relegated in large numbers to our "visiting faculty," the polite designation for part-time faculty members, often referred to as "freeway fliers" because many of them have to teach at multiple colleges to eke out a living and are therefore in virtually perpetual motion, traveling from one institution to another between classes, often spending an uncomfortable amount of time in transit besides putting the requisite hours into prepping classes and grading papers. Freeway fliers are of course desperate for full-time work, most of them, and so if they have any sense they'll be content to take the dregs that are offered them, hoping that their willingness to subsist on whatever crumbs might fall their way will be remembered, fondly remembered, when hiring time comes around again. Often the strategy pays off. More often it does not. Competition for scarce goods, including scarce teaching positions, is the nature of our existence.

When Roly proposed the three/two rule at a department meeting, uproar ensued. It was worse, even, than I would have expected. The three/two rule was an unofficial mandate within the department, a "gentleperson's agreement" if you will, that all of us would teach at least three composition courses a semester and be limited to two plum courses. That way, as Roly explained it, the tenured faculty members, those who had the highest stake in the college and those who benefited most from their employment by the college, would also have a higher stake in transmitting our department's lifeblood. It was no secret to any of us, Roly quietly reminded us, that composition classes kept our department afloat. Without them, we'd need twenty percent of the full-time faculty who now had jobs, rather comfortable jobs, and we would certainly lose a sizable portion of our political leverage within the college at-large, not to mention a sizable portion of our ample department budget. Roly felt that in appreciation of the importance of the composition courses to our department, we should take more interest in them. It was not good form to have the people who spent the most time in the department, and who made the most money and received the best peripheral benefits, involved with the smallest percentage of our students. We could still teach the plum courses, but our first priority should be the detested composition courses. As unpopular as they were with students, we should commit ourselves to making them educationally fruitful, at the least. Not that our visiting faculty weren't good teachers, of course. But they were not full-time employees and didn't even have offices on the campus. Many times students couldn't even find them when they needed them, and the office staff was forced to say, "I can leave a message in her mailbox, but I don't know when she'll get it," or, "I don't know when he'll be back on campus. He has another class on Thursday, but we usually don't see him before then." It was only good professional judgment and good administrative policy to show our commitment to our academic discipline, our institution, and of course our students, by demonstrating our commitment to the courses that brought in ninety percent of our department's funds.

It seemed like a reasonable proposal to me, though I'll confess I would have been unaffected by it. I was already teaching four sections of composition a semester, and one section of American literature. Others in the department agreed that the three/two rule was a good idea. "We should remember that freshman composition is the bedrock of our department," one of them said. "It deserves an appropriate share of our attention."

A vociferous minority, though, responded as though Roly had just proposed the unprovoked invasion of a foreign country, an affront that the well-meaning liberals in our department would have seen as grossly inhumane and a human-rights violation of the highest order. One in particular, the poet James DeCrisco (whose fourth volume of poetry had just been nominated for an *LA Times* poetry award), decided that Roly had finally overstepped the bounds of his elected position (apparently he'd been inching in that direction for some time) and began barraging us all with witty and urbane attacks on our department chair, never explicitly demanding Roly's head on a platter but tacitly discouraging us from reelecting the tyrant who would so casually flout the will of his constituency. To his credit, I thought, Jim never used the phrase "the power of incumbency" in any of his attacks.

The three/two rule was hounded from our midst long before it could be enacted. Those of us who had expressed support for it, or at least indifference to it, were reminded by our colleagues who opposed the rule, several of whom were less witty, less sophisticated, and less tactful than Jim DeCrisco in communicating their disapproval, that we could teach all the composition classes we wanted; but that didn't mean *they* should have to teach them. Various reasons were of course advanced for maintaining the status quo, all of them amounting to excuses to disguise the fact that our colleagues didn't want to teach composition courses, and the fewer they could get away with teaching, the better. Seeing the vehemence of the response to his proposal, Roly withdrew it almost immediately and included an apology for having caused such furor. He hadn't realized, he said, that people felt so strongly about the issue. He was certainly willing to bend to the will of the department because, after all, it was the department that he represented. He was no autocrat in his own mind and did not wish to be perceived as an autocrat by his colleagues. It was our department, he reminded us yet again, and he was just there to serve our interests. But no amount of backpedaling could erase the memory of his crime. He had committed a critical error in judgment, and eventually that error would prove his undoing as department chair. The intradepartmental antagonism began soon after the department meeting at which he announced the proposed new rule, starting with the first of Jim DeCrisco's clever assaults and continuing with the messages from Linda Ham and others. It continued unabated through the next department chair election, in which Roly scraped out a one-vote victory (the closest margin of victory, by far, in his four election wins, I was told). And it lingered to haunt him through the rest of his term of office as our chair, a term of office that would end, finally, after twelve years.

For me, the debacle over the proposed three/two rule was just another version of the lesson I have learned many times in my life, learned again repeatedly in my years of employment by the college, have learned time and again in the years since I left the college, and do not expect to unlearn any time in the future: Human nature is what it is. If it changes at all, it does so imperceptibly and only at speeds that would make the glaciers look like jackrabbits. Moreover, one facet of human nature never seems to change: We're all in it for ourselves—always have been and probably always will be. Darwin recognized it, pronounced it unqualifiedly, and his disciples have been repeating it ever since, with various tremulous qualifications to make the truth more palatable to the dominant intellectual culture in a tender therapeutic age. Hell, even Karl Marx, purveyor of a grand illusion, besotted bourgeois pretender to the proletariat, perpetual parasite, and intellectual forbear of generations of twentieth-century "great thinkers" (he was all those things)—even Marx observed that history is nothing more than the story of individuals pursuing their own ends. His prescription for the ills of the world, the perceived sickness of the modern age, was a sort of bizarre reversion to our tribal roots, an economics of regression that would turn us all into have-nots. Misery loves company, I suppose. He was not even shy about providing a general description of the outright mystifying transformation of "consciousness" required to ensure universal fraternity. All we had to do was get the evil triumvirate of God, family, and private property out of the way, and the "State" could be reconstituted into that fantastical fairyland where nobody owned anything and everybody owned nothing (but the "State," of course, had it *all*). Marx figured, I reckon, that amid the rubble of collapsed capitalism we would all of us be more than happy with our collective primitivism now that we understood (thanks to him and his pal Engels) what we *really* wanted from our lives. Freud took a more realistic view of the human animal—at least he saw that animal as a (quasi)-autonomous being and not just some mindless, faceless, person-less drudge in the witless human herd—and he took Marx and his disciples to task for their superficiality, said they had misdiagnosed the disease and were using the wrong means to treat it. And in that, at least, Freud was amply vindicated by a century of bloodletting in the interest of making the world a "better place" for us little guys. Then he posited his own pallid illusion for the future, placing his own faith in a new modern god to cure a disease with deep systemic roots that Marx had failed to acknowledge. Reason, the good doctor meekly submitted, the power of the human mind to subdue the baser instincts and drives of human nature, might someday, in some distant future, have the capacity to quell most if not all of civilization's discontents.

To me it sounds like wishful thinking at best, at worst more fodder for the next revolutionary to liberate us all by setting us back on the road to serfdom. One thing our glorious visionaries have in common: They hold the squalid masses whence I proceeded, and to which I have returned, in low regard. Where would we, the ignorant horde, be without their grandiose visions to inspire and guide us? Where indeed.

True revolutions are born of desperation and fueled by inflammatory rhetoric and mass hysteria, and when the masses' ire is roused beyond civilization's capacity to contain it, the time has indeed arrived for Katie to bar the door. And let the bloodletting begin.

Personally, I accept the human beast for what it is and neither despise nor fear it. Let the utopians among us imagine a world of harmony and peace, of zestful cooperation and earnest and unbroken goodwill, all under their "expert" direction, of course. Let them imagine themselves the poets of Plato's republic, meditating on transcendence—theirs—while somebody else raises the crops and makes the meals and takes out the slop. Paradise is for those who can get somebody else to maintain it for them. Me, I can handle the truth. I frankly confess not to understand the hysteria provoked in the tender intellectual consciousness by the mere prospect of being poked and prodded—and sometimes dragged—along by the Invisible Hand. I do not accept the fearful proposition that the Hand has impelled us into infamy. Perhaps it has not even impelled us toward it. The process of evolution is noteworthy for its utter indifference in its single-minded devotion to a single end, self-perpetuation, and if where we are now is not better than where we were, it most certainly is not worse. Take a look around you and observe for yourself. You have that luxury.

In my worldview, I suppose pretty much any form of political organization is justifiable—so long as it admits the reality of human nature—the fascistic socialism of the world changers as much as the live and let live of a died-in-the-wool libertarian. But it's the libertarian who promises me the autonomy to make my own choices, to sink or swim for myself. And it's the world changers who presume to tell me what's "good" for me, and who, scarier yet, presume to *know* what's good for me. So I'll take my chances on the libertarian, especially given that the world changers don't have a very appealing track record to recommend them. So what if the slug sitting next to me in traffic has a decent measure of control over his own destiny, and some measure of influence on mine? So what if his outlook on the world is completely different from mine? So what if he has his own values, his own religion, his own interests to nurture and protect? I can live with the consequences. And I certainly prefer them to the alternatives. In my warped worst imaginings, I see a great messiah with a patronizing if benevolent smile and the face of Al Gore, outfitted in jackboots and waving a menacing bureaucracy just above my head, thanking me for the sacrifices I have made for the benefit of us all before climbing into his private jet to whisk off to the next destination and thank the next slug. It's always seemed ironic to me that those who urge self-control for the rest of us are so loath to practice it themselves. But probably it's not ironic at all. It's easier to rule others than it is to rule yourself.

I can handle the truth. And if it doesn't set me free, I'll be content so long as it doesn't imprison me either. The Invisible Hand hasn't swatted us into extinction yet, and there's no reason to believe it will any time soon—let the global warming alarmists rant as they see fit. And if it *should* swat us into extinction, we'll only be going the eventual way of all organisms—or most all organisms—anyway. I can handle the truth.

And as for Darwin, well, he might not be thrilled, but I guarantee you he wouldn't be surprised either.

TWO

There Were Ghosts in the Eyes of All the Boys You Sent Away

Actually, Kayla and I had known each other for some months before we even met, or at least before we *really* met. She was an Administrative Assistant III, a euphemism for the lowest-ranking secretary in our college system. The system is composed of ten discrete "sister" colleges, each one ostensibly autonomous, with its own administration, but also connected to the other colleges via a central administrative division much like the fifty states in their relationship to the federal government. And in much the same way that American citizens complain about the federal government, employees of the ten colleges complain about the central administrative division at the District Office. "What do those button-down types do over there?" you'd hear people wonder. "They don't have any students at the District Office. How do those people justify their salaries?" But they did justify their salaries somehow, and most of their salaries were significantly higher than that of Kayla Blaze, the Administrative Assistant III, lowest creature besides student workers and perhaps janitors on the college food chain. She didn't care. She had just turned eighteen when she took the job. She was fresh out of high school, though still living at home, and even if the job at the college may have looked to most of us like one small step for woman, to her it represented one giant leap toward personal freedom. She'd had part-time jobs when she was in high school, but this secretarial job was her first full-time job, her first foray into the world of adult autonomy and adult responsibility. Imbibing the heady air of the atmosphere in that adult world gave Kayla a rush that would see her through at least the next year of her life. Then she'd have to look for some new thrill to carry her forward. I don't know if she ever found it.

But I was to learn many other things about Kayla Blaze after we collided at Roly McDowell's party, the momentous event in my life that led me to become intimately, intimately acquainted with her. We had been introduced before that—Ellen, our department secretary, had taken Kayla around when she first started at the college and introduced her to everybody in the department—and we crossed paths almost daily, sometimes even brushing past one another in relatively close quarters. But though I'd had occasion to inhale Kayla's perfume, we had not spoken, not even exchanged banal pleasantries that I could remember, so it would be stretching the truth to imply that we had anything resembling an acquaintance, much less a genuine relationship. All I knew was that Kayla Blaze was very young and extraordinarily fetching. She was absolute, rock-bottom proof that sexual attraction begins in some neural or glandular pocket somewhere down in the inner core of our being and then ripples through our whole interior, zipping along nerves like an electric shock along a copper wire, causing tingling, vaguely unsettling reactions at every junction in its path from its point of inception to the level of consciousness on which it finally registers. I could not look at her without wanting her, and I decided finally that it was as much the way she carried herself as what she had to carry that stimulated hormonal activity even without overt provocation. Kayla was tall and thin, with green cat eyes and blond hair that seemed to topple down the sides of her face and spill onto her shoulders, sprawling into loose strands that, when I knew she wasn't looking at me (and she never seemed to be looking at me), used to latch on to my attention and hold it for seconds at a time as I studied the loose strands the way some nerdy scientist studies a virus under a microscope. She had the high cheekbones, narrow aristocratic nose, and fleshy, succulent lips of a fashion model, and the dour, vaguely aloof expression to complement those features. She had round, tight curves, tight in the way only a young woman's curves can be tight, at least without a lot of sweat and strain, and she often wore clothing that could in no way be considered vulgar or meretricious, at least not in my considered opinion, but that definitely showed her physical assets to their best advantage just the same. There was nothing consciously provocative in the way Kayla displayed or carried herself, I decided; the provocation was an unintentional but also unmistakable feature of her bearing. It was in the loose, languid way she had of moving as if she was never in a hurry to get anywhere—didn't know what it was like to be in a hurry—and as if she luxuriated in the simple fact of being in motion. Kayla enjoyed the journey; that had to be it. She couldn't know what it felt like to behold her in motion, the chain reaction of impulses she set off just by walking down a hallway. Or could she? One day I happened into the workroom while Kayla was arched over the copy machine, apparently having dropped something down behind it, and I thought I might have either a heart attack or an orgasm right on the spot. I fled the room before she even noticed me.

At first I didn't think she knew about or understood the tremors she caused. Her behavior was always archly professional, at least where the students and faculty were concerned. With Ellen and the other office staff she'd let down her hair. You'd hear them yukking it up about one thing or another—girl stuff. Ellen was married, but she wasn't much older than Kayla, and she hadn't yet forgotten what it was like to be a young woman. They socialized, too, away from work. I used to hear them talk about it. "We'll be there around eight," I'd hear Kayla say, apparently oblivious to my eavesdropping. And I would wonder who made up the rest of "we." Did Kayla have a boyfriend? If she did, she didn't talk about him. But she was so young; what business did I have thinking about her like that anyway? Besides, there was only one thing I would ever have wanted from her, and even that one thing wasn't worth a sexual-harassment charge. It wasn't even worth the humiliation of being brusquely, perhaps derisively turned away by such a delectable creature.

Having seen Kayla in action, I knew that she had already, even at such a young age, honed the feminine defense mechanism of rejecting advances to a stiletto-sharp skill. It seemed to me she must be so strikingly adept at delivering ego-deflating blows either because she was particularly practiced at it, owing to her looks (she'd already drawn a grown woman's share of attention from men—and perhaps women as well), because she took pleasure in it, or because of some combination of the two reasons. Already she had acquired the knack of dealing out disappointment according to a sort of hierarchy. With the young men close to her own age, students or fellow employees, who approached her shyly, hopefully, politely, but obviously without much confidence of success, she was reasonably tactful and discreet, at least for Kayla (in whom, I would discover, discretion was not a prominent trait). With the brash and the bold, the young men who used apparent fearlessness as their own defense mechanism, the better to appear indifferent about the outcome of their venture (Who cared if Kayla turned them down? There were plenty more where she came from.), or with those who simply seemed to enjoy the hunt itself as much as Kayla seemed to enjoy eluding the hunter, she was evasive, using sarcasm to avoid capture but not to the point of cruelty. With the old guys, though, the predatory types, a couple of fellow faculty members and a particular manager from the fiscal office (a very suave fellow whom Kayla knew to be married with two children), she was downright murderous, carving them up with the ceremonial relish of a serial killer, and with a pleasure that seemed equally perverse. I once saw her wither Keith Hudson with a single sentence, and Hudson was relatively young, not yet thirty, and had a reputation for sleeping with his former students! Debonair expert in Colonial British Literature that he was, he had reason to be confident in approaching Kayla Blaze, lowly secretary, barely out of high school. Shouldn't she have trembled in awe at his mere approach? Shouldn't she have been flattered into spreading her legs for him right there in the English department? And yet she sent him away with his tail between his legs, his ears ringing with an adroitly delivered rebuke from an eighteen-year-old. Didn't she even realize that Keith had a Ph.D.?

 I went to graduate school myself, you know, and I have heard all the feminist blather about male advances, the ghastly impropriety, the "fear" engendered in "victims" by predators (male or female) who have the unmitigated gall to express sexual desire for other people. I call it "blather" because in its extreme form it attempts to deny the undeniable: that the urge to copulate is merely part of our biological endowment as humans—and yes, as men—as natural as breathing. It is merely that and nothing more—neither a cultural fabrication nor a tool of oppression. Not once did I observe any male of any age exhibit anything resembling "stalking" behavior toward Kayla Blaze. None of her pursuers seemed on the verge of bopping her over the head with a club and dragging her back to his cave. A few offered up remarks that some eavesdroppers might have considered "inappropriate," but in these sensitive times "inappropriate" is a word whose definition can be hard to agree on. One thing observers of Kayla's would-be suitors *could* agree on is this: They saw, they came, and they were conquered. They skulked away from the skirmishes with their egos grievously wounded, having been beaten into submission by a girl who was just barely old enough to qualify as a "consenting adult." And I enjoyed watching. There was, I told myself, something gratifying, perhaps reassuring, in witnessing the dexterity with which Kayla evaded her predators. Something had to be inherently right and good about a world in which somebody who should have been so vulnerable turned out to be so inviolable.

But there was another thought that went through my head, not at the time but later. Once it occurred to me, it severely dampened my enthusiasm for Kayla's glib butchering of her pursuers. I could enjoy her triumphs all I wanted, but I could not enjoy them nearly as much once I reminded myself that I too wanted Kayla Blaze, wanted her as much as any fool of any age whose figurative slaughter I observed, and that the only reason I had not approached her myself was that I was afraid to approach her. I'd seen what happened to the others, and I did not want to join them in the long line of walking emasculated. At the time I told myself it was my own sense of propriety that kept me from approaching her. The age difference and all—it just wouldn't have been right. Later on, though, I would come to recognize the truth: I was afraid of Kayla's belittling prowess, and I did not want to be on the receiving end of it. I could pat myself on the back for being "above" chasing her like some leering beast. But the truth of the matter was that I was not above it at all. And that realization, once it hit me, robbed my piety of all its satisfaction.

THREE

An Affair to Remember

Dr. Roland McDowell was married, probably still is, to a firebrand named Rose, a short, noisy, fast-talking woman who was always completely sure of herself and sometimes unpleasant to be around. There were times when Rose's relentless self-assuredness irritated me, her dogged determination to get whatever it was she was after annoyed me. Nobody should be so chauvinistic, I'd say to myself, unless she plans to start a revolution and subjugate a people. But I was never an obstacle to Rose's success, never stood in the way of her getting what she was after, and therefore never locked horns with her. Besides, she seemed to like me, and most of the time I liked her as well. She was irascible, perhaps, but she was also entertaining.

If Roly saw it as his mission to spread education to the masses, and with education enlightenment, Rose also had a sense of mission, but hers was more palpable. She had met her husband when they were both graduate students in English, but while Roly had finished his doctorate and joined the professoriate, Rose had abandoned the academic life for something she saw as more practical. She joined a social-service agency, learned the business, made contacts, and eventually started an agency of her own with various missions: sheltering the homeless, feeding the poor, taking in battered women, teaching English to illegal immigrants, etc. Name a social problem—or, if you prefer, simply a social "condition"—and Rose probably had a hand in addressing it. She had started small when Roly was at a small liberal-arts college in the East, but when he took the job at our desert community college after being denied tenure at the Eastern college, Rose had of course moved with him, and with a larger population base to serve, her various enterprises had grown fast and were apparently still growing. With as many pies as she had her fingers in, it was impossible for her to focus all her energies on a single agency or condition, so as I understood it, she now spent most of her time campaigning for community support from our sprawling metropolis's shakers and movers. Rose was indeed "connected," perhaps even in the way that word connotes in our vernacular, and her extensive connections brought in millions annually to the multiple agencies she controlled. They also brought in a pretty nice chunk of change to Rose herself, from what I could tell, because she and Roly had a beautiful home partway up one of the low mountains that formed a broken chain around our valley metropolis, in a community that no English professor's salary could have hoped to access, at least not without substantial supplementary funds from some other source. Obviously, I was not privy to Rose and Roly's finances, but I had a rough idea what Roly was taking in as department chair, and while it wasn't bad, it would never have bought him the multi-million-dollar dwelling he and his wife called "home." Clearly, Rose's cottage industry was making money, and just as clearly she was profiting personally from it. Each of us can judge the morality of her profiteering for him- or herself. The reality is that she was indeed profiteering, however you want to judge it.

In any event, once a year since Roly had been chair, the McDowells threw a Saturday-night spring shindig at their splendid home, traditionally on the second weekend of spring break, and they invited our entire department, including the office help. The affair could not properly be called a department party, though, because others from the college were also invited, mainly other department chairs and a few administrators (the college president among them, of course—I have already said that Roly McDowell was politically savvy, and his wife was equally savvy, probably more so), as were some of Rose's prominent friends from the community. The turnout, hence, was large and eclectic, and while no explicit pressure was applied to be on our best behavior—both McDowells were far above such boorish injunctions—plenty of such pressure was implied, mostly by ourselves. No humble English instructor wants to be remembered as the asshole who danced naked in the department chair's courtyard fountain—at least I don't think any of us wanted that infamous distinction. Some of my colleagues probably even considered the occasion a networking opportunity, though I tended to think of it simply as a chance to dress up a bit, get out of the house, enjoy a few hours in relatively lavish surroundings, drink a little good booze, eat some good catered food, mingle enough to be seen by the right people (whoever the hell they were), and call it a night. Never did I attend Rose and Roly's "spring fling" expecting more than that, and never was I surprised.

Never, at least, until that night Kayla and I connected.

I showed up around eight o'clock, alone as always, having sipped a bourbon on ice at a bar along the way—a little something just to "take the edge off," as they say—and a crowd of a hundred-plus had already made its appearance at Rose and Roly's, a few of them mixing it up in the living room and kitchen, quite a few more of them gathered in the open courtyard that separated the main living and sleeping quarters of the house, where the food and booze tables were set up, and another sizable group out back, through the breezeway that led to the back yard and a large and pleasant open space. I could hear a jazz quartet playing back there, a composite, it turned out, of student-musicians—three of them—and music instructors from the college—one of him. Rose and Roly always contracted a musical group from the college for their entertainment, and the groups never disappointed. Every year I came away from the party with the renewed impression that remarkably talented people, both students and faculty members, strolled our campus day-in and day-out.

It had crossed my mind to wander out back and enjoy the music and the pleasant evening air for a while, but then I had a vision that dissuaded me. It was a vision of Gino Ciccio, Gailyn Suarez, Jim DeCrisco, and Rolf Holmgren, four of my colleagues, among a small crowd of people dead center in the back yard. There too was Roly McDowell, our host, and the whole group of them were engaged in animated conversation—almost certainly, I surmised, about the institution that employed us all. I wanted no part of that, and since

I reckoned I could not enter or navigate the back yard without being seen and assimilated by that crowd, I retreated to the courtyard where at least my appetites for food and booze could be satisfied.

And there, when I turned, was Kayla Blaze. She was standing alongside one of the long food tables eyeballing the evening's repast, and if I wasn't mistaken, she was whispering asides to a white-jacketed attendant at the table. They must have been funny asides because he was smiling back at her and muttering tight-lipped gems of his own.

Nothing about Kayla's appearance was inappropriate for the occasion. Her manner of dress, as well as her comportment, demonstrated two things about her: first, that she knew how to dress and behave for such a party; and second, that she was a stunningly beautiful young woman who would attract attention no matter where she appeared. She wore a longish (mid-calf) dark blue dress of some very supple material, probably silk, cut low in both the front and the back but not distastefully low. She wore very high heels that straightened her beautiful legs, stiffened her back, and raised and accentuated her splendidly round ass, especially beneath the flowing material of that dress. And she wore a shimmering but not ostentatious necklace and matching earrings, both of which were plainly visible because she had her long hair partly pinned back behind her head, so that only a sort of fringe hung down and didn't quite reach as far as her bare neck and shoulders. In a word, she looked positively regal, and in another word she looked exquisite. The problem with Kayla's dress that night was not the dress itself but what she had put in it—that being the physical person of the virtually edible Kayla Blaze. In a crowd of reasonably well-dressed people, some of them quite stylish, she stood out not because of the way she dressed but because Kayla Blaze, dressed that way, was simply spectacular.

Nor was I the only one in the crowd to notice. In fact, far from it. Glances were being sent her way from every corner of the courtyard, and one or two men were doing more than just glance. A few women may have been gaping as well—either because they were interested or because they were jealous.

Standing near the entrance to the breezeway, perhaps thirty feet from where Kayla still lounged alone beside the food table, I was sipping the wine that I had grabbed on my first pass through the courtyard when suddenly I felt a tug at my jacket sleeve. The tugger was Rose McDowell, elegantly dressed in some kind of fancy blouse and a pair of nice slacks but of course looking like flowered wallpaper alongside Kayla Blaze. "You know her, dontcha?"

"I beg your pardon?"

"Don't play dumb with me, Marty. You know who I'm talking about. I have eyes too, y'know."

"Kayla?" I said.

"That's the bombshell? The one-woman fashion show?"

"Dontchu talk to her almost every day?"

"She answers the phone sometimes. But I don't make a lotta small talk with the secretaries. Only Ellen."

"Well," I said, "her name is Kayla. Kayla Blaze."

"Hmm. Somehow that name seems to suit her."

I sipped my wine. It was unlike Rose McDowell to make small talk with me, especially about Kayla Blaze, when there were so many other, more important fish that could be fried that night.

"I have a favor to ask, Marty." I suppose much of Rose's life had been spent asking favors of one kind or another, and so she was not shy about asking them.

"I'm at your disposal."

"Good. Go over there and keep her company for a while."

"Kayla?"

She nodded, hesitant, it almost seemed, to say the name. "Just for a while," she said. "Until she's ... blended into the crowd ... a bit. If such a thing is possible. I don't know if it is."

"Geez, Rose."

"'Geez?' You want I should ask somebody a little older?"

"It's just not my style, Rose. I don't—"

"You don't like women? Beautiful young women? Astonishingly beautiful young women? Stop me when I hit on the right words, Marty."

"I don't like being somebody's 'distraction,'" I said, putting the word in quotes with my inflection. "Whatsamatter, she make you nervous?"

"As a matter of fact, she does."

"She looks like she's behaving herself just fine, Rose. I don't see the ne—"

"Humor me, Marty. Go over there and put your fabled charm to use. Everybody knows you have it. Roly tells me half the student body at the college is in love in with you."

"Which half is that?"

"Humor me, Marty. Be a pal. I'll owe you bigtime. Just go over there and make small talk with her until all these apes stop gawking at her. Then you can leave her to her own devices and go on your merry way."

I shook my head and showed her a slight smirk. But I also did as I had been asked to do. I wandered over to a spot just a few feet from Kayla Blaze's elbow and pretended to be surveying the sumptuous eats. Meanwhile, my heart was pounding inside my chest like an impending coronary.

When Kayla turned to look at me, things got worse. Formerly, I had just been nervous, but now I felt on the verge of collapse. For one thing, her eyes were outlined with some kind of makeup pencil, and the lashes darkened so that they appeared thicker than they really were (and they were thick enough already), so that when she looked at me—just looked at me, without any apparent emotion in her expression—her eyes seemed not merely to allure but to beckon. For another thing, her lips were made up with dark lipstick, so that they looked even fuller and more shapely than usual, and as I had wondered many times what it must be like to kiss those lips and imagined it must be heavenly, my wondering was only exacerbated at the sight of her close up, the lips so tantalizingly presented to make them stand out and thereby to torture the horny observer who could only ponder them, closer now than perhaps ever before but still distant, not touching. And for a third and perhaps most important thing, I had been sent to Kayla on a devious mission, to confront her for the very first time in our brief acquaintance for a disreputable purpose, to beguile and dissemble, to occupy her so that other gapers might be distracted. It was dishonest, what I was doing—dishonest and distasteful—but I had felt myself nonetheless capable of doing it until the very moment she turned on me and confronted me with those incredible looks of hers. As soon as she did that, I began to worry that instead of charming I might come across to her as palsied and pathetic, a feeble old man (to her anyway), perhaps incapable even of sipping my wine without shaking it out of my glass. I wondered if I could even make my voice sound natural, relaxed and casual, matter of fact, or if instead it would quiver and break like some pubescent boy's.

Before I could find out, Kayla spoke to me: "She sent you over here, didn't she?"

"I beg your pardon?" It was lucky, in a way, that she had confronted me because it made me forget my nervousness.

"You know who I mean. Rosie. Rosie the Riveter. I saw you two talking over there. I know who she is. Ronald McDonald has her picture in his office. She calls him a million times a day. They're lovebirds, those two are."

"You mean Dr. McDowell?"

"Yeah. Dr. McDowell. He's all in love with Mrs. Dr. McDowell. They're lovebirds."

"Well, they've been married a long time," I started to say, but she wasn't listening, and before I finished the sentence she cut me off. "Can you get me a drink?" she said. "I can't get a drink here. That guy over there asks for your ID. I guess there are students around. I got a fake ID but I don't wanna use it here. Too creepy. Maybe if you get me a drink it'll be awright. They won't care. Ellen wouldn't care anyway, but if Ronald McDonald sees me I might get in trouble. I don't wanna lose my job over a drink."

"Well, I don't think you'd lose your—"

"What did she say to you anyway? Did she tell you to come over here and be nice to me?"

"Do you want that drink?" I had started the conversation afraid I might lose control of my bladder, but Kayla's adolescent chirping had a settling effect on me. It reminded me that I was not talking to a goddess; I was talking to a goddamn teenager. "I'll get you a drink if you want it. Just promise me not to be too obvious about it."

"A glass o' that wine would be fine. That white wine. I don't drink wine, usually, I drink beer, or sometimes I drink the hard stuff. But that wine looks kinda good. I'd like to try it anyway."

I sauntered down to the booze table, where the white-jacketed server doubled as bartender and doorman (there was another bar out back by the pool), and though it had to be painfully obvious that I was procuring the wine for the beautiful young woman—the beautiful girl—not ten feet away, he obliged my request for a glass of wine with polite alacrity. I thanked him, turned to the girl just a few feet behind me, and handed her the glass. "It's a pinot grigiot," I said. "What else? I hope you like it."

She smiled faintly first, like a little kid being entrusted with a great responsibility and appreciating the enormity of it, and then she sniffed the rim of the glass as if for poison or other contaminants. "It smells awright," she said, still apparently fascinated that she was being permitted this adult treat right in front of a whole host of people she worked with. It was the very first time in the months I'd known Kayla—if you could say I "knew" her at all—that it had even occurred to me how she must look at all of us: as a bunch of stuffy "grownups," and "teachers" no less. She thought she'd gotten her fill of teachers in high school, and here she was surrounded by them in the workplace. Until that moment it had not dawned on me how she must look at us all.

"It could stand to be a little drier," I said. "But who's complaining about an open bar? I can only imagine what these folks' bar bill is going to be tonight. Not to mention the catering bill for the food."

"They can afford it," she said. She said it matter-of-factly, with an air of authority. "They make plenty."

"I'm sure they do."

She sipped the wine gingerly, still with that expression on her face as though she were indulging some great illicit pleasure. I thought she might make a face, but she seemed to take to the wine fairly naturally. "Not too sweet for you?" I said.

"It's fine."

I had gone back to admiring her extraordinary beauty as discreetly as I could force myself to do. The burble of the crowd was all around us, and I'm sure the gapers were all around us too, but for the first time I felt as though I was actually alone with her.

"So how come she sent you over here?" Kayla asked abruptly. "She didn't trust me by myself? What, was she afraid I'd steal the silverware or something? I can't believe it. One guy at this whole party I wanna meet and she sends him over here to baby sit me. It's the story o' my life."

I was still hung up on the phrase "one guy at this whole party I wanna meet," and I did not respond to her. But I was thrilled, all of a sudden, that Rose had asked this favor of me.

"You look like Dirk Revolver, you know that?"

"Dirk who?"

"Revolver. Dirk Revolver. From that show *Revolver*? It's a *TV* show," she said with mild condescension. What moron wouldn't know about Dirk Revolver? "You look just like him," she said. "I couldn't believe it when I first saw you. I even told my friend Angel, I said, 'We got this teacher over at the college that looks just like Dirk Revolver. I'm not kidding.' She couldn't believe it either. She even went over to the college one day to see for herself. Maybe you saw this Mexican girl following you around like a stalker. Long hair, very pretty? That was Angel. She said she couldn't believe it either."

"So," I ventured, "is it a good thing to look like Dirk Revolver?"

She was halfway through a sip of her wine when I finished the question, and plainly my ignorance mystified her. "Hell yes, it's a good thing. It's about the best thing," she said. "Dirk Revolver? That guy is hot. He's gotta be the hottest guy on TV. Older guy, I mean."

"Ah, so he's the hottest *older* guy. Not the hottest guy period, just the hottest old fart."

"Hey, I like older men," Kayla said, sipping her wine again. She had almost drained the glass off by now. She shot me a look that assured me, for the first time, that she was not trifling with me. Kayla Blaze liked "older men," and I clearly qualified as one of those. But it was better than that. It dawned on me that the chances were good and improving that I would not be sleeping alone that night.

"Can I freshen that drink for you?" I asked her.

"You sure can. Freshen it right on up."

I took her empty glass and visited the white-jacketed young man, who it seemed to me looked a bit envious as he filled it for her again.

When I returned the glass to Kayla, she took it straight to her lips. "You're falling behind," she said. "You better catch up."

"I'm awright," I told her. "Enjoy your wine."

"You're tryin' to get me drunk?"

I only smiled—innocently, I thought—in reply.

"It'll work," she said. And she sipped her wine again. And then again. "It'll work like a charm," she repeated. "God, I can't believe my luck tonight. I got half the old bastards at the college chasing my tail. Blasingame. Rogers. DeCrisco."

"Jim DeCrisco?"

"Is there another one? What, you didn't think the sonofabitch had it in him?"

"I didn't think—"

"Yeah, that's what I figured," she said. "He's a man, ain't he? He's got a dick between his legs. No offense, but you guys are all alike. There ain't any mystery about it."

"Even me?"

She finished off her second glass of wine and smiled coyly. "You can send a boy to school," she said, "but he's still a boy. Hell, I even got Chief Dennis Begay after me. The great Navajo warrior. The great Native American poet. He wanted to take me for a ride on his Harley. Yeah, right. That's not what he wants me to ride on. How." She made the gesture with her hand—insulting, I'm sure. "I'll show ya how. I don't think so, Chief."

She thrust her empty glass at me. "Hit me again. I think I'll get drunk tonight. Get drunk and get laid."

When I returned with the refilled glass, she informed me that a "certain administrator" at the college had even asked her to go with him to his beach house in Mexico for a weekend. He told her he had some work to do and needed somebody to do some research and some typing for him. He offered to pay her for her time, but she turned him down. "When I give it up," she said, "it's because I want to. Not because I'm getting paid for it."

"Maybe he really just needed somebody to do some typing for him," I offered.

"This is Fred Wallace we're talking about," she said. "Just so there's not any mystery about it. He wanted more than typing."

And I was sure, hearing the name, that she was right. "It's a shame you have to be so cynical about men," I said.

"Is it? I can deal with it. You are what you are; and you boys are all alike, every last one o' ya. Anyway, I know it can get me what I want sometimes. Like tonight, I bet."

"Tonight?"

"How 'bout it, cowboy? Feel like gettin' lucky? Angel won't even believe it. Not in a million years. I wasn't even sure if you'd be here. But I thought I'd take a chance. I tol' her, 'He'll probably go. I don't think it'll be just the assholes that show up.' An' I was right, for a change. Do you believe it? I tol' Angel, 'I'd love to get my hands on that guy. I'd fuck him like he's never been fucked before. But he doesn't even talk to me. I don't think he knows I'm alive.'"

She finished off the better part of her third glass of wine before continuing, "An' now, here you are. Right here in front of me. All primed an' ready to take me out for a spin. Are ya up for that, Dirk? I mean Martin? What the hell kinda name is Martin for a macho man like you, anyway? You're too butch to be a Martin."

"Maybe it's time for us to leave," I said.

"Maybe so," she agreed. "This place is too fu-fu for me anyway."

FOUR

A Dream Detoured

A scant few minutes later, having left our emptied wine glasses on a big silver tray by the door from the open courtyard to the front section of the house, I had a gentle grip on her elbow and was steering her through the living room toward the huge atrium inside the front door. The eyes followed us, but I wasn't much bothered by them anymore. I had approached Kayla Blaze at the request of the party's hostess, as a favor to her, and somehow that validated my leaving with Kayla. It did in my mind anyway. Maybe Rose hadn't anticipated our leaving together, especially so publicly, with the party still in full bloom, but I didn't care about that either. Rose always worried about Rose first, and the rest of us got what was left over, and I didn't care about her sense of propriety any more than I cared about her feelings. As a matter of fact, I felt a certain sense of entitlement, tinged with defiance. I was reaping the reward for my bravery, for having risked public rejection and public humiliation—and, I suppose, for having obliged the party's hostess. But that altruistic thought came second, and a distant second at that. The envious bastards could leer all they wanted. In fact, I took some pleasure in their leering. Kayla had made it clear to me that she was only at the party because she'd hoped I would be there. If my exiting with the exquisite Ms. Blaze gave the gaping onlookers something to be jealous about, so much the better.

Out in front of the house the street was quiet and the air was pleasantly cool. I could not imagine more inviting circumstances under which to take to the night. Kayla latched onto my arm as if for support, and we made our way down the long front walk to the street, her heels clicking seductively on the stone path. In those heels she was only a few inches shorter than I was, and she moved with an ethereal grace, even more erect than usual, floating along almost like a one-dimensional image—a hologram, or maybe even a figment of my furtive imagination. Was it even possible that I was leaving my department chair's house with this vision of feminine loveliness, this object of carnal desires? Boys and men across our campus—and, I was sure, far beyond—had entertained sexual fantasies about the beautiful Kayla Blaze. But I was the one *she* talked smut about. I was the one who, if her words were to be trusted, was on the point of having fantasy turned to vivid reality. Somehow, it wasn't right. Things like this just didn't happen in my life. I was a lonely man; I had to admit it. Maybe I didn't have to be lonely, but I was. Often, sitting home alone with my books, I'd contemplated my own loneliness and reckoned it for a choice. And it *was* a choice, but sometimes it was a regrettable choice. Tonight, though, I would not be alone. It dawned on me that the reality of being with Kayla might not measure up to the fantasy (does it ever?). But even just the thrill of anticipation made the risk of disappointment worthwhile. It was worth it just to feel the gentle pressure of her long fingers on my biceps and the easy rhythm of her languid gait. If she was tipsy, she was elegantly tipsy, gracefully tipsy. I wondered vaguely how a girl so young could have acquired such skill. She must be very shrewd, I thought. She must be a very smart girl indeed. "Let's take my car," she said. "Izzat awright with you?"

I consented to take her car and leave mine behind, parked on the street in one of our city's poshest neighborhoods. I'd come back for it in the morning. Hell, the cops could tow it, for all I cared. A night of splendor with Kayla Blaze was well worth the headache and the expense.

We hit the city sidewalk along the street and turned downhill, arm in arm, passing the parked cars of other guests at the party. The sidewalk dropped slowly away from the McDowells' house. Above the house, far on up the hill, were the houses of even wealthier residents of our metropolis. If I'd looked far enough up the street behind us, perhaps two miles, I'd have seen the sprawling, illumined verandah of one of our city's best-known mansions. Such was the splendid company I was keeping that night. Kayla and I were practically within sight of the universally rich and locally famous. Normally, we'd be looking up at that mansion from the base of the mountain like all the other peons. But not tonight. Tonight we traveled in style. Around the McDowells' house were the lights of other scattered houses, spread much farther apart than the houses of us peasants down in the city. Down and away across the street, between two ash trees, you could see the dense spray of lights where the other half lived, our half. It was several miles down to the floor of the valley, the noisy floor of the valley, but it might have been a world away. Up here among the rich and famous, it was quiet except for the distant flutter of voices from the party. I couldn't even hear the jazz quartet, which meant they must be on a break. What I could hear was the steady click of Kayla's heels on the pavement.

We walked on down the sidewalk under the sheltering canopy of a row of mature desert trees, mostly palo verdes and jacarandas, the noises of the party receding behind us. Presently Kayla drew me to a stop by the passenger door of an old Chevy Camaro, a rag top, at least thirty years old and probably older, an antique. I could not see it in the poor light—and besides, I was too preoccupied to notice—but before long I would discover that the car had been dazzlingly painted and sported brilliantly polished chrome wheels. We were on the curb and the car was slightly below us, street level, so that when Kayla leaned back against it her butt was against the window glass of the passenger window. She pulled me to her, and I leaned into her and kissed her, discovering at last that those lips were as pleasant to the touch and the taste as they were to the eye. Only once before in my life, when I dated a black woman named Charla Beldon, a physical therapist with a marvelous physique of her own, had I kissed lips as voluptuous and as tantalizing as Kayla Blaze's. Her tongue found mine and stroked it expertly, and I drew her closer and first reached around behind her head to let loose the hair, so that it tumbled down over my hands. Then I slid my hands slowly down her back, touching her shoulder blades first, then the inward curve of her lower back, and finally continuing south to trace the outward curve of her magnificently rounded behind. She leaned forward again, giving me access, and we stayed locked in a hungry, groping embrace as I worked the hem of her dress upward, found my way beneath it, realized to my boundless delight that there was nothing beneath the dress but Kayla, cupped one gorgeous lobe of her ass in each hand, and pulled her hips into mine with sufficient authority to elicit a low moan from her. Something was going to happen, and it was going to happen right there on the street without delay. I had believed that the consummation I anticipated would wait, that the tension would continue to build—that thrilling, electric, sexual tension—and that we would be prolonging it by driving someplace—my house, I imagined—luxuriating perhaps as much in the anticipation of the climax that awaited us as in the climax itself.

But there would be no waiting now; we could not wait. I broke contact with Kayla's lips only to move my kisses southward, to her neck and shoulders, simultaneously sliding one hand around to the front of her pelvis to stroke with the back of my index finger her mons veneris, and feeling in the process a veritable gush of warm moisture from the hot crease between the labia. At the same time her hips began to buck—back and forth, back and forth—so that Kayla's own spasmodic thrusting delivered my finger inside the crease itself and prompted a much louder moan from her, an urgent moan, verging on a yelp, and the thrusting speeded up as she grabbed both sides of my head and put her lips to my ear and moaned, "Yes! Yes!" I maneuvered my hand to cup the mons and slip my middle finger all the way inside her when somewhere in my consciousness an alarm sounded and suddenly I was aware of voices approaching.

Faster, much faster, than I had entered into the prolonged embrace, I broke free of it, removing both my lips and my hand from Kayla's person and letting her dress drop back below her hips. "No!" she said. "No!" And then she followed that with, "Here. Now. Right now. I don't care about that."

But I had pulled away from her, and I turned just in time to face Walter Herman, former English-department chair at the college, and his wife Beverly, a biologist. They made a staid and dignified couple if ever there was such a thing, and they were walking arm in arm along the sidewalk, Walter trim and gray, immaculately groomed and wearing a dark jacket and slacks, Beverly svelte and youthful for her age (she had to be seventy), in a dress much like Kayla's and high heels, her hair stacked high up on her head and surely dyed to achieve its dark color. Diplomats that I knew them both to be, they said a pleasant "Good evening" and moved on along the sidewalk, though I knew damn well they had known damn well precisely what they were interrupting. They'd been too close to us before we broke apart not to know. Surely, if nothing else, Kayla's animal bucking of the hips had been visible to them, her animal noises audible to them. It figured I would turn just in time for them to make a positive ID. Neither of them uttered my name, but I'm guessing that one of them, at least, recognized me.

"They're gone," Kayla hissed. "Come on." She tried, latching onto my belt buckle with both hands, to pull me to her and undo the buckle at the same time.

"No. Not here."

"Yes," she said. "Here. Right here. Right now. Please."

But I wouldn't yield. "Let's go someplace," I said.

She made a face, but then kissed me, ardently and full on the mouth, before pulling away again. "I know a place," she said. "I'll drive."

FIVE

Love Knows No Bounds (or Damn Few)—or, Nothin' but Mammals—or, The Call of the Wild (Is Answered)

The Camaro rumbled and shook with the deep-throated growl and imposing shudder of a healthy American muscle car, the kind of car I grew up with, never owning because I couldn't afford one but frequently riding in, and, when one of my friends indulged me, occasionally driving. Like the exterior, the interior of the car had been completely refurbished, the upholstery redone in black leather or imitation leather—and if it was imitation leather it was a pretty good imitation. It looked and felt lush. It appeared that all the knobs and buttons on the dashboard had been replaced, or else the originals were extremely well preserved. Probably, they'd been replaced. The stereo was certainly too new to be original, and it bellowed Kayla's rock music through speakers that could not have been stock; they were far too powerful, and the sound they produced was far too rich and full. Shortly I discovered that a "friend" of Kayla's (she seemed to have many such "friends") had installed the speakers—gratis, naturally—placing the two biggest ones beneath the back seat.

We rolled down the hill toward the city, the real city, and Kayla dropped the top on the car immediately and rolled down her window, so I rolled mine down as well. "The interior's all new?" I said.

"What?" She reached to turn down the music.

"I said it looks like the interior of your car has been reupholstered, maybe completely refurbished."

"My dad did it," she said. "He did the upholstery. He did the dash. He did the motor, too. My friend Dan put in the stereo, though."

"It's beautiful."

She reached for a small sign that hung by a leather strap from her rearview mirror, alongside several Mardi Gras-style strings of beads. "She's my baby," Kayla said. And she flipped the sign around so that I could see that it read "My Baby!" in fluorescent letters on a photograph of Kayla's car with her leaning against it.

"What year?"

"Sixty-seven," she said. "Just the one I wanted. My dad found it in Pittsburgh."

"What, did he place an ad?"

She nodded and told me the name of the publication. She said he had found '67 Camaros all over the country, but only one that was just perfect. And we were riding in it.

"This thing's got a four-twenty-seven in it," she said. "Hemi. Holley four-barrel carb. Hooker headers, racing exhaust. This baby'll fly. This is the one I race the boys in. I've never lost yet."

"It musta taken your dad a long time to redo this whole car."

"Six months," she shrugged. "My brother helped him. Some o' the time was just waiting for parts to come in. He gave it to me on my sixteenth birthday."

"He must love you very much," I said.

Her response was to reach over and turn up the radio again. She started singing along with the song that was on, in a voice that was on key if not terribly melodic, and I watched her sing and did not say anything.

We rolled down off the mountain and into the valley and got on one of the freeways. The top was down and the night air rushed in around us and Kayla's hair blew back in the wind. She sang louder as the noise of the wind and the freeway grew louder and the engine bellowed and the radio bellowed along with it. The music was not mine, it was hers, but it was familiar to me and I didn't care for it much. A small part of me wanted just to go home, maybe sit down with a book and a bourbon, or else watch a movie and just fall asleep. But I knew I would regret it as soon as I sat down, knowing I had passed on the opportunity to have glorious sex with Kayla Blaze. It was awkward riding in the car with her, but I knew that the instant she touched me again my nerves would come alive, and then we would be back where we had been before the Hermans so rudely walked up on us. I had a vague and amusing image of Walter Herman doing to Beverly what I had been doing to Kayla Blaze. Then I thought about it and realized they'd probably been doing it for years—I knew they'd been married almost forever—and all of a sudden it wasn't funny anymore. Or rather, it was still funny, but the joke was on me. I'd been going home alone for a long time, sleeping alone for a long time, and it wasn't so damn much fun. Maybe the Hermans knew that—that I'd been sleeping alone, I mean. I didn't see how they could, but maybe they did, and if so maybe they were driving home right now cheering me on. I could hear the conversation in my head. "I hope that boy gets some tonight," Walter was saying. "He sure could use it." And Beverly replied, "That's an understatement. The boy has a biological need that must be met. It isn't natural to live the way he does." "I don't know why he's waited this long," Walter said, shaking his hoary head. And she said, "That makes two of us. Nobody lives forever. And I've never heard of anybody complaining on his deathbed that he had too much sex in his lifetime." "Nor have I," Walter seconded. "I hope she cleans his pipes but good." "As do I," Beverly nodded approvingly. And then, after pondering for a moment, Walter added, "Might make him a better teacher." And his wife affirmed the possibility with another resolute nod of her head. We went through the city and back into relative darkness and started climbing another mountain clear on the other side of the city. I knew where we were going, to a park at the top of the mountain that overlooked the city and provided a spectacular view at night, and I wasn't sure it was the best place to go but I was willing to give Kayla the benefit of the doubt, so I didn't even question her choice aloud; I only questioned it to myself. I wondered why the hell we couldn't just go to my house, where I knew we'd have both comfort and privacy, and get it over with.

Halfway up the mountain we turned off onto a side road that I hadn't known about. Kayla turned down the radio, and we followed the side road around to the back side of the mountain where there were no lights except far off in the distance, and the glow from the lights of the city shined up over the top of the mountain and blotted out the stars but brightened the night sky. Still, it was the darkest darkness we had experienced all night, a darkness that reminded me how bright the lights are in a big city, and as the road narrowed and got rougher I hoped Kayla knew where the hell she was going because I sure didn't. When she turned off even the side road and started back between two palo verde trees, I *really* hoped she knew where she was going. I was also really glad we were in her car, not in mine. And then she switched off the headlights, which scared the living hell out of me, and we bumped and jolted another fifty feet or so and then stopped. She shut off the engine and made sure the car was still in gear and pulled the emergency brake, and after a moment there was a haunting desert stillness about the place that was spooky and romantic at the same time. Off away down the side of the mountain the land flattened out and stretched out dark and expansive into the distance, except where piles of rock cropped up here and there. I think I could have counted on the digits of one hand every individual light I saw in the entire panorama in front of us. There just seemed to be nothing but darkness and stillness out there.

"Come on," she said, opening her door.

We got out and moved around to the front of the car. Looking out across the desert expanse she said, "We need something to drink. Why didn't you think o' that, Dirk?"

"The thought crossed my mind."

"We'll have to make do without it."

"It would be nice to have a little wine up here. Or something. This place is beautiful. I've never been up here before."

In response she reached around behind herself with both hands, undid the clasp on the back of her dress, lowered the zipper just enough to loosen the dress at the shoulders, and then let it fall to the ground at her feet. She stood splendidly naked except for high heels, her ass perfectly round and firm, her long legs perfectly taut and smooth, and when she reached up behind her head to run her hands back through her hair, her small breasts reached up with her and the nipples pointed up and out, as rock-hard as small stones. When I die, I want to take that image of Kayla with me. I believe it will make my life feel complete. Suddenly, I was glad we hadn't gone to my house.

Then she turned to me and pressed herself against me, throwing her arms around my neck and pressing her mouth to mine. I had her entire body to caress then, and I made the most of it, running my hands up and down, exploring every nook and cranny as she arched her back and bent herself into me and tossed her head back, let me kiss her neck and breasts, then abruptly pivoted and planted her derriere in my groin, looking up and back over her shoulder to let me bend slightly and kiss her on the mouth. My hands went searching again, and a moment later she was moaning, her hips bucking again, at first in gentle rhythm, and then harder and faster, and at last wildly, out of control, convulsing in sync with her shrieks of passion or release or whatever it is you experience when you have an orgasm. All the while she had been leaning back into me, trying to keep her mouth against my mouth or my chin or my neck, though it had been impossible for her to keep her lips on me through the whole bronc-riding orgasmic episode. When she finally settled again, with a pleasing shudder, she spun around and dropped my pants to the ground and caressed me, first with her hands and then with her lips and tongue, and then after a long minute she spat me out and leapt to her feet and kissed me on the mouth again, swinging her slender legs up to lock them around my waist.

"Hold it a minute," I said desperately. "Hold it a minute"—though it was a struggle to disengage my mouth from hers. "What about birth control?"

"I been on The Pill since I was sixteen," she gasped, and with a quick thrust of her hips she had me inside her and the thrusting began and the moaning and clutching and groping and neck-biting resumed. I slammed myself into her and into her and into her, cupping her thighs with my hands to hold her up around my waist, losing all sense of time and place and being aware only of her and of me and of the sensation of going into her and into her and into her. I could hear nothing but her noises—not even my own noises—and yet I had the strange feeling there was music being played somewhere, somewhere off in the distance, wafting across the still nighttime air from a car radio or something. I could not even recognize the tune, but it was "I Only Have Eyes for You," or else "This Magic Moment," or maybe it was "Just One Look." I could not be sure, and I did not pay close attention—I was preoccupied—and besides the music didn't last that long. We flatter ourselves that it takes longer than it does, and then we make jokes about it. It's over in the time it takes to cook a two-minute egg—and such. The thrusting and hip-bucking seemed to go on for a long time but it was probably only a couple of minutes, and then abruptly, while the phantom music was playing in my head, she yanked herself away from me and spun around again and sprawled forward across the hood of her car, thrusting her butt in the air to make herself available to me in the enactment of a male masturbation fantasy. Almost instantly I was into her again, as if in fear of losing the moment, and then the music was gone, and she was sprawled across the hood in front of me, her hands stretched out before her as if she might claw right through the metal (I noticed for the first time all night that she had—or had applied—long fingernails that were painted the same color as her lipstick), making more animal noises and then exhorting me, "Come on! Come on!" And the music was gone then, vanquished from my head, and I bore down on her and into her, focusing exclusively on the task at hand (so to speak), the consummation of the act, the consuming, desperate, lunging, frantic plunging toward completion that is the essence and the fulfillment of all human destiny. I felt myself cross the brink—crest the wave, as it were—and in so doing lose all control, disappearing into a blind fury of energy during which I was at the mercy of whatever forces of Nature might apply themselves to me at the moment. I imagine how it must have been for some prehistoric male human ape, or quasi-ape, rushing through that spasm of ecstasy while worrying in some back corner of his mind about predators. And then it was over, the wave had passed, and I pitched forward and pressed my lips to her back and reached forward to clasp her hands with mine, the palms of my hands against the backs of her hands, our fingers interlocking, engrossed in the moment of greatest intimacy between two human beings. "Oh God," I huffed. "Oh Jesus God." And then I went on huffing, trying to get my breathing back to normal, muttering inanities all the while. I could not imagine any moment of human existence so complete or so whole.

Then I was aware of chuckling and felt Kayla's body quivering slightly beneath my lips. I straightened up suddenly and pulled her up with me, and she disengaged from me and spun around and threw herself into me again, the two of us laughing and kissing and caressing each other. I thought for a moment she wanted to go at it again, right then and there, but instead she pulled herself away from me and reached down for the dress that she had stepped out of and left on the ground. She picked it up, shook it off, examined it, brushed it off, then stepped into it and pulled it up and zipped it up and fastened it. Meanwhile I was dressing myself as well. When we had both finished we got back in the car, where Kayla turned to me and kissed me passionately on the mouth before starting the engine. She came all the way over to the passenger side and sat astride me, her knees on my bucket seat, and kissed me for a long moment. Again I thought we might go at it again, right then and there, and I said, "Let's go to my place." And she finished kissing me and spun back over into her own seat, her dress up around her thighs. She appeared happy, and I don't believe I've ever experienced greater satisfaction in my life. At the moment life seemed perfect, more worthwhile than at any other time in all my years. I watched Kayla fire up the engine and then sat back and put my head back against the headrest and took in the night sky. Now, I thought, I know why they make convertibles.

We made our way back around the mountain and down into the city again. "I know a place we can go," Kayla said above the music, which was turned up uncomfortably loud for me. "But we'll have to go to my house first."

"I thought we were going to my house," I said.

"We'll go there later. The night is young."

"It's eleven o'clock."

"Like I said, the night is young. We gotta go to my house so I can change clothes."

We got on a different freeway this time and drove a few miles in the direction of the college and my own house, then passed them both, drove a couple miles more, and got off the freeway. The music blasted the whole time. We drove into an older neighborhood much like my own where the houses were built of block and brick before they started stuccoing over wood frame for all the houses because it's cheaper and faster. The front lawns of the houses were bigger too, and there was more grass in the lawns and less xeriscape. Kayla turned onto a curbless side street and drove up a block and followed the street around a slight curve, and there on the curve was a pleasant brick house with a huge, late-model pickup truck parked in the driveway, and Kayla pulled up in front of the house and switched off the engine.

"Should I just wait here?" I asked her. I really was not in the mood to meet some eighteen-year-old's parents. For one thing, I was skeptical about how I might be received.

"Why?" she said. "Come on in and meet my mother. I know she'll wanna meet Dirk Revolver."

SIX

A Girl Just Like the Girl

Kayla's house, her parents' house, was a sprawling one-story ranch house with a tile roof (not the original roof, I'm sure—I imagine the original roof was asbestos shingles) and a carport instead of a garage. The carport was at one end of the house, wide enough for two vehicles. Attached to it at the end opposite the house was some kind of annex, built solid of brick to match the main house but with a shingled roof instead of tile, perhaps originally intended as a workroom or bathhouse or maybe even a guest house. The annex was Kayla's room, her "apartment" as she called it. It did not have cooking facilities, but it did have its own bathroom in addition to her sleeping quarters.

The main house was immaculate outside—and inside, as I would discover—with bushes and trees for shade and cover, a pleasant paved seating area to one side of the main entrance, and tasteful, subdued footlighting to help you find your way as well as to give the house curb appeal at night. We did not go in through the main entrance, however. We went in through the carport entrance, which gave onto a spacious laundry room and then an eat-in kitchen. Entering and passing through the kitchen, I noticed that the house was both dark and quiet. A lamp was on in the kitchen and another one in the room beyond the kitchen, but they gave off feeble light. We could see well enough to navigate through the house easily, and I could see details on the walls and in the corners, but they maintained a sort of mystery because of the weak light, like the moonlit objects in Hawthorne's famous preface. Shadows pooled in the corners, and the objects in the rooms took on an exotic glow like the objects in a room where the only illumination is provided by a TV screen. You see faces, for example, but they are almost colorless and quite ghoulish in the light from the TV. Often, they take on a bluish tint.

I could hear voices, but they were muffled and I couldn't make out what they were saying. Nor could I tell if they belonged to people in the house or were coming from some electronic device. We passed through the kitchen, Kayla walking in front of me, and into the next room, which was a family room with french doors leading off to one side and a hallway leading off the other side to what were probably bedrooms. Through the french doors I saw a formal dining table, elegantly laid out with candleholders that looked like brushed nickel or pewter and cloth place mats of a color I couldn't make out in the dim light. I remember thinking that Kayla's parents—probably her mother—had good taste. There was no pretense in the furnishings or décor of the house, but there was a sort of simple, dignified pride as if the occupants of the house were concerned about its appearance but not snooty about it. The house was clean and uncluttered so that a visitor would get the impression the occupants of the house were always prepared for company. In the family room were a fireplace and a TV, and a heavyset woman sat on a couch with the lamp on over one shoulder, throwing light down in front of her but nowhere else. She was knitting, and she wore thick glasses so that she could see what she was doing. The TV was on softly and she looked at it over her knitting.

"Doesn't he look like Dirk Revolver?" Kayla opened. "I told you he did."

I couldn't really see the heavyset woman's face, but I suppose she may have been pretty at one time. I couldn't really tell because her face was too much in the shadows. They say if you want to know what a young girl is going to look like when she gets older, you should look at her mother; but if that's true Kayla Blaze is not going to turn a lot of heads when she reaches middle age. I wondered what her father looked like.

"This is my mom. Linda." She added her name as an afterthought. "This is Martin Frey. He's the teacher at the college I told you about."

Kayla's mother greeted me pleasantly, but I thought it was probably to my advantage that the light in the room was poor because she probably couldn't tell that I was perhaps as old as she was and maybe even older.

"Where's Dad?" Kayla asked.

"He's working a double. He should be home by midnight. What time is it now?"

"Maybe twenty after eleven."

"He's still working then."

"My dad works at P & S," Kayla explained to me. "It's a steel fabrication plant. They make steel buildings and stuff."

"Silos," Linda Blaze added. "Sometimes sheds. Mostly large buildings for warehouses and manufacturing plants."

"My dad works a lotta doubles," Kayla said. "Seems like he works all the time."

"He'll be here in just a little bit," Kayla's mother offered. "Aren't you in for the night?"

"We're goin' out to Eddie's," Kayla said.

"This late? Aren't they about closed?"

"Not for another hour'n a half. Jeff'll probl'y be there. Dontcha think?"

"I have no idea. I don't keep track of your brother since he moved out." Linda seemed preoccupied with a stitch, peering intently down at it through her thick-rimmed glasses. Every now and again her eyes would glance up over the glasses at the TV.

"He'll be there," Kayla said.

She noticed her mother's glancing at the TV and followed her eyes and identified the program that was on, some reality show (they're all the same to me), and they talked about it for a minute, perhaps, Kayla demonstrating that she knew the program as well as her mother knew it, so that they could toss names and incidents back and forth familiarly as if the TV people's lives really mattered to them.

Kayla tried to involve me in the conversation but I think she quickly figured out that I had never seen the program before and had no idea what or whom they were talking about.

At any rate, she was only making conversation, passing a few minutes with her mother the way a dutiful daughter should do, and so very soon she announced that we had to get going or we'd never make it to "Eddie's." Her mother again questioned why we would go anywhere so late, and Kayla replied that the night was still young, and then she caught me by the sleeve of my jacket and tugged me out of there. I excused myself politely to Linda Blaze, offering the obligatory "Nice to meet you," to which she responded with a polite nod of her own and nothing else, and then we left that house and I have never been back there since. Nor have I ever seen Linda Blaze again nor met Kayla's father.

We went back through the kitchen and the laundry room and out that door into the carport and then across the carport into the annex that served as Kayla Blaze's comfortably furnished but untidy bedroom. "We gotta hurry," she said. We had no sooner made it through the door into her room than she had reached down for the sides of her dress, swept it up over her head, and flung it on top of a pile of clothes over in one corner of the room. I was not used to seeing her naked yet, and so watching her strip, especially so abruptly and so quickly not to mention so causally, still thrilled me. When she flipped her shoes up on top of the clothing pile, stepping out of one high-heeled shoe at a time and flinging it with her toes up onto the pile, it struck me that she was no longer imposing in my imagination as she had been before, a venomous split-tongued vamp who could like a black widow destroy her mate after copulating with him (or, in Kayla's case, destroy would-be mates who merely attempted to copulate with her); she was just a young girl, a beautiful and well-constructed young girl but a young girl nonetheless. I felt a sudden pang of sympathy or tenderness for her, a protective impulse to father her instead of fuck her.

But it would pass. It would pass quickly when I was reminded that Kayla was neither naïve nor inexperienced.

"This'll just take a second," she had said to the wall in front of her, but apparently it would take a long enough second that the stereo needed to be turned on so that hip-hop music could be blared into the room to entertain me while I waited for her. Without a glance at me she swept up a pair of jeans from the floor and began to wriggle into it, an endeavor that sent another blast of titillating heat right through me as I watched it. But Kayla, surely aware of the effect her antics had on me, feigned oblivion, reaching for a black t-shirt that said "Got a problem?"

in white letters on the front, at the level of her bra-less tits, and on the back "Eddie's Roadside Tavern," beneath which was a graphic I couldn't make out in the dim light (it turned out to be a chopper churning up dust in front of a one-story stucco building, presumably Eddie's), and beneath that was some lettering I couldn't make out either (it turned out to be the tavern's address). She slipped her bare feet into a pair of black deck shoes, which she had to search for in her unkempt closet, to complete her attire for the late-evening foray.

"Just one more second," she said, glancing at me for the first time since we entered the room. She was yanking off her necklace and earrings as she said it. "Let me run a brush through my hair."

If she was brushing her hair to make herself beautiful, she needn't have bothered. That end had already been achieved. But I waited patiently for her, not eager to leave that place anyway, even though the girl's mother was a hundred feet away knitting ... whatever it was she was knitting. I did not really want to go wherever it was we were going, anyway, especially now that I was starting to get the strange sense it wasn't the kind of place I would normally go. I'd have been much more content just to call it a night, preferably with Kayla curled up next to me so that I'd have her there in the morning.

But I was not to get my wish, not yet. I had perhaps thirty seconds to contemplate the walls and the music, and then she came rushing out of the bathroom and hurried me out the door and down the sidewalk and into the shiny little car with the big, gleaming wheels. The engine roared and we were quickly on our way. We got back on the freeway and drove east for some miles, away from the center of our desert metropolis, out into its fringe where the subdivisions get as sparse as the desert vegetation. Kayla drove fast, well over the speed limit, and she blared the music so that conversation was next to impossible. Traffic got lighter, but the possibility of getting pulled over, it seemed to me, got heavier. We did not get pulled over though. We got off on one of several exits to a town in our metropolis that had a reputation for trailer trash and rough behavior. I had been through the town several times but could never remember setting foot there. It was not noted for being exceptionally dangerous if you didn't look for trouble (and I had no intention of looking for trouble), but it was known to be a place where people kept and sometimes carried guns and where they also had a cavalier attitude toward the law and its enforcers. In short, it was known as a kind of lingering remnant of that old Southwestern reputation for mavericks and lawlessness. I did not feel nervous about going there, but I did feel we were stopping at a place I would never have stopped at on my own. I was only going there because Kayla was dragging me there. We drove up an open road past scattered houses and trailers, then through a small business district, the businesses as scattered (and as squalid) as the surrounding houses; then we continued on the open road a mile or so out into the middle of nowhere, and there we were at Eddie's, the very same stucco roadhouse represented on Kayla's t-shirt, where a mélange of pickup trucks and motorcycles and muscle cars, with a few SUVs and nondescript domestic and foreign cars thrown into the mix just for fun, was clustered out front of the place and in gravel parking lots on one side and in back. Eddie's was hopping if the parked vehicles were any indication, and if they weren't enough to tip you off, the hubbub and music were a dead giveaway. The music was coming from a patio out back of the building, and it came to us up and over and around the sides of the building so that the words were lost in the journey, turning into a tumbled blur, but the sound was still loud. We heard the singer's voice, and we heard the guitar screeching and a rhythm guitar banging chords and a bass laying down a line somewhere beneath it all, but most of all, perhaps owing to the direction of the wind or just the way the stage was mic-ed, we heard the drums. Kayla couldn't find a place to park out front, so she searched first in the side parking lot and then around back. At the end of a long row of vehicles in the gravel lot we found a spot fifty yards from the patio and with nothing but open desert beyond it.

Kayla slammed on the brakes and we slid to a stop, and she shut off the engine, the dust now catching up to us and curling in around us, just as the tingle of the night air and the open road started to subside and the noise died away in my ears. "We're here," she beamed at me, and she did not bother to put up the top on the convertible before leaping out and pitching her door closed behind her.

SEVEN

I Got Those Roadhouse Blues—or, American Pluralism

It was hard to keep up with her as she angled across the parking lot toward the back patio of Eddie's. I contented myself to follow a few steps behind her taking delight, occasionally, in watching the hypnotic sway of Kayla's behind in a pair of tight jeans. I was not anxious to get where we were going or even to catch up to her. But as we drew nearer, I became a little more curious about the place that would be, I hoped, the last stop before my house of our night on the town.

The patio of Eddie's Roadside Tavern was perhaps a hundred feet square, enclosed by a low stucco wall that might deter people from skipping out on an open bar tab but not if they were determined enough to scamper off into the desert and take a chance on being run down by Eddie's' security apes. People, quite a few of them, sat on the wall, and others sat at huge round tables on the open patio. In one of the two corners of the patio that adjoined the tavern building itself was a full bar, the bartender exposed to the elements at least that evening (on another occasion I would see a canvas canopy drawn over the bar to shield the bar and its contents, the bartender, and the patrons closest to the bar from the weather). In the other corner was a stage, and on the stage a cowboy band was banging out mostly country and some rock tunes, with even a little hip-hop, as I would discover, thrown in to keep the crowd moving. A dance floor perhaps thirty by thirty fronted the stage, and at that time of night, already past midnight and pushing on toward closing, it was crowded with drunks, most of the males among whom were using the dance floor as a tool to secure more cherished treasures after Eddie's had closed down for the night. It has always seemed to me that there is a certain desperation about the dance floor of a bar or club as closing time approaches, the women feeling the fever of the night and perhaps the influence of the booze, wanting the dancing to go on forever, the men also feeling the fever of the night and the effects of the booze but wanting to get their women off the dance floor and into a sexual liaison with all possible haste. The couples spin and shuffle and gyrate like dervishes, the possessed kind, and the air is charged with an energy that is like no other.

We steered clear of that energy at first or hung on its fringe. Access to the patio from the parking lot was through a ten-foot-wide gated opening, the gate wide open that night, monitored by a t-shirted thug at each end of the opening. "Dan!" Kayla squealed at the thug on our side, then she threw her arms around him. "This is Marty," she introduced me. "This is my friend Dan."

He gave me an indifferent nod and checked his watch as Kayla waited for me to pay the cover charge for both of us. But Dan waved us on inside. "Better hurry," he said to Kayla. "It's almost last call." That prompted her to latch onto my hand and drag me hurriedly in and out among some of the tables toward the back of the patio away from the band and the bar, then pause for a long moment while she surveyed the rest of the crowd, and finally, when she had spotted the group she was looking for, yank me along behind her as we skipped around a couple more tables and stopped at one about halfway up on the dance floor side.

Five people were sitting around the table. A thin Hispanic girl, extremely attractive, also wearing tight, tight jeans but with a bare midriff, squealed with delight on seeing Kayla. She leapt up, pranced around the table, and the two of them embraced. "This is my friend Angel," Kayla informed me.

"Dirk Revolver," the girl blurted out, almost shouting. I could tell she'd had too much to drink, but she was very beautiful. Then she threw her arms around me, and I felt her very large chest against me, and she smelled sweet and perfumy and inviting. "You know I followed you all over your campus one day," she said. "I couldn't believe how much you look like him."

"So I'm told."

"That's Angel's boyfriend, Craig," Kayla was saying, indicating a tough-looking young man in a sleeveless t-shirt with multiple tattoos on both arms. The way he looked at me told me he was very possessive of Angel, smug about having her and determined not to lose her, least of all to the likes of me, a pretty boy in a jacket and tie at Eddie's, of all places. If necessary he would fight me to demonstrate his determination to protect his woman—that is, to protect his interest in her, to keep her for himself. He was not the least bit afraid of a fight, especially not with the likes of me, and he wanted to make damn sure I knew it. His look told me all that, and I am not exaggerating. I have seen those looks before.

"This is Jeff, my brother. He works with my dad."

Jeff was a scruffy young man in his early twenties, tough looking like Craig, with a defensive look on his face but not surly. He stood up and reached across the table to shake my hand, and then he sat back down. "Dad still at work?" he said to Kayla.

She answered him but the music was playing and she did not speak loudly. "Better get a drink," he said to both of us, more or less. "Com'n up on last call. We thought you'd never get here."

"Better late than never," Kayla said almost exultantly. She seemed very happy to be where she was and with whom she was. "Better get us a big beer," she said to me. "A pitcher. Maybe two pitchers."

"They won't let you have two pitchers," the other man sitting at the table said. Nobody had introduced him or the woman who appeared to be his companion. "Not 'less both of you go. They'll give you one apiece. How old are you, girlie?"

He looked to be older than anybody else at the table but probably not as old as I was.

"Old enough to slap you across the face," his companion said. She was a trashy woman close to his age, but I wouldn't hazard a specific guess because I probably couldn't be very sure. I knew that type, and guessing their ages was dangerous. You had to allow for their being rode hard and put away wet, which clearly she had been. I'd have guessed her at thirty-five, which means she was probably in her late twenties.

He looked at me. "Prom's at the high school right down the road." And then he cracked up at his extraordinary wit.

"You'll have to forgive him, Professor," his date said. "He's drunk enough to think he's funny, but you're prob'ly not."

I smiled at her, and she said, "Name's Roxanne. Roxie to my friends. You can call me Roxie. This is J.D. And yes, he was a J.D. in his younger days."

"It's my pleasure, Roxie," I said. I found her very agreeable and very likable. Though our acquaintance proved to be brief, I would never revise that assessment of her.

"The night ain't gettn' any younger," Kayla Blaze nudged me. "And neither am I. Get us those drinks. You can chit-chat with these losers later."

I did as I was bidden by a woman to do—for the second time that night. I went up to the bar and got Kayla and myself a pitcher of beer and two glasses. It was a slow process. In anticipation of last call everybody seemed to have the same idea. The bar was jammed and the crowd was aggressive. My attire drew looks but no comments, at least none to my face. I got my pitcher of beer and glasses and escaped to the table where Kayla was sitting but no chair had been arranged for me. "We couldn't get you one," Jeff explained.

"It's all right," I told him. I stood behind Roxie and off to the side and sipped my beer while Kayla pounded hers across the way.

"So what do you teach?" Roxie asked me.

I told her, and she paid polite attention. The whole explanation seemed to mystify her as if I were speaking Greek—or even Spanish. "Hell, I never even got my G.E.D," she said after a minute.

"You could do that at the college," I told her, but I had the feeling Roxie wasn't exactly the scholarly type. Her days of formal education were permanently behind her.

"Hell," J. D. said. "She wouldn't know which enda the pencil t'use."

"No, but I'd sure as hell know which end to shove up your ass," she said to him. And he laughed more loudly than she did.

Kayla smacked her glass down on the table after draining it a first time and a second. A little beer remained in the pitcher, and I knew she would want it so I left it for her. My own glass was half empty—or half full. "Let's dance," she said. She popped up from her chair and came around the table and got me and we moved out onto the dance floor, where the band's final medley was whipping the crowd into a drunken frenzy. Presumably, the goal was to get us all worked up and then leave us there, so that we left the dance floor and the patio dazed, happily dazed, with the music still ringing in our ears and the adrenaline still coursing through our blood vessels. And the goal was attained. We were on the dance floor for what seemed like hours as the band ground through one number and then fell right into another, the bodies writhing and throbbing and bobbing around us. The band worked us all up to fever pitch, thundered through its final crescendo, and then toppled into abrupt silence and hollered "Good night" and "Drive safely" to all of us.

"You haven't danced in a while," Kayla said to me, rubbing herself up against me.

"Nope."

"We'll change that."

We got back to the table and our little crowd was still sitting there. People all around us were getting up and leaving, some lingering, like my new friends at our table.

Bright overhead lights had been turned on—uncomfortably bright, quite intentionally, I'm guessing, to chase away the slowpokes among us. Eddie's wanted to close. Car engines were roaring to life and headlights were popping on all around us. Harley and Indian motors throbbed off into the distance. Voices chirped noisily in parking-lot conversations. There were no fights, that I noticed.

At our table Roxie was complaining to the others about not getting any child support from whomever it was she was supposed to be collecting from, gesticulating with a lit cigarette in one hand to emphasize the consternation in her words. "All I know is, sumbitch better come across with some cash. I know where he lives, I know where he works, I know what he drives."

"He might be gettin' a visit from the key patrol real soon," J. D. added, holding a car key up to illustrate. "Or I might just have to go right ahead and kick his skinny ass."

"You ain't kickin' nobody's ass," Roxie told him. "You couldn't kick your own ass. Just siddown and shuddup."

"No, you stand up. It's time to go."

"What?" She looked around. "Awright. Les' go."

We did not wait for them. Kayla had already complained to Angel about the beer being taken away while we were out on the dance floor. She wanted something else to drink. She was arm in arm with Angel and they were leading Jeff and Craig toward the exit. I went on ahead of them. At the exit from the patio everybody parted ways. "No Sheila tonight?" Kayla said to her brother.

"Nope. I don't know where the hell she is. I thought she'd be here tonight."

"Goodnight, Dirk," Angel said to me. "Hope to see you again soon." She went off with Craig, who seemed sullen and in a hurry to leave.

Kayla put her arm through mine. "I liked Roxie," I said.

"That trailer trash? Jesus, nobody else would even talk to 'em, hardly. They always do that. They just show up and sit down and start yappin'. Nobody invites 'em; they don't need an invitation, I guess. They just invite themselves. We try to ignore 'em. Jesus, that J. D. is the biggest moron I've ever met. Did you hear him talkin' about beatin' up Ben?"

"Ben?"

"Roxie's ex-husband. He was a Marine. He'll break J. D. in two. What a windbag."

She leaned over in front of me suddenly. "You got beer at your house, right?"

"I got beer. I got wine. I got hard stuff."

"No kidding?" She sounded genuinely surprised as though she simply couldn't accept the fact that she was in the company of a legitimate adult who could legally buy and keep booze in his house. But I would have wagered even then, and I would certainly wager now, that she had already shared the company of a number of adult males. "What hard stuff?"

"I got bourbon. Scotch. Gin. Rum."

"Vodka?"

"Sure, I've got vodka."

"And plenty o' beer?"

"At least a case. Probably more."

"That's all we need for tonight. We're on our way."

We were at the car. Almost everybody else had already left the parking lot. It was just as well. Bar-closing time is not the best time of day or night to be on the road, wherever you live. Let the drunks get a head start on us before we took to the streets.

"I noticed nobody carded you back there," I said, nodding toward Eddie's.

"They know me," she shrugged.

"It pays to be a beautiful woman," I said. "You'll have to show some ID at my house."

"I awready showed you my ID," she sniffed without missing a beat. "I'll show it to you again when we get home. If you're a good boy."

EIGHT

What, After All, Is in a Name? –or, American Pluralism Revisited—or, The Other America

The surname Blaze derived from the surname Blasevitch, or Blasovitch, or perhaps Blasevic or Blazevitch—I don't know because I'm no comparative linguist and I never saw the name written out. Nor did I care all that much, though I did have an English teacher's pedantic curiosity about the name. I suspected it was a Russian surname, given the final syllable, and if I *really* wanted to write it out I'd have to study the Cyrillic alphabet. And Kayla didn't know much more than I did. She said—with maximum indifference—that the name had been shortened when the family immigrated to America, or perhaps some time after its arrival, perhaps owing to the difficulty the natives had in pronouncing the long form, or, just as likely, because the immigrants simply wanted a name that sounded more American. Kayla didn't know for sure and didn't care. "They tell me the name's Polish," she said. "I'm a Polack. You believe that?" She held her face in profile so that I could observe it. "Does this look like a Polish nose?"

"I don't know," I shrugged. "I'm sure not all Polish people have big noses."

"Most o' the people in my family sure do," she said. "You should see my dad. You saw my brother's schnoz, right?"

"I guess I wasn't paying close attention."

"I guess you're just being polite."

"Honestly, I didn't notice."

"My mom doesn't have a big nose," Kayla said. "But she's not a Polack. Her bloodline is English. Her family comes from Cornwall."

"People make fun of English noses too," I laughed. But I could see Kayla hadn't heard that before. All she knew was that her mother—and, I suppose, her mother's people—had smallish noses. That was what interested her.

Some of Kayla's ancestors had stuck it out in New York, mostly western New York. Others had moved west to Cleveland and Eerie, first, then one on to Detroit and another, her paternal grandfather, on to Gary. They were cogs in the great manufacturing wheel that had been the Great Lakes region, a family of hardworking steelers who, as the old expression has it, "built the country." The old expression is not wrong. People like Kayla's forbears, including my own forbears, were responsible for building much of the American infrastructure and then for maintaining it, and they were indeed hardworking people. Building the infrastructure was also good to them, and they lived prosperous lives in cities across the Midwest and Great Lakes regions of the country. When the unions came they benefited, and for a while they were even more prosperous, but as the wages and benefits got better the competition got better too, mostly foreign competition, and the demand didn't get better—at least it didn't get better enough. The manufacturing plants got older, part of the aging infrastructure the immigrants had built, and they were expensive to run, especially as the industries they comprised were more heavily regulated. Eventually the combination of aging plants and government regulation and higher taxes and tighter demand and especially union pressure to increase wages and benefits when wages and benefits could not be increased made cracks in the "rustbelt" as it became known, and those cracks led to the end of many manufacturing jobs. Something else led to the end of those jobs, a rapid upswing in certain new technologies, but it was only one factor among several, and in any event the outcome was devastating, at least temporarily, for families like Kayla's. In the eighties when so many of the steel mills closed, Paul Blaze made the momentous decision to move his family to the Southwest where there was not much heavy manufacturing, the kind of work he was used to, but neither were there unions or high corporate taxes, so companies like P & S were providing plentiful jobs, albeit at modest wages, to transplants from the Midwest like Paul and also to transplants from Mexico like Angel's father, Miguel. The cost of living was low then, and the transplants could buy affordable housing and sit on it as both Paul Blaze and Miguel Hernandez had done, and then when the Californians started migrating in, bringing their California money with them, and when the investors from other states started buying up houses as investments, the demand went up and the supply went up to meet it, and the prices went up (before they went back down, and then later went down *hard*, but that's a tale for another time), and the original transplants, those like Paul and Miguel, were sitting on low mortgage balances and low mortgage payments, and meanwhile their wages had also gone up because the demand for labor in the burgeoning Southwestern metropolis still outstripped the supply (though that too would change and raise no small amount of ruckus in doing so). They lived comfortably, if not lavishly, and if they'd had a little savvy and a little extra cash on them years before when the cost of living was still low—and Paul and Miguel had had both—they'd invested in some additional property themselves and profited themselves from the enormous influx of new jobs and new residents. And that was how a man of modest blue-collar means like Paul Blaze could afford to live comfortably and spend comfortably and treat his family to such extravagances as a fully restored mint-condition dark-blue '67 Camaro convertible.

Yet Kayla did not appreciate her father's hard work or his shrewdness in investing his earnings. One of the first things we established that first night together as we first drank, then screwed, then drank and talked till after daybreak, was that Kayla's home life had been miserable. How it had been miserable she didn't seem able to say—but she was clear and emphatic about its having been miserable.

"Your parents certainly have provided a comfortable home," I told her. "I'd take it any day. Look at this place."

"What's wrong with this place? It's nice. I like it here."

"Your parents' home is nicer. At least if you ask me."

"A nice home isn't everything. Besides, I've seen a lot nicer."

"No argument there," I told her. "But we can't all be rich."

"Awright, *Dirk*." She emphasized the name because I suppose she thought it would bother me that she called me that. But it didn't. "We've established that you like my parents' house. Why don't you go an' live with 'em then?"

"Did they beat you as a child? Is that it? Were they abusive?"

"There are other ways to abuse a child besides beating."

"So they were abusive? They said mean things to you? Like, 'Kayla, you're a dummy?' Or, 'Kayla, you'll never amount to anything?' Or, 'Kayla, you have the nicest ass on the planet?'"

"Don't make fun o' me."

"So that was it? They were abusive? Verbally abusive? Psychologically abusive? Whatever the hell it's called?" "Just shut up and fuck me again."

"I can't. I'm not ready yet. You'll have to find yourself a younger man."

"You'll do awright."

"I could be your father."

"I told you, I like older men."

"That's *another* issue we might have to take up at some point."

"We ain't takin' up any more damn *issues*. You be a good boy and behave yourself and you might get yourself some more o' this." And she took my hand and placed it over her muff, which was covered by a sheet.

"I'm just curious," I said. "I'd like to know you a little bit. Besides there." And saying that, I gave her privates a gentle squeeze for emphasis.

"Ooh, do that again," she said playfully.

"They seem like nice people to me," I said. "Your mom anyway."

"It was just no family life, awright?" she snapped, yanking my hand away from her privates, apparently as a sort of punishment. "You saw it tonight. He works. She sits at home. That's it. That's what I grew up with."

"She never had a job herself?"

"She worked as a secretary when she was younger. Just like me. Then she got pregnant with Jeff and she quit her job and stayed home and she just never went back."

"You lived in Indiana then?"

She nodded. "Then we sold that beautiful house and came out to this godforsaken hole in the wall. You shoulda seen our house back there. We had two acres. It was all trees and grass."

"How old were you when you left?"

"I was five. But I remember everything. And I been back there."

"So you've done all your schooling out here?"

"All of it. Any more questions, counselor? Then get me another beer."

"You didn't give me time. I have more questions. Have you always been this tight with your brother?"

"Always. We hang out together. He's four years older than I am. There's nothing perverted about it. So you get your goddamn mind outa the gutter. We never kissed or made out or screwed or anything. He's just my brother and my best friend—after Angel."

"Did you meet Angel in school?"

She shook her head. "Modeling." It turned out that Kayla had been spotted when she was sixteen by some "talent agent" at a shopping mall. He said he could get her modeling work, and he did, so apparently he was legitimate, not just some pimp trying to hustle her. But she hated modeling, hated it with a passion. "You want a catty business?" she said. "You wanna find the biggest bitches in the world? Hook up with a model. Jesus, you wouldn't believe the back-stabbing."

"But you met some people you liked. Like Angel."

"We both got out of it. Couldn't stand all the shit."

"Well, the world is full of it. Even at the college. You said so yourself."

"Did I? I don't remember. Jesus, who does a girl have to screw to get another beer around here?"

"So what do you think a marriage should be? You said your parents' marriage was miserable. What marriage isn't? Is there such a thing?"

"You're asking me?"

"Is there somebody else in bed with us?"

"I don't know," she shrugged. "I guess it should have a little more romance in it."

"I bet ol' Dirk What's-his-name has plenty of romance in his life."

"Revolver. And you're goddamn right he does. He gets it any time he wants it."

"But he doesn't have a steady girlfriend? A woman to share the burden of daily existence with him? Somebody to help him maintain a home and pay the bills and raise a family? Normal shit like that?"

"Jesus. I'll get my own beer. If I wanted this crap I could stay home with my parents." She got up, magnificently naked, and padded into my kitchen. I heard her open the fridge and then open the beer. She took her time coming back, so she must have been snooping around.

She was gone long enough, in fact, that I got restless and decided to get out of bed. When she finally came back I was out on the patio, having pulled on a robe before I went outside. Kayla, of course, didn't bother to put something on. She just strolled right on outside in her birthday suit. The neighbors were not likely to be peeping over the block walls that separated our houses, but who could say for sure? Naturally, I was turned on.

"How come you have a picture of James Dean on your fireplace mantel?" she said.

"It's just a little print," I said.

"Duh! I thought it was an actual photograph. The hair is naturally blond, but I'm not *that* stupid, awright? I just wondered why you'd have a picture of him."

"I'm surprised you know who James Dean is. Was."

"Never mind," she said. "It's like pulling goddamn teeth to get an answer from you."

"I don't even remember when or why I got that print, but I suppose it's my own little romantic streak showing through," I said. "I suppose that's why I have it."

"The maverick, eh? The loner? All alone in the world?" Kayla was at last intrigued by something I said, sufficiently intrigued to sit down in the chaise lounge next to the one I was sitting in. "Is that it?" she said. "Tell me."

"Aren't you cold? You look like you are."

"Just the opposite. I'm hot for you, baby. My nipples are hard for you."

"How thrilling."

"Come on," she said. "You played twenty questions about my life. Hell, twenty *thousand* questions. Now tell me all about you. All about

Dir—Martin. Marty. Good ol' Marty Frey. Jesus, *Marty*. Start with that name. Tell me all about yourself. How come you're not married, Marty? You're the big believer in marriage. At least you talk like you are. Hard work an' all that shit. An' here you sit, all by your lonesome. With some eighteen-year-old. Damn near jailbait. Hey, Marty, I lied about my age. My birthday's not till next month. I'll be eighteen then. I graduated high school early."

"Jesus," I said, "I came out here to enjoy the sunrise. It's so beautiful this time of morning. Look at that sky. Listen to the birds. My God, it's enough to make life worth living."

"Yeah, yeah, it's lovely. Tell me all about yourself."

"Drink your beer."

"Fuck you."

"I could probably manage that now."

"Hey," she said, "if you ever wanna do a threesome with Angel, I know she's up for it."

"What?"

"I'm serious," she said. "I talked to her about it. She's into it. She's into you, big boy. She's almost as hot for you as I am. She just *loves* Dirk Revolver."

"What about Craig?"

"What about him? What Craig don't know won't hurt him. He's an abusive bastard anyway. Treats her like shit. One o' these days that sonofabitch is gonna get his nuts in a vice. My brother'll take care of it for us."

"So why is she with him? Jesus, I just don't understand this."

"I don't know. Low self-esteem," she said mockingly, parroting the conventional wisdom of every therapeutic thinker of our time. Then, with a shrug, "He gets her into the bars and clubs. Besides, he's a bad boy. The real thing. Sonofabitch has been in prison. Honest to God. You know us girls love bad boys."

"Like Dirk Revolver?"

"You're turnin' me on, big boy. Let's go inside where it's comfortable and screw."

And that is what we did.

NINE

Trouble in the Paradise for Parasites

That was the same spring, my last spring at the college, that the shit hit the proverbial fan. Our family of ten colleges, collectively governed by a central administrative office (our "parent office," if you like that cozy "family" metaphor) and thus comprising a "district," constituted a political entity whose size and clout should not be underestimated. As often as we could, we bragged publicly about our enrolling well more than 200,000 students at any given moment of any given year, and about our impressive track record as a transfer institution, a corporate trainer, and an economical community resource for people who just wanted to take cooking classes or whatever. In roughly forty years of existence we had grown with our community—in other words, we had experienced the kind of explosive growth most institutions of "higher learning" can only fantasize about at this juncture in our nation's history—and had established and maintained a firm niche in the community's consciousness. Unlike the "junior colleges" my parents, neither of whom had the privilege of attending college, scoffed at when they were urging me to break family tradition and attend college myself, we were something of a juggernaut in our community, an educational force to be reckoned with employing nearly ten thousand faculty and staff and with an annual budget surpassing half a billion and approaching a billion dollars. Moreover, our reputation was nationally known among similar institutions, and we were even occasionally permitted to hobnob with the universities.

The personal friend, a university professor herself, who, knowing how I felt about a lot of things, had recommended that I target community colleges for a career, had suggested our district specifically.

Because of our place in the community, and because of the funding mechanism that primarily supported us, we did not experience the financial strain that other colleges and universities across the country faced in the late twentieth century and continue to face in the early twenty-first century. Our money came mostly from property taxes, unlike the universities' money, which mostly came either from legislative and donor endowments or private-sector investments. With a population base that continued to expand like some freakish bacterium in a science-fiction movie, our funding expanded with it, and we enjoyed prosperity that made us the envy of our colleagues across the country. Getting money to travel to a conference, even a conference in Hawaii or Europe, was not a problem for us. Nor was getting money for any other species of professional growth, from a class at a university to a training seminar on our own campus. Such training seminars were plentiful as were other professional-growth opportunities, encouraged by a district that saw these opportunities as one effective way of staying on top of the community-college field. Salary-and-benefits enhancements could also be counted on, partly based on that same rationale that staying on top required "hiring the best," and hiring the best required paying them a decent salary. When money was the least bit tight though—and while it was never tight for us the way it was tight for institutions in less fortuitous locales, it nonetheless got tight by our local standards every now and again—salary and benefits were the first things to incur the administration's scrutiny as naturally they must be since they unfailingly account for an employer's largest expenses.

To combat administrative attempts to curtail faculty power as by curtailing faculty salaries, for example (it is not really difficult in a rationalizing world to equate salary and benefits with quality of education, and perhaps the rationalization is justified for all I know), we faculty members funded our own faculty "association," an organization composed of elected faculty representatives from each of the colleges who met regularly to discuss faculty interests. Like the

U. S. House of Representatives, the faculty association based the size and configuration of its membership on the sizes of the colleges that supported it: Bigger colleges had more representatives, smaller ones had fewer, but every college was represented. Though it was not formally denominated a "union," the association was recognized as such in a court battle in the early 1990s to which I will return momentarily. Union or not, it represented the faculty in negotiations with the administration, though the administration did not call its involvement with the faculty association "negotiation"; it called it "collaboration." But take my word for it, there was marked antagonism between the two sectors of the organization—management and labor—as there always needs to be in any business organization, profit making or otherwise.

As an aside, I can't refrain from pointing out that most of the antagonism to faculty interests came from within its own ranks as I discovered in various episodes that contributed to my gradual self-exile and insular behavior. When one college wanted a program, for instance, it was the faculty at another college that would oppose it for fear of losing that program itself and the accompanying student enrollment (and money and faculty positions) that went with it. When a group of department chairs petitioned the faculty association for more "reassigned" time (reassigned time is time paid a faculty member for doing something other than teaching classes—chairing a department, for instance), it was fellow faculty members, not the administration, who opposed them, arguing that chairs were already fairly compensated for whatever time was required to fulfill their administrative and teaching functions. And most famously and perhaps most perversely, there is the example of residential (full-time) faculty arguing for better pay and working conditions for the visiting faculty, our comrades in arms who taught many of the college's classes, and whose professional responsibilities were not significantly less than ours but who were paid drastically less, on a class-by-class basis with no benefits and no job security. Visiting faculty could be let go at any time without explanation. Every year the residential faculty, via the faculty association, screamed at the administration to give the visiting staff more money, and every year the administration responded that there was no money to give. (Of course, there always seemed to be enough money to hire more personnel at the District Office, where not a single class was held and not a single student appeared except on rare occasions.) Every year the administration negotiators (collaborators?) fell back to the same position: They would increase the per-class rate for visiting faculty if the residential faculty would finance it through a reduced salary-and-benefits increase for ourselves. Naturally, we declined the suggestion—every year.

Darwin comes to mind again. Earlier I used the metaphor of the single college as an ecozone, a biogeographic region composed of various ecosystems with each department of the college representing an ecosystem competing for that ecozone's limited resources. If we expand that ecozone to encompass the entire district, we can now behold an even broader assortment of ecosystems, and the myriad organisms that inhabit those ecosystems, and tellingly observe those organisms locked in a perpetual selfish struggle for whatever resources the ecozone has to provide. I confess, and I suppose I should feel bad about it (but I don't), that I watched these interactions with a certain smug glee, seeing self-interest continually reaffirmed, unabashedly reaffirmed no less, even self-righteously reaffirmed. It was Charlie Darwin insinuating himself into worldly affairs again and yet again, the bearded old man and his disciples so oft-maligned—by the Christian right for unseating that other bearded visage, phantom "maker of us all"; by the "progressive" left for amply verifying that human nature is what it is, every organism for itself. I might have been offended by the melee, but I was too goddamn perversely amused.

Finally, to end the aside and get back to the original subject of discussion, the community colleges in their apparent heyday had the hearty support of their most important constituency, the community they purported to serve, which seemed overwhelmingly to view them as an economical alternative to the high-priced education provided by our universities. Generations of my students' families had proudly attended our college. Nor did they hesitate to admit it. In fact, they sometimes boldly advertised it as they might advertise a family business that had existed for generations. Other students, probably the majority, did not have older siblings or parents or grandparents or other relatives who had attended the school, and they were themselves first- or sometimes second-generation residents of our sprawling metropolis, but they endorsed the colleges as enthusiastically as long-term residents for providing a respectable educational experience at a better-than-respectable price. Now and again I heard snide comments about our school being just an extension of high school, but even the students who made those comments kept coming back. In short, the colleges' place in the community, even as large as the community was getting to be, seemed snug and secure. And two bond issues, roughly ten years apart, seemed to reaffirm that assessment. The two bond issues, each asking for hundreds of millions of public dollars for infrastructure expansion, renovation, or improvement, passed by huge margins. It's not often that you see the public vote with such confidence to increase taxes.

Right about the time I was offered and accepted employment at the college, though, minute cracks seemed to appear in the façade of apparently absolute assurance that the colleges had worn before I came along. The cracks were barely visible, perhaps—perhaps even invisible to the casual observer—but there were early indications that they might cause stress damage sometime in the future. The strife between the administration and faculty association early in the nineties was one indication of paradise lost—but it was an outcome, a symptom. What were the causes? Nobody knew, in part perhaps because nobody even recognized that the body politic was diseased until many years after the first minor symptoms appeared. When it finally became obvious even to the disinterested outsider that all was not perfect in Valhalla, not anymore, two of the symptoms were glaringly visible—sharply declining enrollments in consecutive academic years and an abrupt barrage of disastrous publicity as other symptoms of declining, or at least imperfect, health were noisily exposed to the public. Still, nobody could confidently identify causes. It was speculated that the new president of a large local university was deliberately (and cleverly) stealing our transfer students from us by making his university more attractive (i.e., more affordable) to them than our colleges. It was also posited that proprietary schools—the private schools that have invaded the higher-education market in the last couple of decades—were responsible, achieving the same end (stealing our students) not with lower tuition but with more attractive (i.e., easier) programs. A feeble few even fell back on the old explanation that a healthy economy was robbing us of our enrollment, but they couldn't claim it with much confidence because population growth continued unabated in our desert paradise, and never, under the healthiest economic circumstances, had our enrollments plunged so significantly. Some influence more powerful—and perhaps even sinister—had to be at work.

Things got worse, though, when the other of the two symptoms of malady I mentioned was abruptly exposed. Declining enrollments were cause for discomfort, but the other symptom was downright ghastly to the onlooker's eye and painful to the corpus that exhibited it. A series of front-page articles appeared in the local papers on corruption at the colleges with counterpart stories airing in the electronic media. Offenses ranged widely in severity and frequency, but none of them flattered the schools' collective reputation. One school was accused of funding expensive unnecessary overseas travel for faculty and administrators, ostensibly to develop programs that never materialized. Another was using public money to woo overseas participants to an online program sponsored by the college in hopes of infusing the program with overseas money. The money hadn't started flowing in yet. Administrators involved had committed such indiscretions as lavishly entertaining overseas diplomats—in Las Vegas no less—with public money. At yet another college, low enrollments in a particular expensive program—a program the department chair had campaigned very hard to convince the college to fund—had been bolstered by enrolling family members, friends, college staff members, even fellow faculty members in the flagging program's courses to make the program appear solvent. Once the classes had started but before they had been funded by the state, the phantom students withdrew or were withdrawn. Thus the classes were on the books, but with very low actual enrollments. It was hoped by the unscrupulous department chair who masterminded this particular scheme—he who had begged for the money to pay for the expensive equipment to mount the program in the first place—that the program would eventually become popular with legitimate students, the paying kind, and thus legitimize itself. He never had the chance to find out. And finally, at a different college, another failing program, formerly highly visible and touted as one of our district's marvelous success stories, was simply allowed by its overseeing administrator to continue with very low enrollments—as few as zero in a class—so that the program would continue to appear viable and instructors would continue to have jobs.

These were the symptoms, the manifestations of disease not the causes, and they were highly visible to our constituency and did not enhance our colleges' image. They generated maximum vitriol in some interested quarters, and that vitriol showed in letters to the editors of various local publications as well as in calls to talk-radio hosts around our metropolis, letters and calls condemning the individual colleges, the district as a whole, certain individual administrators by name, higher education in general, and even public education as a whole. Respondents used the various indiscretions as weapons to attack their personal pet peeves. One guy's worried about a general decline in morality in America, another about the poor caliber of the educational professional, another about the detrimental effects of illegal immigration (by whatever name you wish to call it) on public education. Etc. Etc. Largely, though, and more tellingly, the symptoms of our disease generated simply appalling widespread apathy. Nothing was the response. No comment. No interest. At our first department meeting after the initial series of articles permeated the local press and soon after the state's attorney had very publicly announced a more widespread investigation of our institutions, Roly polled us all on the attitude about the scandal(s) in our classes. There was little to report and nothing of consequence. Most of our students appeared not even to know about the news stories, and if they did know about them, they didn't care. The stories only showed the great Darwinian enterprise continuing on about its business. Business as usual. No changes anticipated until the next ice age or maybe the next sizable meteor crashes into us. And no improvements are likely even then. Evolution does not denote progress; it denotes only evolution.

No matter how little the public seemed to care about our ethical and even legal violations, though, district employees reacted with hyperbolic zeal as if each of us were protecting his or her own personal reputation. It is the kind of overreaction typical of educators, at least

American educators in the early twenty-first century. Invective was hurled at the media for taking such glee in exposing our little flaws. "The media and the public are always quick to point out our faults," an anthropology instructor wrote on the district's employee listserv. "One would think they would be just as eager to publicize our many contributions to the betterment of our community. They are not. This is one of the perils of working in public education in a country that always has its eye on the Almighty Dollar, even at the expense of its own soul. Hail, Capitalism!" Never mind the non-sequitur (capitalism breeds contempt for education?). It's not the thought that counts; it's the emotion behind it. Similar shots were fired by other faculty and staff members. Only one had the guts to defend us publicly, though, identifying himself in a guest editorial in one of the papers as an instructor at one of the colleges. And he was censured by district officials for his "unauthorized" and "ill-advised" response.

Officially, the district itself, through its primary mouthpiece, the chancellor (our top paid official, appointed by his bosses, the "governing board," a collection of five elected and unpaid citizens from different geographic regions of the community)—the chancellor offered meager, sometimes embarrassing rhetoric (embarrassing in that it came from our top official and made us sound not only guilty but stupid); it suspended several administrators and fired two college presidents; and it promised repeatedly that we would "clean house." "It is inevitable in a political entity as large as ours that there be indiscretions, and that some of those indiscretions will go unnoticed until they are brought to the attention of the proper authorities," he wrote not to the papers but to his underlings, again on the district listserv. "Let me herewith affirm our commitment to delivering a quality educational experience to our entire community who seek it out. Let me reaffirm also that the District will make every effort to find and correct violations of the public's trust."

It was Darwin who was again reaffirmed, again vindicated as the chancellor made every effort to reassure the public and regain its trust—by saving his own hide. He made a nice public showing, recorded for posterity by local TV cameras, of cutting loose the two college presidents, both of whom were known to have caused him prior discomfort in his tenure as chancellor. And he announced a new initiative involving a so-called "blue-ribbon panel," a panel composed primarily of private citizens with no ostensible personal interest in the colleges. The panel would conduct an extensive audit of all the colleges, more extensive than our overworked internal auditors could even imagine performing; it would make recommendations for restructuring and improvement; and it would of course open up all its findings to public scrutiny. Not only that but the chancellor also announced he would personally oversee the installation of a new "civic responsibility" initiative for all district employees—which, if you read between the lines, simply meant that all employees would henceforth be required to attend seminars that would dictate appropriate behavior to us. The absurd premise that all you need to do is tell people what's wrong to do and they'll refrain from doing it—the same idiotic premise that underlies all those ridiculous anti-drug and anti-smoking TV and radio commercials that we taxpayers pay for—undergirded our fearless leader's response to the public disclosure of "alleged improprieties." Only in education, I thought, could the shit get so deep and nobody even question it.

Inside criticism of the chancellor was rife, especially from those who had been loyal supporters of the two fired college presidents. It had been popular when the chancellor was installed in his office to hail the appointment as a great triumph for our district's "diversity" value—since he was black—but now all of a sudden diversity didn't matter quite so much. He was a turncoat, scrambling only to keep his own job, willing to sacrifice anybody around him to do it. Rather than boldly stand up to face the charges against us, to defend our honor in the court of public opinion, he had meekly submitted to public bloodlust—before a single indictment was even handed down no less!—and offered up a pair of sacrificial heads and a promise to do better. Of course, no employee that I know of voiced this criticism loudly enough for the chancellor to hear it. But John Q. Public, with nothing personally at stake besides a few tax dollars, was equally perceptive in assessing the chancellor's actions and less timorous about expressing his perceptions. Again the editorials whizzed and whirled, asking loudly and publicly where the chancellor was while all the indiscretions were occurring (it was his store to mind after all) and calling for his head on the same platter as the two college presidents' heads. The governing board convened in a "special closed-door session," and when it emerged from that session it voiced its continued support for the chancellor it had appointed along with its own promise to make sure he did a better job of minding the store in the future. When I left the district's employ, the chancellor was still occupying his top-floor office.

Officially, the faculty seemed interested in distancing itself from the administration while at the same time responding appropriately to the "crisis." "We are in mourning," the faculty association vice president wrote in her "Open Letter to the Faculty," distributed electronically on the faculty listserv. "In thirty years with the District I cannot remember a time of greater sorrow or strife within our family. But let's remember that in times of sorrow or strife, families pull together." Without endorsing either the chancellor's "blue-ribbon panel" or his "civic responsibility initiative," she announced the faculty's own "professional ethics agenda," an effort "to encourage and promote cooperation and ethical behavior among faculty colleagues." In the true spirit of cooperation the "agenda" hoped to promote, it would begin with a series of faculty meetings on the various college campuses, convened and presided over by our local faculty association representatives, at which the initial topic of discussion would be "What is professional ethics?" Once a definition of professional ethics had been articulated at each of the campuses, a "formal definition" could be synthesized from the various college definitions. And when *that* definition had been drafted and approved by the entire faculty district wide, the next round of discussions could begin to determine how we as "professionals" could be induced—through cooperation not coercion, mind you—to uphold the ethical standards prescribed by the definition. The entire process might take ... years? Decades even? I'm sure it's still sailing merrily along toward *something* of substance, something that actually accomplishes *something*—years after it was conceived—unless it has been forgotten, succumbing to the weight of its own inertia like so many similar "initiatives" before it, a victim of the sprawling bureaucratic complex that spawned it. Ah, the public sector—where so little actually gets done, and so much energy is expended in doing it!

It may be needless to say that I did not attend our own campus's initial meeting to determine what is meant by "professional ethics." I did, however, receive a report on the proceedings from a similarly skeptical colleague who made time in her schedule for the meeting because as she put it, "I could use a laugh." Predictably, she said, the first half-hour of the meeting consisted primarily of those on our campus most in love with the sound of their own voices' pontificating about "ethics," including a brief but fascinating, not to mention thoroughly pompous, discourse on Aristotelian ethics by one of our college's philosophers. The second half-hour, though, was considerably more entertaining as the whole affair degenerated into a bitch session about office and classroom assignments, department policies, real and apocryphal contract obligations, and annoying colleagues. She couldn't wholeheartedly endorse the session for its entertainment value, but the second half-hour had been worth the price of admission. Overall, she felt comfortable assigning it three stars out of a possible four.

TEN

We Are Family (and Don't You Forget It)—or, The Devil Wears Pravda

The first media bombshell about inappropriate, unethical, or even illegal activity by employees of our district exploded in November, reportedly after the newspaper that detonated it confided to district officials that they were about to set it off. The officials were offered an opportunity to respond publicly to the charges against us immediately after those charges were leveled, but—again according to hearsay, but it's reliable hearsay—they naively, foolishly, or just plain idiotically turned it down. I suppose they thought that if they kept a low profile the whole thing would blow over more quickly than if they tried to defend our honor publicly. It's like pretending to be invisible to ensure invisibility. It didn't work. The second media blast came the following February, and it was the more damaging of the two explosions, the one that highlighted potentially *illegal* activities and instigated the state's attorney's grandstanding investigation. Uniformed and plainclothed sheriff's deputies were on our campus and other campuses, evicting personnel from their offices and removing confidential files. The "scandal" became a concrete reality to employees who had only witnessed it from afar as a sort of vague abstraction that affected other people. Now these employees, themselves under no suspicion, could personally feel not only the medias' but the law's scrutinizing stare, and it made them downright uncomfortable. The phrase "police state" was bandied about our campus for a week or two, always with an air of righteous indignation. How could such a thing be happening to such devoted public servants as all of us were? But the cops meant business; there was no doubt about that. So you'd better not trifle with them. Blow all the hot air you want—but keep your damn hands in sight.

The faculty's "ethics agenda" began then, and those initial meetings were held to determine what we should and *shouldn't* be doing on company time. I'm sure the entire debacle was a prominent subject of discussion at Roly McDowell's annual party, but I was preoccupied—at my hostess's behest, let me remind you—and didn't get in on the gossip.

I was nonetheless not much surprised when, two weeks after Roly and Rose's shindig, Gillian Greenback paid me a visit in my office. It was late in the afternoon—late by our standards anyway. Visit a college or university campus at two or three o'clock of a weekday afternoon and you'll likely find that most of the higher-paid help has already cleared out. The door was open when her head appeared. She asked if she could close it behind her.

"Be my guest." I indicated the straight chair by the door, an institutional straight chair of the excruciatingly plain variety, not too pretty and not too comfortable, so that students who visited me would be discouraged from settling in for too long when I was trying to get something done. I didn't need to point the chair out to Gillian, obviously, but I did so out of politeness.

No sooner had she plopped down on it than she was leaning toward me casually, a behavior I was accustomed to seeing in Gillian and found mildly annoying. It assumed a familiarity, an intimacy, that I wasn't willing to grant, and I resented her haste to assume it. Gillian was a classic representative of a breed in academia that I found particularly distasteful: the tenured female (it could also be a male, I'm sure, so don't be too quick or too smug to write this off as mere contemptible "sexism") who is married to a successful spouse and therefore enjoys a very materially comfortable existence while simultaneously exploiting the privilege of decrying evil capitalism and extolling the virtues of "socialism," though specimens of this breed are rarely if ever clear about the details of the "socialism" they have in mind for us all. The breed is often recognizable by its appearance: expensive hair and nail treatments, designer clothes, jewelry that no proletarian could ever hope to afford. As a graduate student, I once overheard two well-heeled Marxists chatting amiably in the hallway about which high-priced luxury SUV was the best purchase. When I reported the conversation to a fellow graduate student whom I knew to be struggling to support a family while attending graduate school and working full time, he offered me a gem that I've been pleased to repeat from time to time ever since. "Naturally," he said. "They can afford to be Marxists."

Gillian, then in perhaps her late forties or early fifties, enjoyed the added bonus of being an old hippie who could dress like a gypsy, a particularly stylish one; continually exhibit her reverence for cultures other than the dominant culture (she had a particular affinity for "Native" cultures—she liked to burn incense and play funky tribal music in her writing classes, arguing that it stimulated "creativity"); and decorate her multi-million-dollar house, even higher up on the mountain than Roly and Rose's, with "Native," "African," and "Caribbean" art. She could profess great affinity for tribal cultures while being blissfully ignorant of aspects of those cultures besides the ones that appealed to her—the "warm, fuzzy" aspects as another cynical colleague once put it. And she could denounce capitalism as both "inhumane" and "dehumanizing" (I'd heard her use both those descriptors at one time or another) while looking down on the rat race, drink in hand, from her spectacularly expensive patio. I'd been to her home once—had only been invited that one time and then of course only along with our colleagues from the department—and I knew that while she only lived in a different zip code, she might as well have lived on a different planet. Her husband, Burt, an agreeable sort though he seemed to regard academics as a rather peculiar breed, not to be taken very seriously, maybe somewhat like teenagers who have profound sentiments about the world and about life but have little experience with either, was a land developer who had made numerous wise professional decisions in his rise to prominence among the city's moneyed gentry. He had several large indoor shopping malls under his belt, along with quite a number of strip malls, more than one of which bore his own name, and others of which bore the names of persons and things related to him, including his pet, all three of his children, his ancestral home, and of course his wife (hers was—still is—called "Gillian Place," and it's a small upscale shopping center patronized by women with plenty of money to spend and plenty of free time to spend it). But his coup de grace, his crown jewel, his pet project—the project that "made him his money"—was an entire planned community in the foothills on the southern fringe of our metropolis that he had envisioned, planned, and then brought to life. The community had grown and prospered, and it was now a sizable autonomous suburb and a very desirable one at that. That development alone had made Burt many millions of dollars. It had paid for the beach house that Gillian referred to as "the San Diego house," and that she offered out to faculty colleagues—for a price, of course—at select times of the year (a gal's got to pay the rent, doesn't she?). It had probably paid for the Mercedes convertible that Gillian drove to work. And it had put all three of Burt and Gillian's children through prestigious universities so that they too could fully enjoy the fruits of capitalism, perhaps while denouncing the tree that produced those fruits. It's okay though. They could afford to be Marxists.

And yet, though it will seem unlikely, I liked Gillian. Or at least I did not entirely *dislike* her. Like other rich liberals who mean well, she had an ingenuousness about her, an earnestness that was impossible to despise even if it was equally impossible to admire. At least it was impossible for me to despise her. She *liked* her students. She *liked* her colleagues. I always believed she wanted the rest of the world to be educated and prosperous just like she was. It was just that she had absolutely no concept of the gulf that really separated her from us. She loved ideas, loved the way they looked and spoke to her in her mind even if they didn't necessarily make sense. They made sense enough to her—in her mind—and she rarely had to worry about their affecting her in the world outside her mind. And so she could bandy ideas about all she wanted. They wouldn't hurt anybody.

Gillian and I had always gotten along tolerably well mainly because I kept my distance from her. I watched her toss her ideas around with those who took them seriously, always with a flurry of long, sandy hair and "tribal" jewelry, and I smiled and stayed back and retreated to my office if necessary to avoid her line of vision. If her chirping bothered me, I quietly closed my door. I didn't want to offend her; I just wanted to put her out of earshot.

When she came to my office two weeks after Roly and Rose's party, the only way to put her out of earshot was to get rid of her. I wasn't sure how to go about that. Searching my memory, I could not recall a single prior occasion on which she'd parked her rich rump in my office, so I was unpracticed at getting rid of her.

"I saw you at Rose and Roly's," she chirped. "Wasn't that fun?"

"It was indeed. They have a beautiful home."

"Burt and I had a great time. I think we were the last ones there. A little group of us."

I nodded amiably. I knew something must be amiss. Chit-chat with Marty Frey wasn't something Gillian typically penciled into her daily planner. I wasn't nearly important enough to merit such a casual visit from Gillian. So something was up. And I had a pretty good idea what it was.

"Wasn't that jazz quartet amazing?" she continued.

I agreed that it was, and I quickly related the story about the first time I'd heard a quartet from the college play at Roly's house—asking them how long they'd been together and being told they had never played together before that night.

Gillian heard the story with a kind of dazzled smile. She wasn't really listening. She didn't want to hear it. She wanted to press on, get to the reason for her visit. And yet she didn't want to appear rude.

"You left early," she said as soon as she thought it acceptable.

"I did." It was coming. I knew now that it was coming.

"With the girl who works at the front desk. The new girl."

"Kayla," I said her name. "I left with Kayla."

She raised an eyebrow but trying to be inconspicuous about it. "You're seeing her, aren't you?"

"I am." Every goddamn night as a matter of fact, I thought. But I kept those words to myself.

"She's so young," Gillian mused. "How old is she?"

"She's eighteen. Nineteen in another month or so."

"Wow." She looked surprised, but I wasn't buying it. I had a feeling she knew exactly how old Kayla was even before she walked into my office. "They're so ... naïve at that age. I know I was. I remember I was at Amherst and I fell in love with my literature professor. Frank Carson. God, I remember him." And she looked off into space, this time with a different kind of dazzled look on her face, a look of fond remembrance, of tender nostalgia. I was half tempted to ask her if she was fondly remembering him with his cock in her mouth.

"He was so ... sophisticated," she continued. "So worldly." Again she was looking me in the eye, leaning too far toward me, striving way too hard for a familiarity I didn't want to grant her. She had pretty eyes though; I'd give her that. In fact, she had a pretty face. And she smelled good. I could see why that sophisticated fellow, Frank Carson, had wanted to get that long-ago version of her in the sack—as I was already sure he had succeeded in doing. I had figured that out the moment she started telling the anecdote. A lesson was going to be conveyed here, and I was to be the learner.

"A young girl at that age is trusting," she said to me in a different voice, one that wasn't dazzled with nostalgic romanticism. The lesson was beginning. I was being taught. "Or at least they used to be. Some of them still are, I guess. But it's a different world now. Kids are a lot more jaded than they used to be. Still, young women like that, they look for love, and they think they know where to find it. An attractive older man like you ... you have a lot to offer a young girl like that. At least in her mind. It depends on how she was brought up, of course. I don't know anything about that. But I know how she feels. I've been there. I know she has a very unrealistic—"

"Did you sleep with him?" I interrupted. I was not subtle about it. I suppose I lacked Gillian Greenback's extensive social skills.

"What?"

"Frank Carson. Did you sleep with him?"

"That's a rather personal question, Marty."

"Oh, come on. And your asking me about Kayla isn't personal? We're adults. Pretty advanced adults, to be truthful. I won't tell. It was years ago anyway."

"Yes," she said abruptly. "I slept with him. Many times. We had an affair. He was married."

I looked at her in a way that was intended to convey nothing at all, but she read it her own way. "Don't look so smug, Marty. I was young. It was a long time ago. The sixties—you know. Free love."

"I didn't say a word."

"Your mouth didn't. But your eyes did."

"I have no interest in offending you, Gillian. But you're offending me with these questions. Awright? What you want to know is if Kayla and I are fucking. That's the word for it. Fucking. Having sex. Intercourse. Whatever. There are a million euphemisms for it. You probably know as many as I do. Maybe more.

"The answer is yes. We are. Often. And in many different ways."

"Don't be crude, Marty."

"Then don't ask me about my sex life. Truthfully, it's none of your business."

I had not had a flare-up of any kind with a colleague in years, and—truthfully—this one was exhilarating. I felt myself coming alive along all my nerve endings the same way I had felt that first night with Kayla.

"Awright, Marty," she said, in a manner that suggested she was ready to remove the kid gloves and put on the boxing attire. "Maybe it's none of my business. And maybe it is, in a way. You're having an affair with a secretary in our office. A girl half your age."

"Less than half."

She shook her head in disbelief. "Less than half. Thanks for that correction. I wish I could be as nonchalant about this as you are. But I can't. You're not using your head, Marty. Not the one you're supposed to think with anyway."

"Pardon the political incorrectness, but while she is not twenty-one, she is both free and white."

"That's vulgar, Marty. We both know where that expression comes from. What it means. I'll kindly ask you to leave it ou—"

"And I'll kindly ask you to leave my office if you have a problem with the way I talk.

"Let's cut the crap here, Gillian. What Kayla and I do is called fucking. We're doing plenty of it. And even if she reminds you of a student—or whatever your problem is—she's not. She's completely legal and completely consenting. And frankly, I'll be damned if I know why you're making this your business."

"You've seen the papers, Marty. You've watched TV. You know what's going on. I know you keep your head buried in the sand, but tell me you don't know about the problems the college has been having."

"Of course I do."

"Then you know we have an image problem right now. We've gotten nothing but bad press for months."

"Don't forget *The District Daily*," I said holding up a finger to stop her. *The District Daily* was part of the administration's idiotic knee-jerk response to our critics. It was an online "daily" that published nothing but happy-go-lucky news about our wonderful accomplishments: "Student Wins Merit Scholarship." "Women's Track Team Places Second in Nationals." "Former Art Student Opens Own Gallery." A propaganda sheet, in other words. And a shameless one at that.

"Now *you* cut the crap, Marty. You wanna be another headline in the paper? Keep it up. There is pressure on us now like there has never been before. Pressure to behave ourselves. To conduct ourselves like professionals."

"And I resent the insinuation that I am *not* conducting myself like a professional."

"Our sexual harassment policy specifically states that romantic relationships between employees are prohibited."

"No, it doesn't. It doesn't say 'prohibited' because it can't enforce any such prohibition. It wouldn't even try because it would lose. All over this campus—this district—people are fucking. Administrators fucking instructors. Instructors fucking instructors. Staff fucking faculty. Faculty fucking students."

"I get the picture."

"I just wanna make sure. Because I know it and you know it. Both of us could name names. The district policy *discourages* these relationships. It could never enforce a prohibition."

"Then consider your own professional responsibility, Marty. She's eighteen, for Christ's sake. You're ... what ... forty?"

"Close enough. And what does that have to do with my 'professional responsibility' as you put it?"

"You have a power relationship with this girl. She's a secretary in your office. You're a person of authority. You're exploiting your advantage over her."

"Oh, for Christ's sake, Gillian. Spare me the rhetoric. This isn't a women's studies class. I'm not one o' your goddamn wide-eyed undergraduates. I'm not exploiting her any more than she's exploiting me. It's mutual exploitation—the way o' the world. Ask your precious Marx."

"My precious Marx?"

"Just don't bring this my way anymore, Gillian. It's not illegal. It's not 'exploitation' any more than your"—I started to say "your marriage to Burt" but then thought better of it—"any more than your being personal friends with Roly is exploitation," I finished. "Are you taking advantage of him just because you two are friends?"

"That's not the same thing."

I agreed with her—sort of. But her being friends with Roly was the best I could do on the spur of the moment. "It's close enough for me," I said. "My point is, that girl knows what she's doing. She's not half as naïve as you make her out to be. And what we're doing is absolutely legal and none of the college's—or your—business."

"I disagree," she said. But she stood up to go. She knew she was getting nowhere with me and she saw no point in pressing the matter further. She had several moments into the conversation, when things were starting to get a little testy between us, dropped out of the phony intimate posture and leaned back away from me, stiffening her back in a gesture, probably unconscious, of mild hostility.

Now she was through with me—pretty much. But after opening the door to my office she turned to me. "You need to reconsider this, Marty. For your own sake—the sake of your career—you need to think about it."

"I've thought about it plenty," I said. "I know where I stand. I know where my career stands. I'm not doing anything wrong and my career should not be in jeopardy. And that's all there is to it."

She shook her head but started to close the door. "Oh, by the way," I added. "Next time, please tell Roly to do his own dirty work."

ELEVEN

Tropic of Cancer—or, Wild Nights—
Wild Nights!—or, Girls Just Wanna Have Fun—
or, Libertarianism Meets Libertinism

Every night of the week Kayla Blaze stayed with me, starting with the night of that initial encounter at the McDowells'. She didn't always start the night off with me, but she always finished it with me. Some nights, many nights, she went out first, out to some bar or some club or some party at a friend's house—or more likely at the friend of a friend of a friend's house. Kayla Blaze was never at home with good ol' Mom and Pop or never seemed to be. I never returned to her house, but then I never had to. She wasn't there either.

Some nights I went out with her but only when she conned me into it. We returned to Eddie's; we went to a dance club, a place I had heard of that was popular with the kids, called Apollo West, where they played hip-hop music and the rich boys showed up in their rich-boy clothes, and a girl like Kayla never paid for a drink. We visited a neighborhood joint named Joe's Paradise Club, a favorite with her brother Jeff and some of his buddies from the fabrication plant; I even went to one party with her where I was paranoid about running into some student of mine from the college, but the crowd turned out not to be a college crowd and the only person I knew there was Angel. I wanted to be with Kayla, actually enjoyed spending time with her, in my own perverse way, as if she were some object of curiosity, a person from some category I didn't often mix with and enjoyed being peripherally exposed to, though had the exposure become too extensive I probably would quickly have tired of it. I enjoyed being with her and her crowd, in fact, in precisely the same way she enjoyed being with me, though she didn't know it then and wouldn't have admitted it if she had known it. She was infatuated with an image, the image of Dirk Revolver, and if he wasn't a detective with a gun in his pocket he was at least somebody from a category she considered vaguely exotic and certainly remote from her own experience. Our first night together Kayla had confessed to me that she was completely mystified by my colleagues at the college. They were even more foreign and strange to her than her high-school teachers, and those teachers had been foreign and strange enough. I had been foreign and strange to her too and probably would have stayed that way had fate not acted in the person of Rose McDowell to thrust us together. Now I was still foreign and strange to her, she said, but she knew too that I was "normal" down underneath it all. Her goal appeared to be to get me to be more like her by dragging me off to as many clubs and bars and neighborhood dives as I would tolerate.

But she was also trying to change for me. I didn't recognize it at first, obtuse bastard that I am, recluse that I am, who mostly keeps to himself and shuns excessive involvement with the world. I didn't realize that Kayla was trying to domesticate herself, and she was doing it for me. Home had never been the place she was most comfortable, and she spent as much time away from it as possible even when she wasn't working. She had a certain few TV programs that she watched religiously, and that she apparently discussed with her mother as though they were talking about close family members, but beyond that she took little interest in TV or movies. She said they bored her. In fact, the only reason she had started watching *Dirk Revolver* was that I looked like him. She felt some kind of vicarious connection with me through that program—so she said. It was her mother who was the TV addict. Her mother had "no life" in Kayla's words, and so she sat on that same couch we had found her on that Saturday night and did her knitting and became intimately involved with every TV program that happened along. Kayla, meanwhile, was out on the town, had been since she was old enough to use her stunning good looks and a fake ID to get into the clubs.

But that was changing now; Kayla was trying to change it. I was too stupid to figure that out. I knew she abhorred the life her mother lived—was chained to in Kayla's view—and I recognized with my fancy, formally educated mind that Kayla's own life, constantly on the go and apparently chained to nothing or nobody was a conscious (or nearly conscious) response to that abhorrence. It reflected her determination not to become her mother. I knew that. I recognized it. I'm a smart guy, and I can figure these things out. But I did not see how Kayla's hanging around my house was an effort to be more like the woman she thought I would want her to be, the domesticated woman who enjoys her man's company at home even if that woman began to look to her more and more like her own mother. I did not see that until very near the end of our time together.

She even started cooking for me after a week or so, coming up with simple dishes she had learned from her mother. "Can I use your kitchen tonight?" she'd say to me outside the English building on the campus when she was sure, somewhat sure, nobody was listening. And of course I let her.

Cooking was something she was terribly insecure about, but I reassured her, telling her that she seemed perfectly competent at it. "Hell, you're a better cook than I am. I've lived alone a long time, and even then I've never spent much time in the kitchen."

"You're a dude," she said. "Dude's never like t'cook. That's why they get somebody like my mother t'do it for 'em." "Really? I've known men who love to cook."

"Yeah, those fags on TV. That's not the same as making dinner for your man every night. Night after night after night."

She was right; it wasn't the same. Cooking for pleasure, or as an avocation for your own personal satisfaction, is nothing like the obligatory cooking my mother did every day and night just to keep the family fed. Cooking for her was a job. Our family did not have the means to check out the latest fashionable restaurant every evening. My father had his job, and she had hers. And it was not a bad arrangement. Neither of them ever complained much about it, though had they been different people they might have complained. He had the kind of job where you punch a time clock to get paid, and there's no covering it up if you're late, even a minute late. And if you're late too many times you get fired. And if you're too sick to work you work anyway because if you don't work you don't get paid. Often, hearing certain of my colleagues at the college complain about our working conditions, I had been so repulsed that I couldn't go on listening and had to remove myself from the setting for fear I wouldn't be able to contain my anger.

"You've always got your nose in a book; that's your excuse," Kayla said. "You don't even watch TV hardly. Just sports sometimes. You hardly ever go out. You're the strangest dude I ever hooked up with."

Later that night we would have sex. In fact, *every* night we had sex—or at least most nights—vigorous, sometimes adventurous sex, the most invigorating sex I'd had in my life with the most continually willing, continually enthusiastic, continually ready partner of my life. Kayla behaved as though sex were simply a matter of course; it was just what couples do at night. They don't talk about it; they don't argue about it. One of them does not spend time trying to coerce the other into having it. They simply engage in it as if they were cleaning up the dinner dishes or putting the kids to bed.

Even on the not-infrequent nights when she went out on her own, with friends perhaps but without me, having reluctantly accepted the excuse that I had work to do to prepare for the following day's classes or that I had some papers to grade, she would show up at my house sooner or later, and I'd get laid. Often, in fact, those nights yielded the best sex of our relationship because some circumstance had put Kayla particularly in the mood. One night, for example, she did not show up until nearly two in the morning. It was the one night I can remember when I started to question whether she was going to show up at all and even whether she might have lost interest in me altogether. Kayla was a strange experience for me; perhaps the thrill for her had gone as quickly as it had come. I had already fallen asleep, with that thought on my mind, when I heard her let herself into the house with the key I had given her, creep back to my bedroom, and wordlessly undress. With the homeowner's ear out for prowlers, I had let myself remain only semi-conscious as soon as I realized the intruder was Kayla, and my eyes were not even open when she crawled into bed. But the next thing I knew she was on her knees above me, taking me into her mouth. I had some work to do. It turned out she had visited some all-male revue with Angel and was feeling particularly randy.

Most nights, though, especially as her "domestic phase" began and then started to become more prevalent, she would simply show up some time after dinner or have dinner with me and then lounge around the house waiting for me to finish whatever I was working on and then have sex with her. She waited patiently for the most part, though there were nights when she goaded me with querulous needling like a spoiled child (the spoiled child that she was, I suppose). More often, she used a subtler and far more persuasive method of getting what she wanted. She would simply tantalize me into having sex with her. One of her favorite methods was to make herself comfortable for TV watching by taking off her own clothes and putting on one of my dress shirts (we both had a particular favorite) and nothing else. Then she would lie, usually flat on her belly, either on my bed or on one of the couches (depending on what room I was in) with her long legs stretched out behind her, her rump minimally covered by the hem of the shirt. When she had decided the time was right, she'd start making some kind of innocuous movement—bending her legs at the knees, for example, so that the toes on both feet could play with each other and at the same time ever-so-slightly arching her back and perhaps rhythmically letting her rump rise and fall, not provocatively, or at least not overtly provocatively, but as if she were doing it unconsciously, to the beat of some song in her head. I knew better. But the strategy always had its desired effect. Another technique she used was the infamous "bubble bath." She'd profess boredom while I was doing whatever it was I was doing and ask me if she could take a bubble bath. Of course she'd leave the bathroom door open, and after a while, if I hadn't already happened by and been tempted into the bathroom by my own rampant lust, she'd call me in and ask me to wash her back or massage her shoulders. This method, though less subtle than the "shirt" method, was equally effective. But her least subtle tactic of all, naturally as foolproof as either of the others (or any other method she devised), was the "lotion" technique in which she'd complain of an aching back, whine that I was selfish if I didn't immediately attend to it, promise that she would only need me for about fifteen minutes, and then, when of course I consented, strip down to her thong underwear and lie down on my bed for her treatment. What began as a genuine therapeutic massage naturally ended in a different form of therapy, and the procedure always lasted longer than fifteen minutes.

Often, at first, I wondered what Kayla's parents must think about her spending nights at my house. Her father I hadn't met, but her mother had struck me as the kind of mom who would take some interest in her daughter's well-being even if she didn't try to control her behavior. Surely, in the little time that Kayla did spend at home, her mother had to be warning her about getting involved with a man so much older than she was or at least asking her prying questions about what she was up to. She could not possibly sit casually by while her youngest child and only daughter conducted a torrid affair with a man more than twice her age. Could she?

Kayla said she could. "I'm an adult," she told me. "I'm not jailbait. I'm legal age. Arntcha glad about that?"

"Don't get upset. The question wasn't supposed to offend you."

"Well it does offend me. You'd get offended too if somebody treated you like a child when you were an adult. Don't tell me you wouldn't."

Part of me was tempted to challenge her definition of "adult" even at that stage of our relationship when I was accepting it myself, tacitly at least. But apparently I wasn't ready for that yet because I refrained from it. "Don't get upset," I repeated. "I'm not saying you're not an adult. I'm just saying I'm concerned about what your parents think about me even if you're not."

"You're afraid my old man'll show up here with a shotgun some night?"

"That wasn't exactly what I was thinking, no."

"You're Dirk Revolver," she said. "You can take care o' yourself."

"I'm sorry I ever brought it up."

"Look," she said. "My parents don't care. They love me an' all; I know that. But they recognize that I'm a full-grown adult with rights of my own. I don't even live in their house exactly. Jeff's been out on his own since he finished high school; now I'm getting out on my own.

They know that. They expect it. They don't shove their nose in my business."

"Awright," I conceded. "Awright." I was not entirely sure I believed her or at least not sure I believed her entirely. But she had given me no reason not to take her at her word. In fact, she never would.

TWELVE

Another View of Kayla

For my part, I had begun to be pressured by a strange and unhealthy fantasy, a nascent fantasy that I would be able to vanquish from my thoughts before it grew to take on any sort of concrete shape or substance and before its hold grew too strong on my imagination. Briefly, though, it had a place in my mind, asserting its influence almost exclusively when I was alone at home with Kayla watching her paint her toenails, for instance, or put on her makeup of a morning or even just idly lounge on the bed, her legs gracefully crossed at the ankles. I found myself entertaining strange notions about the possibility of a future with Kayla Blaze. And it was not simply that I submitted to the warped, misguided expectation that she would remain young and lustful—or even just lustful—and fill my nights forever with exhilarating sex. I was never quite that deluded by my own romantic attachment to Kayla. Mine was a practical delusion if still a delusion. I understood, for example, that I wouldn't even *want* her to fill my nights forever with exhilarating sex, that I would get bored with it even if not with her (and probably I would get bored with both); that I was bored with the sex already, sometimes, or if not bored with it then simply not interested in it. There were nights when I didn't really want to be tempted by the magnificent charms of the endlessly alluring Kayla Blaze, that incredible male erotic fantasy realized in the flesh. Or at least I told myself I didn't want to be tempted. There'd be a particular book I was reading, for instance, and maybe I'd committed myself to finish two more chapters, but if I finished them it would be late and Kayla would still want sex and I would give in, and then I'd be dead tired in the morning. So the book would fall by the wayside at least for the time being. I could simply refuse to have sex with her, but then she'd work her subtle magic on me and I'd give in—which meant I really *did* want to have sex with her; I was only lying to myself that I didn't.

Like everybody else, I played mind games with myself. I analyzed one possible motive and then tried to look at a string of causes and effects leading up to the motive—like a Darwinian cesspool where the conditions are suddenly right to create life. Voila! The motive makes sense. I looked at other motives the same way. But I didn't just stop there. I picked and chose among the motives that not only made the most sense to me but also made me feel the best—or perhaps the least vile—about myself. Very human.

Ultimately, it didn't matter a damn whether I was lying to myself about not wanting sex with her every time she offered it. She might not always want it herself. Maybe she'd get old and plain like her mother and neither of us would want it. Or maybe she'd just get tired of it herself, the youthful fascination would wear off, the "kid with a new toy syndrome," and she'd be bored with it and I'd be bored with it and she'd either just stop showing up at my house, if the day of mutual boredom came not too far down the road, or, if that day didn't come for a while, we'd end up stuck together, perhaps even married, and then she'd retire to her own diversion—knitting, perhaps—and I'd retire to mine, and we'd exist in mutual isolation from each other the way Kayla's parents existed, at least if their daughter was to be believed.

No, it was not the absurd belief that Kayla would remain endlessly appealing and endlessly available to me that caught and briefly held my mind's eye. It was a stranger fantasy than that, the strange fantasy that she might after all make a suitable life partner for me. It was not so incredible to believe that I might actually crave a life partner. I was lonely; I recognized that. Kayla had brought me another kind of stimulation than the merely sexual. I wasn't even sure *she* had intended that—I didn't know yet anyway—but she had brought it with her whether she meant to or not. I was getting older, and it was not impossible to believe that I might choose, finally, to "settle down," to find myself a long-term companion in the tradition of those long-dead Victorian gentlemen who are so unpopular with the PC crowd. Having established myself in a career I was now prepared to establish myself in a marriage. I was a man of suitable social position and acceptable means—

Hell, that wasn't it. Not exactly anyway. Like all human desires, this one was far too complicated to be explained away by simply attributing it to some social convention, despite the intelligentsia's obsession these days with offering such trite explanations. The real truth, or at least the more real truth, was that I had never wanted the complications and attachments of a long-term relationship, at least not a marriage, and so I had lived my vagabond's life and been happy with it, or at least content, or maybe just restless not *knowing* what the hell I was looking for. I was not some Victorian gentleman building something substantial that I could share with a partner; I was a child of the sixties (in spirit if not quite in body) muddling along in search of "satisfaction," "fulfillment," "self-realization"— whatever you want to call it—and not having a clue where to find it. I was one of those idiots—there are scads of them in academia— who believe that whatever is can't possibly be enough, that there must always be something else, something better. But I could not discover what it was that was better, and then, I don't remember precisely when, I realized that there really *was* nothing better, there was only something different; and that, I believe, was the instant, the precise moment in time (I'm being melodramatic) when I acknowledged that my loneliness was real and acute and not some self-absorbed pedant's notion of a "social construction." It occurred to me in conjunction with this revelation, this sad epiphany, that having a life partner might actually be desirable after all—for me personally, I mean—and not just some archaic social contrivance (contrived for whatever reason—I won't get into that). Hell, maybe I needed somebody after all—or if I didn't *need* somebody, maybe it would be nice to *have* somebody at least. And it was not long after I began mulling over my loneliness, accepting the reality that I was not happy—that I was in fact quite unhappy—that Kayla blazed into my life.

So it was not so incredible that I would consider the possibility of marriage even after years of calling it out of the question, of developing the studied habit of living like a bachelor and believing it was the only life for me. What was incredible was that I would consider marriage with Kayla Blaze, that I would regard her, the child in a woman's body, as a potential candidate for the life-partner position. Kayla, who appeared to be bragging when she claimed she'd never read a book in her life. Who seemed to feel that nothing in life was more important than finding out where the party was and whether a fake ID would pass muster to get an underage person admitted. Who was infatuated with me because I reminded her of a goddamn TV detective. And yet I did begin to fantasize about her that way, at least in those dim, unguarded moments when I was willing to let sentimental sap take precedence over rational thought.

And was it really so unreasonable when you look at it closely? After all, Kayla had symbolized more to me than just a piece of ass right from the beginning. She was smart; I had recognized that before I ever laid a hand on her—or inserted any other part of my anatomy in her. And she had a cynical, mistrustful nature that appealed to me precisely because it so closely reflected my own. Moreover, she was not daunted or beguiled by the veneer of respectability and decency a Ph.D. can apply even to the worst degenerate. She understood formal education for what it is, a process, a rite of passage but by no means a measure of moral progress. The stuffy pricks at the college didn't have her fooled, for all their highfalutin blather, and she was not too intimidated by the adult world to let them know it. I loved Kayla's ass, all right, but I also loved her sass, even if it came across so much of the time as nothing more than adolescent petulance, a sort of brash, unfocused, and immature flailing at the world's indignities. But we could work on that. She was only eighteen, wasn't she? The aging process works many wonders on behavioral defects. It can with a little luck—and perhaps the right guidance—turn a spoiled child into a mature and responsible adult.

I was afflicted with a mild case of what I have for years called Aylmer's Disease, after the character in the Hawthorne short story that so splendidly shows it for what it is. It should not come as a surprise given my prior adolescent yearnings to "change the world" and "make it a better place." Symptoms of the disease are common in teenagers and even very young adults, and they're charming and even desirable in that demographic up to a point. In ostensibly mature and responsible adults, they're downright ugly and occasionally dangerous even resulting sometimes in a fatal conceit. In these advanced cases—again enormously common in the halls of academia—the disease manifests itself as a condescending view of others, including a jaundiced and patronizing view of their rites, entertainments, dreams, and principles; an absolute certainty in the correctness of the afflicted's own worldview; and, in the worst cases, an unwavering belief in the afflicted's own absolute right to impose his or her worldview on others no matter what the costs. In my younger days, my more ebullient days, I even exhibited signs of that last, perilous symptom. Thankfully, though, the maturation process had all but eradicated the disease, vanquished it from my system. *All but* eradicated it, I said. Apparently the process was not complete for here it was, haunting me again in the contemplation of a lifetime with the irrepressible but also woefully juvenile Kayla Blaze.

Still, it didn't amount to much as long as it remained my own private fantasy, occupying its own remote corner of my consciousness and staying there where it belonged. But I've never been one to leave well enough alone, and unfortunately, a scant six weeks or so after Kayla and I first collided, sending minute but brilliant sparks into the night air, I was tempted by a poignant moment to initiate the conversation that was better left imagined, scripted in fantasy and kept there, inviolate. We were having a cocktail before dinner, a fairly late dinner, sitting outside on my patio absorbing the quiet of the evening and looking up into the darkening sky. "I love the night sky," Kayla said dreamily. "It makes me feel peaceful."

"Me too." Contemplative moments were rare for Kayla—no, let me put it less smugly, lest I sound too much like the academic I used to be—it was rare for Kayla to reveal her contemplations to me, and I was intrigued.

"Back in Indiana you could sit out in our back yard and look up through the trees and see the stars out over the lake. That's what my dad said anyway. He said those stars were out over Lake Michigan and you could see 'em so bright because it was dark on the lake."

"Was your house right on the lake?"

"Hell no. Ten miles. Lake Michigan's huge, Professor."

"I stand corrected and enlightened."

"You sit corrected and enlightened."

"You're right. I am sitting. Want another drink?"

She shook her head, her eyes still wistful. "God, I loved it back there," she said. "When my dad said we were moving out here, I cried."

And here it was that I was seized by the regrettable impulse. "When you look into the future, whadayou see?"

"Nobody can look into the future, Professor. All that shit is fake. That crystal-ball shit. Sorry to bust your balloon. You should get your money back."

I said nothing—content, perhaps, to let her sarcasm end the conversation and maybe even the fantasy with it—but she could not suppress her own compulsion to reflect. "I don't know what I see," she said. "I'm eighteen. I don't know what to see. I don't even know what I'm looking for.

"I see kids, I guess," she continued after a very long pause. "I can tell you that much. I definitely want to have children."

"Well, that's natural, I guess. I think everybody wants kids, down deep."

"Even you?"

"Probably even me. I'll get to be seventy and look back and say, 'Shit, I shoulda had kids.'"

"You could adopt."

"I wouldn't. If I'm going to have the little bastards, I want them to be mine." I looked at her. "Selfish, I guess."

She shrugged. "Isn't everybody? Adoption is never anybody's first choice. At least nobody normal. Just frigid bitches and dike movie stars."

I laughed. "Should we check on our fabulous steaks?"

"You can check. I'm too comfortable."

I went and checked and came back and sat down. "Give 'em five more minutes. Maybe a little less. I got 'em cookin' real low."

"They sure smell good."

"I should check on those potatoes."

"They'll be fine, Professor. Relax."

I sat back and sipped my drink and looked up at the stars again. "What about a career?" I said.

"What about it? I thought you awready had one."

"I meant for you."

"Ah. For me. A career for me."

"You said you liked math in school."

"No, I hated math. I just hated it less than everything else I had to take."

"I see. So a career as an astronomer is out of the question?"

"Maybe not. I love the stars."

"Yeah, but astronomers need to know a lotta math."

"I never understood that. Why do ya need math to look through a goddamn telescope?"

"They do more than just look through a telescope. It's math that helps them figure out the stars, for example: how they move, how far away they are, how big they are—"

"For Christ's sake, Professor, I know. I know all this. I ain't gonna be no damn astronomer. Jus' drop it awready."

I dropped it awready.

"How come you're so goddamn interested in my future anyway?" Kayla asked me testily. "What's it t'you?"

The steaks weren't even ready to come off the grill, and already she had me backed into a corner. I didn't have the spine to come clean with her, so naturally I hemmed and hawed. "I'm—just—wondering," I stammered. "Can't I do that?"

"Sure. Now let *me* wonder. What's in *your* future? Huh? Kids? A wife maybe? You gonna change jobs? You always bitch about the one you got. How you don't feel like it's 'meaningful' or whatever—whatever the hell that's supposed to mean."

"Let's just drop the subject. Forget I brought it up. Dinner's damn near ready anyway."

Fifteen minutes later, though, when we were enjoying our own version of the romantic candlelit dinner, a convention Kayla claimed to abhor, condemning it as "sappy" yet participating in it with what appeared to be both enthusiasm and pleasure, I brought the disdainful subject up again though only after Kayla had done some subtle maneuvering to bring me around to it. "I just thought you could do well in school," I told her. "That's all. I thought maybe you had some career plans. You work at the college. You can take classes for free."

"Whoop-tee-doo. Maybe I can do well in school. But I'll hate every minute of it. You're tellin' me I should suffer through four years o' that crap when I don't even know what I wanna do with it?"

"I'm telling you no such thing. I said to forget I brought it up."

"Christ, you always bitch about that place an' those people, an' here you want me to go get a degree. Make up your goddamn mind."

"It's got nothing to do with that place or those people. That's just a stopping place and faces you see along the way. A means to an end."

"Well it's not a means to my end."

"I can see that. I said to forget I brought it up."

She appeared unwilling to do that though. After a minute or so of uncomfortable silence, during which I watched her grind relentlessly away at the same bite of steak, utensils in hands (one in each), and during which I also noted that her eyes were filling with tears, she appeared to be overcome by the contemplation of our discussion, swallowed hard and with some apparent difficulty, then chucked her utensils down on her plate, plucked her cloth napkin from her lap and flung it there on top of them, and stood up abruptly. "I can't eat this stuff. I don't eat like this. I live on fast food."

Then she turned on heel and huffed away from the table and out of my house, and all I could think of as I watched her go was how goddamn good she looked in that dress and those heels that she had worn to work that day.

Later that night, though, I was in bed reading and she came in without a word, slipped off the heels and out of the dress, and climbed in bed with me.

THIRTEEN

A Strange Turn of Events—or, Enemy of the State?

In the final week of that semester something happened that prompted an abrupt and necessary change in my life. In some ways, too, it may have decided the matter with Kayla Blaze once and for all. I still have not figured out whether it decided the matter for better or for worse. I suppose—no, I know—that in the end it doesn't really matter.

In the fairly brief interim between my unbidden visit from Gillian Greenback and the grand revelation that changed my life, the attitude toward me around my department seemed to undergo the slightest shift as if my colleagues were keeping a secret from me. That sounds like paranoia, I know, and maybe in part it was, but it was also something more than that. Actually, it's fairly simple to analyze and comprehend. I had pulled a fast one on everybody, in a manner of speaking, and it had caused the whole lot of them to revise their overall assessment of me. In some cases, perhaps, but not many, the reassessment was favorable, in a sort of perverse, green-eyed way. What I was doing, the sin I was committing, was one that others wanted to commit but were not being permitted to commit. Kayla had denied them if they'd even had the temerity to approach her. In most cases, though, the reassessment of my conduct and my character implied disapproval or even condemnation. Gillian's view almost certainly represented the view of the majority, an austere moralistic condescension that bordered on the puritanical.

I was violating a sacred trust of sorts, the PC version of a sacred trust. All that lacked was a panel of stern Puritan judges to render a binding official judgment against me.

The change in attitude showed not in the things that were said but in the things that were unsaid, the sharp looks that were sent my way despite the smiles that still accompanied them, austere, puritanical smiles, pinched smiles, the kind of smile you show somebody you don't really feel like smiling at but feel compelled by circumstances or decorum to smile at anyway—like the cop who smiles pleasantly in through your open car window prefatory to asking, "Do you know why I pulled you over this evening?" Those were the smiles I was seeing now. For years I'd had a penchant and a reputation for keeping to myself, but every now and again I'd emerge from my office—at the quiet end of a long hall, the end farthest from the chair's office, the front desk, and the secretaries' cubicles—to join in the kind of water-cooler banter that people in offices engage in. I was happy to chatter away about how many papers I had to grade or how my students seemed to have lost all energy and were slogging listlessly through the semester or, when the conversation got personal, how I liked a certain restaurant or didn't mind cleaning toilets (that's right, the conversation actually took place, probably in response to the charge that as a man I would regard myself as above such tasks) or how my brother in Ohio was a water engineer who said he'd never move to our part of the country because of the nightmarish water situation. There were of course a thousand other banalities that left my mouth and crossed paths with the banalities that were received by my ears. If the conversation turned remotely serious, though—say, political or religious—I quickly returned to the privacy and insularity of my office. I had nurtured a reputation for being personable, charming, and absolutely innocuous. At least that was the reputation I believed I had made for myself. People found me sufficiently agreeable that they would not look at me as a potential adversary—I was just too doggone easygoing and perhaps too doggone apathetic—and at the same time they wouldn't pick me to hide behind in some noxious internal struggle in our department. They would write me off as a "decent guy" and look for stronger, more assertive allies. I was, essentially, a nonentity in the department, a nobody. And that was *perfect* as far as I was concerned. It advanced my plan to retire from the college in complete anonymity. I was well on my way to achieving that end—if, that is, I simply stayed in the job, biding my time like a good public servant until retirement.

Given my relative invisibility within the department, my affable, innocuous presence and my ready sense of humor, I'd always been a candidate for mundane, typically jocular conversation with virtually any of my full-time colleagues, any of the visiting staff (whether or not I knew them or they knew me), or any of the office staff, including the student workers. Like the grinning, poorly dressed uncle you only see at family get-togethers, about whom you know so little and perhaps don't care to know anything more, I could be counted on for a few minutes of genial conversation about absolutely nothing of significance just about any time you happened to be stuck with me and didn't know what else to do besides pretend you were actually interested in my existence. It didn't matter if you were a lesbian gender-feminist with a socialist agenda or merely a statist anti-bourgeois "liberal" (I think we only had one person in our department further to the Right than that, and he was hardly ever around for water-cooler conversations), I could give you a few minutes of decent, innocuous, and generally light-hearted chatter on any subject of no import. When the discussion turned to more pressing and more revealing topics, though—say, Bush's invasion of Iraq (the bane of our nation) or Hillary's potential candidacy for the presidency (the salvation of our nation), I scampered back down the hall and took my opinions with me. Through such maneuvering I was able to draw and keep about me a shroud of semi-privacy and semi-secrecy. Nobody knew who I was—not really—and I liked it that way.

In our department we had one token conservative, Jared Willow, a cleancut young man, early thirties with a recently conferred doctorate (his focus was on fiction of the American West, if I remember right), a wife, a small child, and another child on the way. And we had one mere wretch, Raj Patel, long ago transplanted from India to the States, wizened and withered and overdue for retirement but refusing to retire both because he had nothing else in his life and because he was an old skinflint who lacked faith that the millions he had accumulated by pinching pennies and investing them wisely would see him comfortably through what remained of his life. I joked that he would die in the classroom but that none of his students would notice. It would have been politically correct to accept and respect Raj because he was from the Far East, and the rules of political correctness dictate that people from the Far East are to be not merely accepted but respected since they represent a non-Western (and therefore superior) culture. Unfortunately, he presented a difficult case because he was so hopelessly politically incorrect himself. He had a penchant for offense, especially for public offense, and I remember department meetings in which he blatantly but offhandedly offended women, the Irish, and Mexican-Americans, among others, with comments that would at one time not have been broadly regarded as offensive because they reflected what Ellison alluded to as the realities that gave rise to the stereotypes, but that in a PC culture were sufficient to mortify their auditors almost as much as a personal insult or slap in the face. Perhaps the faint of heart even left those meetings nauseous, on the point of physical illness, as when the Harvard president induced illness by merely remarking that biological differences between men and women might prompt fewer women than men to enter the hard sciences. Such was Raj's power to offend, and yet he should have been on the politically acceptable list because he was not a Western male. Therefore, he was in a position much like that of the black woman who for religious reasons opposes gay marriage. What was worse, he was a classical liberal whose views on concrete issues were often politically correct (he hated both Bushes, for example). In other words, he should have been all right—but he wasn't. And so, according to the rules of PC in higher education, he was one of those troubling anomalies like the black property owner in the Flannery O'Connor short story who proves so difficult for the story's protagonist to fit into her hierarchy of Christians lining up at the pearly gates—he should be among the last to enter heaven because of his race but among the first because of his respectable status as a property holder. What's a good Christian—or in this case, a good PC advocate—to do? Raj's junior colleagues (for we were all junior to him) had no choice but to write him off as an eccentric and an anachronism. Had he been born in more recent and "enlightened" times, he would surely have held more acceptable viewpoints. At least one had to believe that—it would give one hope.

Jared was the department conservative who kept an extremely low profile and was besides a softspoken, inoffensive sort in person and therefore difficult to hate. Raj was the department relic, the old eccentric who could not be taken seriously. Others in the department had their niches, and others still, like me, simply stayed out of sight as much as possible and kept our opinions to ourselves. I was not uncomfortable leading this existence, and I certainly preferred it to taking my colleagues seriously and to being taken seriously myself. What would happen that spring would jar me back to the realization that certain politically incorrect opinions even of my own could not afford to be suppressed, that certain opinions are indeed worthy of personal and professional sacrifice, even of fighting for. I am reminded of yet another literary appurtenance, a character in a certain Camus short story who tries to hide from the malevolent world only to have it seek him out. You can run as they say, but that don't mean you can hide.

In the meantime, though, I had already cast myself in a new and unfavorable light as the pedophile who was holding the child Kayla Blaze hostage and molesting her every night. Nobody *said* anything, but they knew, and I knew they knew.

I knew what most of them thought as well behind those pinched smiles. People who are jealous or resentful are jealous or resentful for a reason—because they are passing judgment—and most of my colleagues had revised their kindly previous assessment of me. Maybe I was not so innocuous after all. It may even have crossed their minds that I was not entirely PC, for all my apparent harmlessness and decency. And that would indeed be an eyebrow-raising violation of local protocol. It was like suspecting an orthodox Jew of not keeping kosher. What kind of trafe was I trifling with?

Kayla, sharpy that she was, also knew what they knew about us, and she took shrewish pleasure in it. "You shoulda seen that bastard Ciccio look at me today," she said one night. We were in bed, and she was sitting up watching TV. "He's a jealous sonofabitch," she said. "He wants what you got."

"Maybe."

"I know that look. He's thinkin', 'When do I get my turn?' The sonofabitch."

"They know, don't they?"

"Of course they know. Everybody who was at Ronald's party knows. Ellen knows."

"Did you tell her?"

"I didn't have to tell her." It was clear she resented my obvious suspicion that she couldn't keep her mouth shut, that she just had to make the affair known to the people at work. Her shunting me off to bed and then managing to get me back there, repeatedly, was a form of conquest, of mastery. It showed that all of them—all of us—with our fancy education and smug attitudes were not superior after all. When the clothes came off we were no better than she, the humble secretary, and we could take all our pretense and shove it up our collective ass. In fact, maybe this minute triumph of hers was all the more delicious since it was I, the innocuous Marty Frey, not much help in reshaping the world but not bad to look at, whom she had taken down this time around, knocked off his fancy pedestal and compelled to take his rightful place among the ordinary vermin. Marty Frey the nobody was a regular animal after all. *Naturally* Kayla would want her power publicly if tacitly acknowledged. "She was at the party," she said sullenly.

"Awright," I told her. "I'm not accusing you."

"The hell you weren't."

And she was right, of course.

I had not said anything to her about my little conversation with Gillian Greenback and didn't plan to. I did not want to risk a disruption of the excitement that working in close proximity to my lover now brought me. For me there was a certain thrill in every chance meeting with Kayla at the college now. Bumping into her before—as she returned to the department from the records office or the copy shop, for example, or as I was rushing out of the workroom with photocopies for a class as she was strolling into the workroom to make copies— bumping into her before had brought a moment of intense discomfort, an unsettling tension in the pit of my stomach, knowing as I did that

I wanted her but being nervous about even engaging her in mundane conversation, worrying as I did that a wrong word from me might provoke her to chew me up and spit me out the way I had seen her do with others. But now every meeting brought joy, an electric shock of delight more intense, and certainly more pleasing, than the nervous tension I had felt before. I could barely contain myself, sometimes, could barely keep my hands off her.

In fact, sometimes I *didn't* keep my hands off her though I would have kept them off her had discretion proved the better part of valor—or rather, had I been disciplined enough not to let my erotic impulses rule me. I had been blasé about my job before, tired of it, bored with it, and feeling unfulfilled in performing it no matter how much I enjoyed my students (and I did do that). But now every workday brought the virtually guaranteed prospect of seeing Kayla, of seeing her officially in precisely the way I had seen her before for nearly an entire academic year but of knowing that I would see her again when the day was over, and when I saw her then there would be nothing officious or stuffy or formal about our seeing each other; we would enjoy an intimacy I (and presumably she) had with nobody else on the campus. This satisfaction alone brought a new sense of fulfillment to my professional life—or, to be accurate, it returned excitement and anticipation to my formerly listless days. And then Kayla brought an even greater excitement to the routine of showing up for work every day. She came and saw me in my office on her lunch break, and we had sex there, quiet, thrilling, daring sex. Less than a week later we pushed the outside of the envelope even further. We had sex on the lecturer's desk at the front of one of our building's auditorium classes, and we did it only fifteen minutes before Jim DeCrisco was to use the room for a literature and film class. I'd had the room during the previous period, and as soon as my last student was out the door at the end of the class Kayla hastened in, locked the door, pulled up the skirt she was wearing and flung herself forward over the desk. I couldn't resist. The mere impulse to flout the college's image, its reputation, its sense of dignity and propriety and respectability, its sense of mission and self-importance, its goddamn environment of political correctness—that mere impulse was as strong as or stronger than any hormonal urge to get my rocks off. DeCrisco had a key; knowing that made the experience all the more exciting. Let him walk in on us, the bastard. What would he say? In fact, he did walk in but only as Kayla was walking out.

He knew, though, as they all knew, all of them who were interested in knowing, who paid attention to department gossip. They knew, and most of them looked at me disapprovingly. They would still let me be one of the department shut-ins. They simply seemed, all of a sudden, to avoid me. Water-cooler conversations still occurred when I initiated them, but my colleagues cut them short now. In the past, I had been the one to excuse myself politely and wander off. Now they were the ones to avert their eyes and leave, sometimes smiling, sometimes offering me a curt, accusatory glance of reprobation—and sometimes doing both. Nobody but Gillian had the inclination or the guts to broach the subject with me—or else nobody but Gillian was put up to it by our department chair. But I could guess what their eyes were saying. What you're doing isn't right, and it isn't proper, they warned me. Nor is it politically correct. It can't end well. Surely you, the innocuous, unimposing wallflower Martin Frey, casual and unthreatening and affable, the department Luddite who never involves himself in the meaningless but fierce battles for dominance within our department, who seems not merely to tolerate but to like everybody he works with (regardless of race, creed, sex, or national origin)—surely you must realize that you are putting your professional neck at risk for a piece of ass. And they might be right about that, I believed, despite what I had told Gillian Greenback. If they couldn't come after me for fucking a department secretary, they could surely find other excuses to come after me. All they needed was the right opportunity and the motive. But I didn't care. A small but not insignificant chunk of my consciousness, I realized, did not really care if the affair with Kayla Blaze cost me my job, directly or otherwise.

FOURTEEN

The Affair Goes South—Approximately

Kayla turned on me a few weeks before the end of the semester. More precisely, she turned on me immediately after our little tiff over her plans, or lack of them, for her future.

Actually, I'm overstating the change that took place. The affair did not end immediately after Kayla and I had our little discussion and she walked out on me in tears. It just took on a different and unpleasant cast at that point. Whereas before there had seemed to be no mystery about what the two of us were doing together—as I told Gillian Greenback it was called "fucking"—the uncomfortable conversation about the future seemed to add a new and not-entirely-welcome dimension to our love affair. It is a bridge I have crossed with other women in the past, a bridge we all come upon sooner or later in our romantic relationships—gay or straight, old or young, male or female. At least so I've heard. Some have suggested that it's s symptom of the sickness that plagues fat, indolent America in the age of narcissism, and maybe they're right. Mythologies have been created about the phenomenon in American popular culture and perhaps in other cultures as well. I've heard about the Three-Month Rule, the Four-Month Rule—various "rules" that are applied to relationships by various analysts, all of the analysts basing their analyses on their own experience of the world (and the experiences of their friends, school acquaintances, and often certain loudmouth drunks they've met in bars), all of the "rules" involving arbitrary but fixed time frames (i.e. "three months" as opposed to "a hundred days"), and all of the talk indicating a perfectly understandable, perfectly human anxiety about the level of commitment one ought to make to a particular relationship. It's an imprecise science just like sociology (well, maybe not *that* imprecise), and it goes to show how much freedom we in the modern industrial world enjoy when we can indulge the luxury of such angst. I doubt that people in ancient tribal societies could afford to trifle with their mating habits quite as much as we do. But I could be wrong.

Kayla and I arrived at the uncomfortable where-do-we-go-from-here? juncture right around the month-and-a-half mark. Once we were there I regretted our having gotten there so soon, but Thomas Wolfe was right even if he was a tad verbose in expressing it, you really can't go home again. We tried, but it just wouldn't work. It's like inadvertently opening that surprise birthday present from your mother. You can try to pretend you didn't see what it was—you can try to unremember—but it's a hopeless pretense.

And so began the period of being uptight and cranky with each other. I had lobbed the first round when I proposed that Kayla attend college and become an educated woman—for all my disparaging of "educated" people precisely as she pointed out. Her return fire came mostly in the form of accusations that I was some kind of social oddity because I didn't find her favored forms of diversion amusing or at least not half as amusing as she found them. I'd rather read than enjoy the entertainment and the company at Eddie's. I'd rather sit and contemplate the peace and quiet of a spring evening by my pool than grind to the thump-thumping beats at the club. I'd rather get a full night's sleep of a weeknight than go out and "have fun" and pay for it the next morning. I'd rather spend time *alone,* in many instances, than spend it either surrounded by the din of voices and music—or even the comforting strains of some TV program. Why, I did not even take her up on the offer of a threesome with Angel (though I did think about it), a sure and certain indication in Kayla's view that I was not only a social misfit but an unmanly one at that. It became plain to me that I was the strangest case Kayla Blaze had ever encountered and that she eyed me with the same kind of prurient curiosity that motivated me to wonder about her. Who the hell is this guy? she was thinking. And all the time I thought I was the only one who didn't understand our relationship!

At first, though, she had been indulgent. The strange world of the academic mystified her, for all her obvious disdain. She resented us, and at the same time we intrigued her. Why would anybody want to spend his or her life *studying*? It had been painful enough being put through ten mandatory years of school and two more that she had submitted to only because she didn't want to be a Total Loser herself. Why the hell would anybody voluntarily invest time in reading, contemplating, and writing about things that were so remote from and irrelevant to common human experience? We were all of us aberrations, even those among us who seemed "almost normal" (that was the expression Kayla used). She did not respect us, and yet she had a certain regard for us, a kind of awe, the kind of awe you might reserve for, say, a priest, a man sworn to a life of celibacy and self-denial and loneliness based on an incomprehensible leap of faith. She could not help but admit a kind of mystified respect for our devotion even if she considered us as people bizarre, almost ridiculous.

"You're all the geeks who loved school," she sneered one night when she caught me reading Aristotle on rhetoric. She had picked up the book while I was bent over my keyboard, and I hadn't noticed that she was even in the room much less that she had seized my book and was looking through it.

There aren't any pictures, I almost sneered back at her. But this was in the first month of our love affair when she was still indulging me and I was still handling her ego with kid gloves, lest she go away and leave me before I was through with her and deprive me of her extraordinary physical gifts. "Believe it or not, I hated school" was what I said. "It seemed like such a ... waste of time—so much of it."

"So now you're a college professor."

"Go figure. My students get a kick out of it too. I tell 'em I have no idea why I do what I do. Except that I enjoy the material—and their company."

"That's the whole reason you took all those years o' school?"

"That and the fact that I didn't know what the hell else to do, I guess."

"You were one o' those 'perpetual students'?"

"No. I had different jobs. I went to school on the side. Later."

"But you never figured out what you wanted to be when you grew up?"

"I guess not."

"Have you figured it out yet?"

"I don't think so."

Before I confronted Kayla about her future, I could take certain liberties with her present. If I didn't want to go out with her, I told her I had work to do. And she bought it even when it wasn't true or was only obliquely true. She would absolve me of blame (it was my job, after all), show me the closest thing she knew to affectionate warmth, cheerily run off for a few hours herself, and of course return to my house to provide me with a happy—no a blissful—ending.

But after that night I sent her away indignant with what I considered innocent questions (well, not entirely innocent questions), she came to regard me with no small measure of suspicion and resentment. She still fucked me, mind you. She still went out alone, came home alone, and slept with me—but she had an attitude about it.

"Hey, look, I'd rather go out with you than spend hours reviewing three Emerson essays. Believe you me."

"Yeah, I'm sure you would."

"I mean it, Kayla. Have you *read* Emerson?"

"I'll be at Eddie's if you change your mind. Your sweetheart Roxie'll be there, I'm sure. She's been askin' about you."

"Give her my regards."

"You could give 'em yourself. Haven't you read this stuff before? Didn't you say you've read it a dozen times awready?"

"At least."

"So why d'ya need to read it again, for Christ's sakes?"

"Have you *read* Emerson, Kayla?"

"'Have you *read* Emerson, Kayla?' 'Have you *read* Emerson, Kayla?'" she mimicked, and did it well, even capturing my inflection almost perfectly. "I've never *read* Emerson," she hooted. "An' I ain't gonna read Emerson. But I will be at Eddie's having myself a good time. In case you wanna study that—find out what that is—get off your ass and leave Emerson and come with me."

But I did not go with her that night, or on many other nights, and our relationship developed an unpleasant edge that told me the end was near. It had been ridiculous of me to contemplate a "future" under such circumstances. This was not *Pygmalion*. Life is not *Pygmalion*. Shaw was a ridiculous socialist with utopian fantasies. He did not inhabit the real world and could not rightfully claim to comprehend it. He did not know Kayla Blaze.

One night she came home drunk and angry and the sex we had was a wrestling match. She fell asleep afterward, then awoke me in the early hours of the morning to go at it again. I was tired, and I was not in a good mood. I was feeling at odds with myself and my life again (still), at odds and purposeless, and the last thing I wanted was a run-in with Kayla, which is what this desperate grappling match amounted to. When it was over, with her half dressed, looking as though she'd been assaulted (but still extraordinarily attractive, naturally—Kayla was a young woman who looked every bit as delicious when she woke up in the morning as when she went to bed the night before), I pulled away from her sullenly. "You know what our problem is? Once we leave this bed we don't have a damn thing in common."

"Is that what our problem is?"

"I think so."

"You 'think'? You don't *know*? You're a real genius, Professor."

"This is hopeless." I got up and went in the bathroom and came back out wrapped in a towel.

"Fuck me again," she said.

I wanted to. "I can't," I said.

"I bet you could. Let me see what I can do."

"No. It isn't that. Cut it out. I'm going for a swim."

"Like that? Naked? Let me come with you."

"No."

"Come on. Let me. I'll be good; I promise."

"Jesus," I said, "this is hopeless." But I wasn't sure what I meant.

"Is it?" she said. She was pouting then.

"Come on," I said, abruptly (not to mention irrationally) eager to make amends. "Come with me."

"Fuck you," she said. "This is hopeless."

I leaned down into her and pressed myself against her, kissing her forcefully on the mouth and working on her clothes with one hand while holding her down with the other. And that was the day I called in sick and canceled three classes, and Kayla called in sick, and I'm sure everybody in the department who was interested figured out where we were and what we were up to.

FIFTEEN

Rebel Without—or, "Rebel from the Waist Downwards"

"I can't figure out why you're angry," I said to Kayla Blaze. "Angry at the world, I mean. At least when you're angry at me I usually know why. But I can't see why you'd be angry at the world. It just doesn't seem like you have much to be angry about."

"I'm not angry. I'm pissed off."

"There's a difference?"

"People like me don't get angry. We get pissed off."

"I see." I did not see, and I didn't really feel compelled to humor her. I just said something to say something.

"I have feelings too."

"I see."

"Cut it out. You're patronizing me."

I see, I almost said. But I caught myself.

We were sitting out back by my pool, and night was fast descending. Virtually all the color had bled from the sky and there was only a pale light hanging up behind the trees as a backdrop. I have a queen palm behind my pool and sometimes when darkness is falling and you look up at it, you see it etched against the sky like a silhouette on a deep blue background. With a little imagination—well, perhaps a lot of imagination—you can turn the back yard into a tropical paradise, an island paradise remote and untroubled and serene. You can make yourself feel, that is, as though you're lounging on some isolated tropical beach. The reason it comes to mind now is that Kayla Blaze had a license-plate holder on the front bumper of her car, her beautiful car, that had a painting of an empty beach, a placid sea abutting it, a starry night sky, and a palm tree silhouetted against it. You had to look closely at the picture in the license-plate holder to make out the details, but they were there, and the tree in that painting looked very much like the one behind my pool—at least the way the one behind my pool looks sometimes of a dusky evening.

We had spent most of the day in successive rounds of an ongoing sexual free for all. Never had I had sex so many times in one day, and not for a very long time had I spent the whole day in such complete disregard for the routines of everyday life. We had eaten only cold fruit from my fridge throughout the day, snacking when we were hungry. The rest of the time we lounged about. I even watched a couple of Kayla's TV programs with her. There was one about kids living a "real life," extremely contrived, a "real life" played out exclusively for the fawning cameras and for the edification of bored children across America. The other one was something about being paid to do the most disgusting things imaginable. Contestants did them for the money—but not really; they did them because a sizable TV audience wanted them to do them, and they didn't want to disappoint that TV audience. The shows reminded me why I didn't (and don't) watch TV. I do not want to lie on my death bed remembering that I once invested half an hour of my life watching people eat live crickets. Kayla, on the other hand, glanced at me frequently to ensure that I was watching, to content herself that I was enjoying whatever "shock value"—or whatever the hell it was I was supposed to enjoy—from the interminable silliness, the interminable reminder of our boredom at the ease and comfort and leisure of modern life.

Neither of us had donned more than the scantiest attire. Kayla had spent most of the day stunningly sporting my dress shirt that she fancied. She had not worn anything else all day, and she had only disrobed to swim or screw me.

I was sore and tired. I did not think I'd want to have sex again for a week (but by the next day I was ready). I had suggested to Kayla that we prepare a feast for dinner and stay in, and she consented to it. For once, I think she was happy not to go out.

And yet it was not contentment that I felt. I felt not sated and happy but vacated, washed out, empty, as if whatever zest for living I normally felt (and I can't say that it was much) were contained in my jism—and right now my jism was at low ebb.

"I'm thirsty," Kayla said. "Get me another beer."

"I'll get you a beer," I said. "But answer my question first."

"What question?"

"What are you pissed off at?"

"Are you still on that?"

"Just curious. Humor me."

She did not seem put off by the question. She just didn't seem to have an answer. "I don't know," she finally shrugged. "All the bullshit."

"Bullshit?"

"You know what I mean. You bitch about it all the time. The bullshit. Those people. Just the bullshit of life. It drives me crazy."

"I'll get you your beer." I went inside the house and got her a beer and when I came out she was swishing her foot around in the pool above one of the steps. I watched the painted toenails trace a consistent pattern in the water. Then her foot broke the pattern and she simply swished it back and forth.

"You know what I think?" I said to her.

"I can hardly wait."

"I think you're bored. In fact, I think your whole generation is bored. Maybe mine too. Maybe everybody is just bored."

"I hate it when you get like this. You don't make any sense." She said nothing else for a long moment, but I didn't talk either and it must have bothered her. Out of the blue she said, "Don't you feel like a bum? You missed class today. Right now they're having classes over there. Thousands of people running off to classes. And you're not there. Marty the professor doesn't do his duty. Marty the bad boy."

"You're bored," I said. "Just like all those yo-yos over there." By "over there" I meant the same thing she did: at the college. Specifically, I meant my colleagues at the college, about whom we were both of us, Kayla and I, always complaining. She complained just as much about them as I did. In fact, she made fun of the whole lot of us, me included. We were geeks, all of us: people who read books and talked about things that were not important as though they mattered a great deal to everybody. We were a fringe group, the lot of us. We occupied our own strange little territory out on the fringe of society where normal people, people like Kayla Blaze, could generally ignore us. She would have ignored us too except that she couldn't because she had to work with us.

"Bored, bored, bored," I repeated. "Life's just too damn easy. You've got nothing better to do than bitch."

She pretended not to have heard me. We were having separate conversations. "Don't you feel guilty?" she said. "Doesn't it make you feel like a bad boy?"

"Nothing to do but bitch," I said numbly. I wasn't even talking to her really. Not anymore. I was talking to myself.

"Okay, Einstein. Whatever you say."

"Yeah. Whatever I say."

I sat down next to her on the edge of the pool and put my foot in to swish it around. I followed the rhythm of her foot with my foot and mimicked her humorless expression.

All of a sudden she stopped, so I stopped. "I'm a rebel," she said. "I always have been. Probl'y always will be."

"Izzat so?"

"It is." She shook her head defiantly as if to reinforce her claim. Tossing her hair back, she looked like some model in a rock video—an eighties rock video.

"So what are you rebelling against?"

"The bullshit," she said smugly. She seemed convinced of it, too. "I'm rebelling against all the bullshit."

SIXTEEN

The Internet Is a Marvelous New Invention That Will Bring Us All Together—or, Roadblock to the New Republic—or, It Takes a Village?

The next morning I was going through my email, catching up on all the exciting news I'd missed in my day's absence. There was of course the spam, the junk mail: hot stock tips; advertisements for penis enlargers, fat burners, drugs for treating "sexual dysfunction"; beachfront property available in Costa Rica; an old classmate of mine who was trying to track me down, and with whom I could quickly be put in contact for a modest fee. There was the guy with the funny name in a Far Eastern country, who wrote in a broken, very non-standard but comprehensible English about the unfortunate relative of mine, whom I hadn't known but who it so happened had been a millionaire in far-off [Fill in the name of the country.], and who had died tragically but in dying had left a fortune to his long-lost [Fill in the family relationship.] The writer of the letter happened to be an attorney who had represented my relative and who was authorized to release my relative's millions to me for a small fee [Fill in the amount, usually something in the low thousands.] I was reminded of the rich brother in *Death of a Salesman* who had walked into the jungle at seventeen and emerged scant years later a wealthy man. I never knew I had been so lucky.

There was the district spam, too, as I called it, the mountains of messages from fellow employees that were so rarely of any real concern to me. It consisted of notices about upcoming events to make us all better "leaders" or better "teachers"; of notices about new online services available to us from our human resources department; of announcements of new legal or personnel policies we needed to be aware of, especially in the new "climate" (a climate of scrutiny and suspicion though we were to pretend that no such climate existed and that we were all instead "pulling together"); of pleas by department chairs for faculty members (visiting faculty, of course—they needed the money) who could teach a section of physics or math or English or whatever the department chair needed; of announcements of upcoming events at the colleges—plays, musical performances, sports events, and the like; of announcements of glorious accomplishments by faculty or students at the various colleges so that we could hear more about the "positive side" of what we did; of announcements from various textbook reps about new products we should try (textbooks and online services in other words); of announcements of new courses we should take (or convince our students, friends, or family members to take) to learn amazing things well worth learning; and, of course, there were the obligatory announcements of upcoming meetings, or simply of tacit support or endorsement, for the gay-and-lesbian rights group, Hispanic Heritage Month, Women's History Month, African-American History Month, or whosever month it happened to be at the time. I don't remember. All the months in celebration of this group or that group tended to bleed into each other after a while. Much of the district spam, probably most of it, came from people who worked in the District Office, a largish office building where not a single student could be found except on rare occasions when they were summoned there for criticism or for praise by the great governing board itself; where button-down corporate types came and went all day looking very important indeed; where the budget was larger than the individual budgets of almost all the colleges (to pay all those button-down types, presumably, and keep them comfortably ensconced in far nicer digs than we at the colleges enjoyed); and where people had to look busy and important, I suppose, to give the impression that they *were* busy and important and to justify their existence on the district payroll.

My delete key found itself furiously busy that morning until it came across a particular notice that interested me. It was a press release. I saw who the sender was and knew that I would read the message rather than immediately delete it—in fact I would file it away for possible future reference—but then after I read the headline on the release itself my blood started to chill, and the more I read the colder it got.

For several years, as long as it had existed, I had been on the listserv of a particular non-profit organization, fittingly based in Philadelphia, that concerned itself (and still does) with violations of the First Amendment rights of students, faculty, and staff at American colleges and universities. It was hardly a secret to me that the PC generation of scholars, who matriculated in the 1960s and wanted to force "tolerance" on us—for our own good or, better said, for "society's" good (so as not to confuse the two, which all too frequently do not coincide, as Freud also astutely pointed out)—the PC scholars had been busy for years constructing appropriate mechanisms for stifling unpopular opinions on their campuses: speech codes to control what students (and employees) could say and about whom they could say it, harassment policies that were so ambiguous they could admit virtually anything as "harassment" if the administration chose to label it such, educational programs designed to make students and employees alike more "sensitive" by ramming certain viewpoints down our throats. It had struck me at first as tenderly, almost humorously ironic that the generation that had once vilified The Man and trumpeted the rights of the individual in our society had now *become* The Man (or—so as not to be sexist because we all know from our reeducation classes that sexism is bad—The Woman) and was doing everything it could to stifle the rights of the individual, a la *1984*, having recognized, I suppose, that sanctioning individual rights is the surest way to despoil any utopia. One cannot have a perfect world unless one has it forced upon him (or her—so as not to be sexist because we all know from our reeducation classes that sexism is bad). Human nature won't permit it. Human beings free to choose will take that option, and they will not all choose the same things. Even those who do choose the same things will not all choose them for the same reasons, and those who choose different things will obviously have reasons of their own. The one constant in all human interaction is that we will choose for ourselves and/or for those we deem it appropriate to benefit.

It had begun, as I said, almost with a sense of bemused irony, a bewildered disbelief that people older than I was and more formally educated could embrace with such zeal ideas so inimical to personal freedom. Didn't those who trumpeted the virtues and insisted on the absolute necessity of "academic freedom" surely recognize the noxious paradox of simultaneously muzzling dissenters? There had to be some joke in all this. But the joke, I found out, was on me and on others of similar beliefs as I discovered that the assault on freedom was being zealously endorsed and supported, out of naïve ignorance or out of bald disdain for their fellow human creatures, by a fair number of those in my profession who seemed caught up in the Zeitgeist of the times, perhaps without regard for the implications of their religious quest. When I began to hear the horror stories of those who challenged the new status quo only to have their academic freedom stifled in the name of "tolerance," of protecting from offense those who howled "harassment" merely at being offended, and of proclaiming a new "freedom" that was not freedom at all except for those who would decide what it permitted and what it precluded, I lost my sense of humor over the whole matter and adopted a reclusive, sharper-edged cynicism. At the same time, I became more vigilant and certainly more cautious.

I had my reasons. I saw young graduate students embrace the ideology of the new academic elite with all the vehemence and veneration of Hitler *Jugend*. I heard from the academic elite vague ruminations about the "limits of free speech," the implication being that freedom should belong only to those properly trained to manage it (and that would include the academic elite themselves, of course). I heard the suggestion made, in all seriousness, that speech should in fact be "filtered" by the elite to make it acceptable to the masses. I read scholars who claimed that personal freedom was not a key determinant of "happiness" and that the common herd might find itself more fulfilled if it had fewer choices about where and how to earn its keep, more taxation, and more choices made for it by the government. I watched and listened as a fresh-faced, bright-eyed young woman, a Ph.D. in geography and a tenured colleague of mine, showed not the least trepidation in proclaiming in support of the college's "sustainability" agenda that the people must sometimes be "forced to adopt the right behaviors," suggesting that *we* were in fact the right element of society to determine which behaviors should and shouldn't be adopted. I heard frequent suggestions, subtle and unsubtle, that "the people" must be taught the proper way of interpreting events both historical and current, must be, as an author once put it, "led to the proper conclusions" whether or not those conclusions were supported by the facts. I heard these things or overheard them, and I was disturbed.

But I was not disturbed enough, obviously, to protest. I sat in my office; I met my students; I ridiculed the politically correct crowd from the safety of sympathetic company, including the company of Kayla Blaze. Sympathetic company was hard to find in that environment, but it was not nonexistent even among my colleagues. But they too kept their mouths shut to preserve the peace and, especially, to protect their own professional hides—with the exception of Raj Patel, whose indiscretions were chalked up to eccentricity and perhaps incipient senility. The closest ol' Marty Frey ever came to a public expression of his disdain for the hubris and sanctimony of the world changers, the social engineers, was perhaps a rare oblique jibe, a sniggering wisecrack that had the rhetorical force of an adolescent's puerile posturing. I risked nothing, or damn little. At most I raised suspicion that I was cynical and not wholly devoted to the cause of "transforming" the world through my students and my highly privileged status as a "molder of minds" from the bully pulpit of the college classroom. I uttered no word and took no action that might jeopardize my comfortable sinecure or even, for that matter, my reputation as the innocuous Marty Frey, quirky, complacent perhaps and even a tad reclusive—but harmless overall. Even the affair with Kayla Blaze, shocking though it surely was to some delicate sensibilities around the department, cried out for castigation but not necessarily condemnation. If I had converted myself into a bad guy all of a sudden, it was only because of poor judgment not because of heretical tendencies. I may need straightening out, I may need the prudent counseling of a sympathetic (if patronizing), wiser, perhaps more "enlightened" colleague—Gillian Greenback—but I did not warrant extermination. Properly managed, I could be redeemed.

And now this thing came, this avatar, not more than a hundred words in length, this demonstration that even here in my own neighborhood the religious zealots of the PC movement were prepared to translate their sanctimony into action. They meant business, and they were fully convinced of their own righteousness. They had exercised their totalitarian impulse, no doubt, without the slightest compunction and with the absolute certainty that their own gods smiled on them for it. My reaction was not entirely unanticipated, not entirely strange to me, as I had felt similarly reflexive responses to news of other minor tyrannies in institutions far and wide across the land. But even I was surprised at the strength of the reaction, the depth to which the chill penetrated me on reading about this new tyranny, this local tyranny, so local that I was willing to bet I was personally acquainted with at least one or two of its perpetrators. More than anything else, though, I was surprised at the sudden sense of certainty and the clarity of vision the revelation inspired in me. It's not that much of a stretch to say I felt like one of William James's shuddering converts, vivified by a sudden recognition that had the gripping intensity of a religious epiphany. James, that stuffy pragmatist, shrewdly observed that a religious conversion needn't be "religious" at all—it needn't, in other words, include the embrace of a higher power or transcendent being. The embrace of a principle or ideal will suffice—for me as much as for the social engineers to whom I seemed to be reacting.

A Nietzschean will to power? Well, if you insist. But if you do, bear in mind that mine was not the will to power of any collective, of Hegel's great organic State, for example, that authoritarian monster appropriated by Marx and legions of his ideological descendants, from Mussolini to Lenin to Wilson to Hitler to Roosevelt and well beyond. Mine was not the will to power even, of some cohort of district administrators or an academic department or indeed a whole college or a whole *legion* of colleges brimming with elitist idealists. Mine was the will to power of the individual übermensch, his ire sparked to flame and then to blaze at the audacity of the totalitarian beast. Mine was the will to resist. What lunatic, what parade of lunatics, can put faith in the "collective will" without recognizing it as the ultimate and necessary path to smothering oppression? Go ahead, figure the odds for yourself. Figure the odds that six-billion-plus little übermensches will all direct their individual "will to power" toward the "common good"—the common good determined for them, of course, by the dominant übermensches—without considerable force of persuasion or just considerable force. It's not for nothing that the twentieth century's numerous organized efforts to make the world a better place—for *somebody,* presumably—left enormous piles of corpses in their collective wake, and I confess that I felt more than just mildly irritated that the self-righteous bastards held me in such contempt as to conceal the truth from me so as to avoid resistance. And resistance I'd have given them all right. I'd give it to them still. Call it the will to power. Call it whatever the fuck you want. Freud rightly recognized its source as the perpetual, irresoluble conflict between the individual übermensch and the society of his own making, the society created both to keep him safe and comfortable and to keep him in check. If the individual will to resist society's strictures is strong enough, those arbitrary strictures will not contain it. No social contract can claim that kind of absolute authority.

I had not felt self-righteous myself in quite some time, and the feeling felt strange to me and took some getting used to. For years, it seemed, I had been adrift, moving forward through time but without a strong sense of purpose. Nothing that transpired in my aimless journey through life was of any real consequence "in the grand scheme of things" because there was no grand scheme of things. I suppose my own cynicism was the biggest contributor to my own apathy, my own willingness just to let the world slide by without standing up for something. I didn't believe in God or transcendence or moral absolutes or even a moral system of any kind that can be defended except on the principle of self-interest—the recognition that I need a moral system for my own protection, and so I am more than happy to afford that same protection to you. I could live with that; I could even be happy with it. But the happiness, or at least the sense of contentment it provided, better than mere resignation, hardly had the exhilarating energy of a passionate commitment either. Rabid ideologues may often be deluded, but their delusion also inspires them. Few things stimulate hormonal activity like devotion to a cause.

It hadn't helped matters much that I was less than thrilled with other aspects of my life—my career path, for instance. And I was alone, I lived alone—alone by choice but no longer a happy choice. I did not have even a smart-ass girl like Kayla Blaze to share the existential burden of meaninglessness with me.

Around me, meanwhile, were ideologues who burned with the passion of self-righteous self-certainty, the religious conviction that they knew what was "right" not for themselves only but for everybody. A dangerous conviction, for it breeds only contempt for those who don't share it or who embrace other convictions with the same fervor, and when it's sufficiently powerful and sufficiently sustained, it leads most often to oppression and violence. But it nurtures the spirit; it fuels passion. I had felt passion for nothing and then only for a girl who reprieved me from monotony and endlessly provoked and then indulged my primal urges, who provided both stimulation of my senses and gratification of my desires. Any rush is better than no rush at all besides the rush toward the grave.

I had managed at times to get myself worked up, sometimes even to fever pitch, when I read about the suppression of dissent or heard about it in the news. The commitment to free expression was in me, in principle it was in me, and it had always been more than mere pretense. And yet, when suppression arrived in my own back yard—even in the innocuous electronic format in which it had arrived—the strength of my aversion, the powerful sense of conviction I suddenly felt, took me by surprise. That strength and power derived, I suppose, from some quirk of my personality, some hitherto undetected or at least unprovoked character trait. Or it was the latest in a long line of actions and reactions spawned by some initial urge or desire or fear buried deep in my subconscious, so deep it lay there unrecognized and unremembered until circumstances conspired to stimulate it and in so doing, by some equally unrecognized route, to stimulate me. I came from the masses, the shabby proletariat, and felt a deeply rooted antipathy for elitists and elitism. That was part of it, I suppose. I distrusted authority in all its incarnations and always had. That was part of it too. And perhaps, in the back of my mind, was the mere instinct for self-protection. If they were muzzling *him* now, who was to say they might not find it expedient to put the muzzle on *me* later should I summon the intestinal fortitude to publicly express a dissenting view? The best defense we all have against oppression is the legal right to speak our minds publicly. And every violation of that right nudges us that much closer to losing it. Having lived and worked among academic elites long enough to assess the strength of some of their own convictions, I no longer doubted that they were capable of obliterating the individual and his rights if their glorious cause called for it. And right here in my inbox was tangible proof that my suspicion was justified.

Ultimately, though, it mattered little what initiated the reaction at least for the time being. It mattered much more that the reaction itself was palpable and strong and almost annoyingly persistent, culminating in a feverish adrenaline rush and an advanced heart rate reminiscent of that one time, and one time only, I was goaded by a former girlfriend of mine into experiencing the rush of a cocaine adventure. It was my turn to have a sense of purpose. I felt the way a soldier might feel on the eve of battle—not some uncommitted conscript but a warrior type, a genuine fanatic without doubt that the cause he supports is just and right—knowing that the time for engagement has arrived and there is no dodging it, no means of avoiding it except through cowardice, withdrawal, a failure of courage.

It had not occurred to me yet, though I would apprehend it later as I puzzled through the matter and puzzled through it again, that there is a sharp line to be drawn between the mere embrace of some fuzzy ideal to assuage guilt and validate your personal existence and personal need and the steadfast commitment to a principle you feel is true, just, impeccably sane, and supremely defensible. But is it worth sacrificing for? That is to say, is it worth making a *personal* sacrifice? The cynic in me recognized that the legitimacy of an ostensibly altruistic impulse can only be measured by the size of the sacrifice required to exercise it. Talk, in other words, is cheap. A principle is not a principle until it is tested. Whatever quirk in my character had instigated the flutter in my stomach and frozen the liquid in my veins, it had also instilled in me the unequivocal certainty that the time had arrived to take a stand. And the thing that surprised me was my own unqualified, even eager acceptance of that conclusion.

But I did not pat myself on the back for my enthusiasm. Cynic that I was and am, I could not share my colleagues' reverence for altruism, even my own pallid version of that abstract virtue (if virtue it be). My reasons for it were still my reasons—*my* reasons. I was tired of the job anyway. Wasn't I? I was bored perhaps. I needed a cause to inspire me. I had lived most of my life without such a cause, but now I needed one. My survival depended on it. Survival? That was excessive. Sanity? Well, maybe. Mid-life crisis, perhaps? That was entirely plausible. But I could not deny the strength of the feeling that possessed me any more than I could entirely account for its existence.

SEVENTEEN

A Man for All Seasons—or, Un hombre para todas las estaciones del año—or, Question: How Does the Sedition Act Stand on Bespectacled Math Dweebs? (Answer: With Both Feet!)

The headline that sent creeping unease into my stomach that quiet late-spring morning—and then as I contemplated it sent my innards into a deep freeze—announced that a mathematics instructor at one of our sister colleges had been suspended without pay, and his termination was pending, for sending out a copy of George Washington's 1789 proclamation making Thanksgiving Day an official American holiday.

Warren Kefauver, the math instructor whose Washingtonian indiscretion had occasioned his censure by, and potential involuntary departure from, our district, was a man with a history. If you looked at it from the district's perspective, it was a sordid history. From my perspective, it was a gloriously American history. Either way it was a troublesome history.

As a math instructor, a guy who could throw those x's and y's up there on the board with the best of 'em, Kefauver was fabled to be quite good. That's a bigger accomplishment than it sounds like. College math departments across our great nation have the reputation of being populated by foreigners whose math skills are extraordinary but whose teaching skills don't necessarily equal their math skills and whose accents impede instruction in any event; by pedants and nerds who either don't like teaching basic mathematical concepts to bored, mandated students, most of whom share neither the nerds' proficiency in math nor their interest in it, who are easily bored and frustrated with the students, and who don't care much about their success or failure and therefore don't object to a high failure rate; by incompetents (who might also be foreigners or nerds or both) who would like to see their students succeed but don't know how to teach them; and by a small minority (rumor has it) of gifted and enthusiastic teachers who recognize and accept their students' math shortcomings and are nonetheless capable of coaxing a respectable measure of success from a respectable percentage of the students. My understanding is that Kefauver was, probably still is, a member of this last group. He made a strong showing on the "rate your professor" sites. I know; I checked.

What had drawn the ire of our district's administration and was on the verge of getting Kefauver canned was not his teaching; it was his politics. About two years before the Thanksgiving Day incident that was threatening to get him fired, he had crossed wires with the wrong people in our community and bought himself some trouble. Kefauver was apparently not only a man of conservative political beliefs and therefore already a rarity in higher education; he was also unafraid to express those beliefs. I don't know if he kept to himself in his office as I did; but he did not keep to himself on the Internet. He put himself right out there. On his own webpage, accessed through the college's website and sponsored by the college, he had links to numerous articles on the subject of illegal immigration—or whatever it is appropriately called. The latest PC term I've heard is "undocumented residents," though applying politically correct terminology to this issue or any other issue has absolutely no substantive effect on the issue itself. By any name the issue remains what it is. Kefauver's views on undocumented residents were politically incorrect. He believed that the rising tide of immigrants from south of the border was having a detrimental effect on our state's economy and its quality of life. At least that's what he believed if the articles linked to his site reflected his own beliefs because all the articles (at least all those that I checked) expressed that view.

What got Kefauver in trouble was not his views per se though. Many people in our state, which was and is heavily populated by undocumented residents, shared his views. What got him in trouble was that somebody complained about him and his views. The newspaper claimed that "students and fellow employees" were "offended" by Kefauver's politically incorrect views. I have good reason to believe, however, that it was a few of Kefauver's own colleagues who brought his noxious webpage not only to the administration's attention but to the attention of a certain large and powerful special-interest group composed of a number of movers and shakers in the community, especially the Hispanic community, who decided that Kefauver's views should not only be excoriated; they should be suppressed. The group filed a lawsuit against our district, and the lawsuit was reported by the local media though it was not given much prominence.

Kefauver, invoking academic freedom and the First Amendment, triumphed in the suit. More accurately, the suit never made it to court because the district stood behind Kefauver and his First Amendment rights, and the special-interest group decided it could not win and probably would not look good to the local public in losing. As quickly and quietly as the incident arose, it subsided and apparently disappeared.

The memory of it lingered, though, and it was the after-effects of the threatened-then-withdrawn lawsuit that caught my eye and then agitated my stomach. In retrospect, I imagine a cabal in a plush meeting room at the District Office working out the details of a pact. (The members of the cabal are smoking cigars, by the way, in my imagination. I don't know why; that's just how I picture cabals. They're sitting around a long table, over which the lights hang very low, so that only the table is lit while their faces are shrouded in darkness, and they're smoking cigars.) The pact is an agreement between the district's top administration and a powerful special-interest group to quell the threat of further skirmishes by controlling the content of employees' websites and email messages. That sounds like a reasonable proposal. Organizations that sponsor websites should have some control over the content of those sites, shouldn't they? Just as they have control over the content of other materials produced under their purview. But let's not forget that the community colleges were, and are, a publicly funded entity, supported by everybody's taxes not just those of special-interest groups that make loud noises. So if the organization continues to endorse certain political viewpoints while denouncing or suppressing others, the issue of who should have control over what the organization produces might not be so clearcut.

And so it was in the case of Warren Kefauver. A few months after the minor eruption over his offensive website, we received word via the district listserv of a new "administrative regulation" aimed at curtailing inappropriate use of the district's Internet facilities including email and webpages. The regulation, about which we were notified by our legal department, sounded innocuous enough. For one thing, district employees had been complaining ever since the Internet came along about the high volume of emails we all received, so many of which did not really concern us and were therefore more hindrance than help. I could certainly attest that I received more than my share of unwanted emails, probably at least fifty of them every day. Every day I spent a certain amount of time going through my inbox and deleting everything I didn't need or want. And for another thing, our faculty tended not to take administrative regulations all that seriously anyway. Our contract with the district administration had been negotiated through the faculty association, recognized as a legally binding contract in a court of law, and updated annually in negotiations between the faculty association and the administration. That contract dictated the terms and conditions of our employment, and as far as we were concerned it told us what our rights and responsibilities as district employees were. In the case of a conflict between the contract we had negotiated and an arbitrarily imposed administrative regulation, the contract would win out. At least it had won out in the past.

Since the hiring of our latest chancellor, though, we on the faculty had witnessed a growing tendency by the administration as a whole to consolidate and strengthen its power base and to erode the faculty's in the process. For one thing, the administration was growing. More and more button-down types took up residence in the corporate center known as the District Office. A "vice chancellor" of this was added here; a "director" of that was added there. The number of suits, and the layers of administration, were growing, and the administration made gesture after gesture, most of them subtle, to whittle away the autonomy of the individual colleges and increase the power base of the central administration at the District Office. A power play was on.

Part of the power play entailed the suits' stiffly issuing more administrative regulations such as the one that monitored the use of email and other district resources for the dissemination of information. The district could now control which messages by its employees were disseminated to the masses and which were suppressed. Again, this might sound reasonable since the district is supplying the resources but remember that it's the taxpayers who are ultimately supplying those resources and remember too that even after the new administrative regulation was in place, the district still permitted the dissemination of information that might have offended some people and that *certainly* must be considered politically sensitive. So complacent claims that the district had a "right" to control the information its employees circulated were suspect at very best, at least if you adhere to the belief, as I do, and as the district proudly proclaimed in its mission statement, that it was dedicated to "inclusion," to representing the entire community and not just select segments of it. It could not tacitly endorse one point of view by permitting its widespread dissemination via district email and then self-righteously suppress another point of view. It couldn't—and yet it did.

Warren Kefauver initially abided by the new administrative regulation, like a good little soldier in the war against intolerance. Somebody told him his links to "intolerant" and certainly inflammatory articles on undocumented residents had to go, and he obliged by removing them—or else they were forcibly removed for him. All I know is that they disappeared. I checked his website soon after the administrative regulation went into effect. The chilling truth hit me then: The regulation was hardly innocuous. It was being used as a tool to suppress dissenting views. It was a mechanism for censorship. It was the thin end of the wedge.

But I kept my mouth shut then like a good little soldier in the war against "intolerance." And so did Warren Kefauver, at least for a while. Kefauver knew censorship when he saw it, though, as did I, and apparently it didn't sit well with him. He witnessed the continuing onslaught of district-approved emails on topics that were politically sensitive but apparently approved by the district autocrats because they reflected the district's alleged commitment to "inclusion." But the censorship clearly didn't sit well with him because one fine day, out of the blue, he decided to practice that great American tradition known as dissent. The occasion was Thanksgiving, another American tradition, approximately a year after the administrative regulation was issued and a year before the district came under media scrutiny for alleged ethical and legal misconduct. The medium of expression Kefauver used to dissent was George Washington's happy proclamation of an annual day of thanksgiving.

It was the most splendid rhetorical ploy I had witnessed in my residence at the college, and I remember chuckling aloud when I read it. Recognizing censorship when he saw it (and was oppressed by it), Warren Kefauver had decided to practice the time-honored American tradition of dissent not by ranting and raving about oppression but by offering a subtle gesture of support for his own political agenda. It would take a pretty shrewd affirmative-action lawyer to argue convincingly (in the court of public opinion not the Academy—in academia, the prejudices are so strong that it takes no argument at all to convince academics of the guilt of certain parties) that George Washington's proclamation was "hate" mail. And many Americans, even some of the employees of our own district, would regard Washington not as an emblem of oppression but as an icon of personal freedom, the right to a viewpoint. Moreover, since many Americans (again, outside academia, a world unto itself) feel strongly that Thanksgiving is a sacred day insofar as it represents the bounteous good fortune they feel they as Americans enjoy, the message would have a powerful emotional appeal with a certain audience (most of it, again, outside academia). Kefauver's strategy was brilliant. He was making a statement about personal freedom, the right to free expression, without visible rancor and without libeling anybody (except, of course, by a ridiculous stretch of logic, the Native Americans, but if you buy that argument, then you too are assuredly guilty of practicing "hate crimes" of a similar nature against *somebody*). And he was using an icon of American freedom and American dissent to do so. It dawned on me at the time that he might be too bright to be an academic. Perhaps he should consider a career in the business world.

It did not, however, dawn on me that he might be fired for his dissenting gesture, and so I filed his message away on the hard drive of my computer—just in case, since I had learned that it was *never* a bad idea to file away those messages that might come in handy as evidence somewhere down the road—and then I went back to work, amused that somebody besides me had noticed the hypocrisy of an organization that pays lip-service to "inclusion" and "diversity" and then goes on about its merry way excluding and limiting diversity to its authoritarian heart's content. He had noticed it, and he had brought it to the district's attention as well—if the district powers that be were even smart enough to understand the gesture.

But it was not, of course, reading the press release that detailed Kefauver's suspension and pending termination that sent me into a numbing shock. It wasn't that I believed our administration incapable of such lowbrow unethical behavior. Rather, I went both numb and cold because I knew my own hand was being forced, and I recognized instantaneously that the repercussions for me personally would not be insignificant.

EIGHTEEN

The Crucible

After I read the press release I sat in my office and thought for a long while about what to do next. I could hear Keith Hudson down the hallway yukking it up with Mary Bonner and Ellen laughing with them. It was the end of the semester. Summer was coming. Mary and Keith were going off to England to teach in our study-abroad program. They'd enjoy five or six glorious weeks inhabiting English pubs and other English cultural venues. With any luck Keith would find a female student to become his admirer and keep him company when the class and the trip were over. Ellen would be rid of us all until the summer session started, and then she'd have fewer of us to baby sit until she took her own vacation in August. A reprieve from work and stress was on the horizon, and the mood in the department was jovial. Life was good.

Kayla was probably out there, too, but she did not care about the time of year or who was around to make work for her. She never talked about the breaks for students or faculty or what was going on at the school except that people made work for her and she did it. Sometimes she did it grudgingly, but she did it. She wanted to keep her job because the job to her symbolized freedom, mobility, opportunity, independence from her parents. But it was still just a job and nothing more.

After a while I got up and sneaked out the door at the other end of the hallway, away from the main desk. We were between classes and the campus swarmed with humanity, mostly young humanity. I went down the sidewalk to the parking lot and walked to my car and got in and started the engine and backed out of my parking space and jostled with the other cars in the between-classes traffic, waiting forever for access from one of the college's massive parking lots to the street. I sat at the stoplight and grew impatient. Important things were happening in my own life and the world, and I didn't have patience for waiting in a line. Then the light changed and I was out on the street and away from the campus. I drove home and called Ellen and told her I'd had a relapse of the terrible flu that had swept over me the previous day, and for the first time in my career I was going to have to cancel classes on successive days. It bothered me, especially during the last week of classes, but the flu that had seized me would not relent, and I did not feel up to meeting my classes. I gave her instructions for one of the classes and told her just to let the other two know I'd be back on Friday for their last meeting of the semester. She understood. Ellen was always very understanding. In truth, of course, she understood even more than she let on. She understood, for example, that I had spent the previous day romping with Kayla Blaze and that there was something incomprehensible about my suddenly coming down with the "flu." But she understood even better that it didn't pay to ask too many questions. Ellen was good at her job and didn't pry.

Not ten seconds after I hung up with her the phone rang again, and of course it was Kayla Blaze. "I wish you had a cell phone," she greeted me. "I don't know why you have to be so weird. You could come into this century with the rest of us."

I said nothing in reply, and she said, more indulgently, "What's wrong? How come you went home?"

"I got some thinking to do," I told her.

"'Bout what?"

"Nothing. I'll tell you later."

"I hope so."

"I will. You're coming over tonight?"

"Don't I always?"

"I mean you're not going out first?"

"Do I ever go out anymore? I'm a regular homebody now."

That was a backhanded criticism, an implicit reproof for my not taking Kayla out and entertaining her the way I should do (if I had any sense), but I was not in the mood to respond to it and all I said was, "We can talk about it tonight."

She was suspicious. "Is it about us?"

"Whadayou?—No, it's not about us. Not like that anyway. I'll tell you about it tonight."

And so I did. Uncharacteristically, she came straight to my house that night instead of stopping at home first to change clothes and chat with her mother (and sometimes her father). She was at my house by five-thirty and found me sitting in the kitchen drinking a bourbon on the rocks.

The drink surprised her. I don't know why. She knew I had at least one cocktail or maybe a glass of wine or a beer almost every night. It was perhaps in part a consequence of living alone and of spending so much time alone. I'm sure that by somebody's definition I was and am an alcoholic. "Are you drunk?"

"This is my first drink. I've been sipping it for half an hour. I might be drunk before the night's over though."

I told her the story of the persecution of Walter Kefauver, and she was remarkably, astonishingly unimpressed. "That's why you came home early?"

"They suspended this guy two months ago," I said. "About the time you and I met is the time they were telling him to hit the road."

"So?"

"He's been ouda work for two months, Kayla. Without pay."

"My heart goes out to him. Jesus, you nearly scared meda death t'day. I thought something terrible was wrong. I almost left early again myself. I told Ellen and she said I probl'y shouldn't push it 'less you told meda leave. She said Ronald McDonald is all watching me now since I'm fucking one of his teachers. She says he's watching both of us."

"You've told me that."

"I'm telling you again. I almost left work today thinkin' somethin' terrible was wrong with you, and then it's just some guy you don't know loses his job."

"I might lose mine next."

"What's that supposed t'mean?"

"Means I have to do something is what it means. I can't just stand by and watch this happen."

"Oh, Jesus. Don't we have enough trouble awready? Without that?" She took a long swig of her beer.

"We got no trouble at all. None. You're legal and I'm legal and what we do on our own time is none o' their business. We're not in any damn trouble at all."

"That's not what you said before. You said we hadda be careful."

"It is what I said before. We do have t'be careful. We can't be fucking in my office. We can't be fucking in the classrooms anymore, for Christ's sake. But they can't do a damn thing to us unless they catch us doing something inappropriate at work."

"Which they coulda done various times now."

"But they didn't. They haven't. And they won't. Because we're not going to give them anything to get us in trouble over."

"Jesus," she shook her head. "Listen da your tune now. You were the one that was all paranoid. I told you what they say about the teachers around there: You have to get caught screwin' a student on your desk in front o' class to lose your job."

"Well, it depends on who's telling the story. Some say you have to be high or drunk when you're fucking the student in front of your whole class. And some say you can get away with fucking a student, but you'd better not be fucking a sheep. And some say even a sheep won't get the job done."

"Listen da you. Now you're all smug about it. And before you were all nervous."

"They can't touch us, Kayla. As long as we clean up our act at work."

Something occurred to me suddenly, and I looked her hard in the eyes. "Is that why you like all this dangerous stuff at work, Kayla? You *want* them to catch us?"

"I like the risk," she grinned at me peevishly. "It gives me a thrill. A rush."

"Well I don't get a rush from it. Or a thrill. Not anymore."

"No, but you get a thrill from losin' your job over some asshole you don't even know."

"No, I don't. I don't get a thrill from it."

"Then why do you do it?"

"Because I *have* to."

"And why do you *have* to?"

"Because it's the right thing, that's why."

"The right thing? What the hell is that? Mr. I-don't-give-a-shit-about-anybody and now all of a sudden you gotta do the right thing?"

"You're some 'rebel,' Kayla Blaze," I smirked at her. "You call yourself a rebel, but you don't know what the hell you're rebelling against. Then I tell you a story about a real rebel and you run away and hide."

"I ain't hidin' from nothin'," defiantly. "Go ahead and do whatever it is you're gonna do. See if I give a shit."

She sounded just then like exactly what she was, a petulant teenager with insufficient drama in her life so that she had to create her own drama to make life interesting. I could not help but feel flippant about her, regarding her again, if briefly, as the piece of ass who enlivened my nights and not as the young woman with whom I was more intimately involved than I had intended to be. I felt "all smug"—for the moment—precisely as she had characterized me, and I let it show in my voice. "Relax, Kayla. I won't do anything that'll get me fired. They can't fire you for having an opinion."

"They fired *him* for it, didn't they?"

NINETEEN

You Take the Low Road

I had resolved that before I made my futile gesture of support for Warren Kefauver, whatever that gesture was going to be, I would give the faculty at the colleges a chance to redeem itself. I had to act quickly, though, because time was running out, the semester was almost over, and the district administration was running the old end-around for which it was famous. It was perpetrating unpleasantness on an employee right at the end of the school year when the faculty was just about to go on summer break and was consumed with final exams, final papers, and of course final preparations for that three-month hiatus that only people in education enjoy. When dirty work had to be done and there was a chance it would raise the faculty's ire, the administration did damage control in advance by trying to sneak the messiness past the faculty at the end of the school year—when we weren't looking. Nonetheless, news of Warren Kefauver's impending dismissal had to have reached faculty ears in our district—hell, it had reached Philadelphia, well over two thousand miles away—and so it was not only the administration that was keeping the news a secret from the rank and file. The faculty association had to be aware of Kefauver's case and probably involved in it, and the association too was keeping secrets from its membership. And that is what truly irritated me. From the administration I could expect low tricks and high intrigue, an us-against-them mentality that put me decidedly on the side of "them." They were management after all. We were labor. If that made us not precisely the bad guys then it made us at least the guys you don't come entirely clean with. But the faculty association was alleged to be on our side, the side of its members. And even if Warren Kefauver wasn't a dues-paying contributor to the association he could expect its protection in a time of persecution by the administration. The association protected non-members on the rationale that it was best to maintain solidarity against our common enemy, the mighty bosses in administration. Darwin at work again, I suppose.

And so it was strange that the association, ostensible advocate for our beleaguered colleague, was mum on the issue of his suspension under such circumstances. Faculty members in our district had brought the district's wrath upon themselves before, often for much more severe ethical or policy crimes—sometimes even crimes that were actual crimes, against the laws of our state or our country—and they had received the protection of the association even though it was often provided so quietly that the accused faculty members weren't aware of the crisis. Was Warren Kefauver being afforded that same support? Just a year before, for instance, a faculty member had committed plagiarism in a way that was not merely illegal; it was patently stupid. The faculty association had come to her aid, and the district had finally settled the matter out of court to avoid unpleasant publicity, settled to the tune of hundreds of thousands of dollars; and here was a man being fired for expressing a personal opinion on a district listserv. He had cost the district absolutely nothing except the unspeakable agony of a presidential proclamation. He couldn't possibly be canned for that. Or could he? Surely our colleagues who represented us on the faculty association would be the very first to point out, loudly, the absurdity of such an action.

The silence from the association was eardrum numbing though. I waited until the end of the last week of classes and still heard nothing. Finally, on the Monday of finals week, I decided to make a move. In the interim, I'd been almost constantly in a sort of obsessive frenzy, a mental hand-wringing anguish so consumptive I could barely bring myself to fuck Kayla Blaze. Something needs to happen, I kept repeating to myself. Something must be done, and if I don't do it I will forever hold myself in contempt. It was strange, my going from feeling so little to feeling so much, and my agitation nearly drove Kayla berserk. On Saturday night, in fact, she went out without me and almost didn't bother to show up at my house that night, finally stumbling in, drunk, around three-thirty. I was barely aware of her presence and responded to her sexual pestering only after she had shown much persistence and even then only groggily. I had missed her right up until the time I fell asleep and then missed her not at all, enervated as I was by the expenditure of so much nerve-tingling frenetic energy, consumed by guilt not over something I'd done but over something I'd failed to do. When I finally slept I slept like the dead, the energy burned right out of every nerve so that every organ felt on the verge of shutting down and every appendage felt leaden, drained of life. Kayla could not be dissuaded, though, and after she finally tempted me—tormented me—awake, we performed numbly, her numbness coming from booze, mine from exhaustion, and then I fell soundly asleep again and didn't wake up until noon the next day. Kayla spent the better part of Sunday afternoon on a raft in my pool and went home late in the evening, purportedly to spend the night in her own bedroom for a change because she couldn't abide my nervous company. But apparently she couldn't spend the night apart from me, either, because she was back around midnight, her clothes for the next day in a shoulder bag that she often brought with her to my house. She had changes of most everything in my dresser drawers, but she always kept her work outfits at home.

On Monday morning we were both cranky, still tired, but I planned out my day and prepared to take action, starting with a phone call to my local faculty-association representative. I had the phone to my mouth before I realized I didn't know who my faculty-association rep. was. I had to find out from Juan Hernandez in the office next door. Our rep. was Gillian Greenback.

This tidbit of information might normally have deterred me from carrying out my plans now that Gillian and I were no longer on friendly terms (at least I figured we weren't), but in this instance I was too determined to be turned from my mission by anything less than physical restraint. What I did do, though, was wait until late in the afternoon by the college's standards to let the place empty out a bit. I was wary of a possible confrontation, an unpleasant encounter as bad as or worse than the one we'd had over Kayla a few weeks before. Since by three o'clock every afternoon the office hallways were pretty much deserted, I was taking the chance that Gillian would have followed the herd home. But when I finally steeled myself for the walk down around the front desk and then down another long corridor to where she and a number of the other members of our "Old Guard" were stationed, her office door was open. I popped my head in and said, "Got a minute?"

She had been poring over a volume of poetry, and she looked up pleasantly but with a sort of weary expression on her face. It was not me who beset her, made her feel put upon; it was the defeat of Roly McDowell in the most recent chair election, an end to the McDowell dynasty after four terms. The defeat two weeks before had come as a shock to many of us in the department, I think, accustomed as we were to having Roly in the chair office. I suppose Roly's detractors were shocked at the failed "power of incumbency" while his supporters were shocked that a majority of our colleagues could actually be unhappy enough to vote him out of power in favor of James DeCrisco, whom most members of the department seemed to find abrasive. DeCrisco was a loner much like I was but an irritating one. Nobody I talked to had expressed concern that he might actually win. I had been confident enough in his defeat, or perhaps I had been apathetic enough, to write Raj Patel in for department chair. It was a strange bit of humor when I thought about it in retrospect, at least if I valued the quality of my professional life in the department. And yet I was at the time of the election endowed, perhaps, with a certain prescience, a foreknowledge that my days at the college were numbered. At any rate, I did not feel bad about the vote I cast even after I heard the election results, though some colleagues were crestfallen and Gillian had moped about as though she'd been personally betrayed. I wondered how long it would take her to recover if she recovered at all, or if she'd end up expressing her disgust by transferring to another college. (She transferred a year later as a matter of fact.) For the present, she seemed barely to have retained the will to live. It would take a Caribbean sailing trip that summer, or maybe a walking tour of New Zealand, to restore her flagging spirit.

"I just have a quick question for you," I said, still shadowing her office doorway.

"Shoot." Her tone was not saccharine but it was nauseatingly pleasant under the circumstances—the circumstances circumscribed by our recent set-to and Roly's recent defeat, which she took as a personal affront. In fact it was worse than saccharine because it rang so damn phony. "Don't take me literally," she said—as if she meant it. "What's your question?"

"It's an association question," I said.

"Fire away. Ope ... there I go again. I'm the association rep. What's the question?"

"It's about Warren Kefauver."

I think the look of her face darkening gave me the most perversely satisfying pleasure I've had in years. It was very much like watching a balloon deflate, quickly deflate, when it's been punctured. "Come in and shut the door, Marty."

I could see that she was far more pained by my broaching the subject than I was by broaching it. I'd had reservations about approaching her in person—even thought about emailing her instead just to avoid face-to-face contact—but now I was glad I'd knocked on her door. "I can come back another time, Gillian. You look busy."

"There won't be a better time, Marty. Sit down. But please remember the walls around here have ears."

Her office, unlike mine, was dimly lit for effect, so that most of the light in the room was from a desk lamp that cast a soft glow on the workspace directly in front of her. She had some kind of Far Eastern theme going on, up to and including incense that burned in a holder on her desk, and some sort of settee of a very dark wood with a plush cushion and exotic-looking throw pillows strewn about its surface. In more convivial times I had considered jibing her about being a concubine in a harem or maybe a geisha, but now I did not feel that comfortable with her and I did not make a joke. I sat down between two cushy pillows and sort of folded one to my side.

"Go ahead, Marty. I'm bound to represent you—no matter how distasteful I find it. Ask away."

"What is being done on his behalf?" I said bluntly.

"We're paying his legal fees," she said. "The association attorney can't represent him because it would be a conflict of interests."

"I figured as much." That meant the complaints against Kefauver had come not from students or administrators but from faculty members. There were five complaints of "offense" by "fellow employees" according to the Philadelphia press release, but what that translated into was five of the math instructor's colleagues hating his guts or else just hating what he stood for and wanting to sell him down the river. They wanted him and his unpleasant opinions gone from sight.

"It's a sensitive situation," Gillian admitted. "We're on both sides on this one. We are supporting him as best we can under the circumstances."

"Under the circumstances."

"Yes," she said flatly. "Under the circumstances."

"Awright," I said, preparing to stand up. "You've told me what I needed to know."

"Oh, Jesus. What does that mean, Marty? What did you 'need to know'? Why did you 'need to know'? Tell me," she said. And then: "Please."

I stayed seated. "I have been in contact with a certain organization in Philadelphia," I said. "An organization that advocates for the rights of individuals in such cases."

"Oh, for God's sake. I knew Kefauver was a right-wing neo-con nut-job. I never expected you were." She put her hand to her forehead, shielding her eyes as if she were truly traumatized by the revelation that I was a "right-wing neo-con nut-job." It was as if I'd just revealed to her that I'd butchered her family.

"I didn't know I was a neo-con *or* a nut-job," I said. "Well, maybe a nut-job. I'm no neo-con."

"Please, Marty, what do you have in mind? I told you, this issue is sensitive. It's a hard case. Either way we turn we're going against our own."

"I'm sure you're traumatized, Gillian. I'm sure it feels like fratricide."

"Don't mock me, Marty. I'm not in the mood."

"I'm sorry to hear that. But this guy's rights have been violated. Grossly violated."

"He broke the rules. He violated an explicitly stated policy. A policy that's very clearly spelled out."

"Cut the crap," I said. "The only thing 'clear' about that policy is that it gives *them* absolute control. Anything they say violates the policy violates the policy. And anything they say doesn't violate the policy doesn't violate it. Don't hide behind the goddamn rules on this one."

Gillian sighed. "That doesn't make this case any less sensitive. I would hope you can appreciate that."

"I'll tell you what I can appreciate," I said. "Kefauver isn't PC. And since it's an influential segment of the Hispanic community that he's offended—just by having the balls to express a dissenting opinion, mind you—he's alienated the district on this one as well.

"I can hear our fearless leader right now. More closed-door sessions. 'Cut that cracker lose. He ain't takin' me down.'"

"Maybe you should tone it down a little, Marty," she said threateningly. "It's one thing to be cheeky. It's another to insult the chancellor."

"Is it really? And where's the line between the two, Gillian? Is it wherever you and your PC cronies decide it should be?"

"Oh, for God's sa—"

"Oh for God's sake is right," I said venomously. "Come down off your high horse. Don't be so damn smug. If this were Enron, you'd be screaming bloody murder. If it happened anywhere in the private sector you'd want somebody's head. Evil capitalism, you'd be shouting. Evil greed. Terrible, terrible greed.

"And if Kefauver were being punished for speaking out in sympathy with illegal immigration you'd be trumpeting his praises from one end of the city to the other.

"Check that. This wouldn't happen in the first place if the guy were speaking out on behalf of illegal immigrants."

"He's a right-wing nut-job," she protested fiercely. I think she may have forgotten her own warning about the walls' having ears.

"Ah, let the truth be spoken. I can imagine how that discussion must have gone in the association meeting. 'Jesus, we gotta defend the sonofabitch. He's one of us—technically. But can't we just look the other way? Maybe we could arrange a little accident.'"

"Stop it, Marty. *Now* who's being smug? We're representing the sonofabitch. Even though he doesn't deserve it."

"How gallant of you all. God forbid anybody should take a stand on principle and show a little pride in it."

"I'll leave that up to you, Marty. You can be the champion of righteous indignation. Poor persecuted white man. Picking on those evil brown-skinned, illiterate laborers."

"Fuck you, Gillian." It was out of my mouth before I could stop it.

"I *beg* your pardon?"

"You can beg all you want. You're the last person in this department I'll let mock *me* like that. You spoiled bitch. You go home to that mansion on the mountain every night, and yet you have the nerve to insult me and mine? Go fuck yourself. You don't know what hard work is. You don't know what suffering is. And I seriously doubt you know what sacrifice is."

She was in tears. They just seemed to erupt all of a sudden. I don't think I could have reduced her to tears—I certainly hadn't intended to—had it not been for the cumulative effect of our precious district's public humiliation, which Gillian among others seemed to take as a personal disgrace; the defeat of her close friend in the chair election, which she seemed to take as a personal insult; and now the insolence, the insensitivity of her "right-wing neo-con nut-job" of a colleague, which she seemed to interpret as a physical threat. "Should I call Security, Marty?" She already had the phone halfway to her mouth.

"What? No. Of course not."

"You're scaring me, Marty. I mean that very sincerely."

"Put the phone down, Gillian. I didn't come here to physically attack you. You know that."

"This verbal assault's bad enough," she sniffed. "I'm not accustomed to being assaulted by my colleagues."

The innuendo in her voice was easy enough to read. Most of her colleagues were more civilized than I was. They discussed their differences rationally, calmly, and professionally no matter how striking those differences might be. The word "barbaric" carried with it ugly and non-PC connotations, but there was something "unenlightened," or perhaps "unevolved," about a person who conveyed his feelings through contemptible masculine—no, that wasn't PC either—through the contemptible brutality of unrestrained aggression. A better man would know how to control his temper and still voice his opinion.

I could stomach a little condescension from her, especially given my regrettable outburst, but her license to patronize, the license I was granting her because I felt bad about losing my temper, came with a restriction. She'd best not try to ride it too far. "I don't much like being insulted by my colleagues either, Gillian."

"Then I apologize," she said.

"And so do I." I meant it too. I did not dislike her—not really. Well, maybe I did, but that did not mean I wanted to insult her. My plan had been to confront her, but I had also meant to show some class about it. Few times in my life have I told somebody to fuck off, get fucked, or fuck him- or herself, and I have never felt anything but miserable about it after I did let it happen.

"My God," she sniffed, having drawn a tissue from the box on her desk and started dabbing at her eyes with it. "You must think I'm some weak-minded woman."

"No."

"It's a woman's curse," she continued as if she hadn't heard me. Perhaps she hadn't. Or perhaps she'd heard me but didn't believe me. Or perhaps she didn't care one way or another because she was on her way to making a point and didn't want to be deterred. She was a teacher after all. "A woman's period is popularly called her 'curse,'" she went on. "But it isn't. This is her curse. You bristle and glare and swear and get your back all bent out of shape. And me, I bawl like a baby." She put the tissue to her nose and wiped it, trying to be delicate and cultured about it. She was no pig; that was my domain.

"I wasn't thinking about that," I said. "I was only thinking about Kefauver."

She wadded the tissue up in one hand and smirked at me. "Do you *know* Kefauver, Marty?"

"No. Don't know him. Don't even know what he looks like. Don't care."

"He's a pompous little dweeb," she said. "A skinny, bespectacled little math nerd. Arrogant. Condescending. Just—arrogant. That's all. He's nothing like you. He's not pleasant. Not gracious. Not charming."

"I bet he never told you to go fuck yourself."

"That wasn't you talking, Marty. I know you better than that. At least I'd like to think I do."

"He has a right to an opinion, Gillian. As much as any of the rest of us."

"Don't do anything stupid, Marty. Please don't. There's no call for it. He has the support of the faculty association."

"And that's why he's being terminated?"

"We'll do what we can for him, Marty. We'll do everything we can for him. But we're schizophrenic on this. It's us against us on this one."

"I don't know why. I thought 'we' were the ones who always shot our mouths off about 'academic freedom.' Did I miss something here?"

"Freedom has its limits, Marty. You know that as well as I do. Even academic freedom."

"Then it should have limits for everybody. The limits shouldn't just be on the guy who's a math dweeb and whose opinions we don't like."

"Please, Marty. You're starting to raise your voice again."

"I'm sorry. I should leave." I stood up. "I don't wanna turn this into a shouting match again. I'm sorry, Gillian. I'm sorry I said that to you."

"Apology accepted. Forget about it, Marty. And Marty?"

I had the door open already. I turned to look at her. Her voice had that patronizing quality in it again. She was being "nice" to me and I detested it.

"Forget about Kefauver too," she said. "I promise you we'll give him the protection he deserves. If you go off half-cocked about this you'll only weaken the faculty."

"I'll take that into consideration," I said.

I left then and crept self-consciously up the hallway back in the direction of my own office, nervous that somebody had overheard us and regretting it if they had. They were such nice people, really, such well-meaning people. It wasn't as though they really meant anybody any harm.

TWENTY

A Place to Come To
(with Apologies to Robert Penn Warren)

The next day I mostly went about the business of ending the semester appropriately, which was the business I was getting paid to go about. I finished grading a final batch of papers from a composition class; I read a few revised essays from students who were trying to improve their final grades; I graded a small batch of literature essays that served as the final exam assignment for that course.

I received visitors, too, as I did most days—students, often those who had finished their last final exam or final paper of another grueling semester and were just looking to let off steam, to relax and know me not as somebody who would pass judgment on them but as somebody whose company they enjoyed, and to whom, for better or worse, some of them looked for advice.

That Monday's quartet was a potpourri that partially but not entirely fit the description of finishing students who were coming in for a breather before they left me behind them in their lives. Three of them were students I'd had before but only one I'd had that same semester. The other two came from farther back in the past. The fourth was somebody I didn't know.

She was a young woman who came to see me about a composition class she wanted to take in the summer instead of waiting for the full semester in the fall, and she wanted my advice about whether it was feasible given her busy schedule, a schedule that included a full-time job and another summer class and—I guessed, for it was unlikely she would ever divulge this; it was not in her best interest under the circumstances—a social life of some kind, probably a fairly active social life given her outgoing personality and the easy, confident way in which she comported herself with a total stranger, an older total stranger at that, a social life that probably also included a boyfriend who wondered why she had to devote so much time and energy to school when he had made it abundantly clear he existed only to adore her and indulge her every whim. Or maybe he was not that boyfriend; she seemed too sure of herself and her purpose in life for that boyfriend. More likely her boyfriend was the supportive boyfriend who had his own life and saw her when he could and didn't complain that it wasn't enough. One could never be sure about these things. What I was sure of was that the young woman wore a short skirt and crossed her legs at the knees and recognized that I was attracted to her as I recognized that she was attracted to me, smiling that toothy, inviting smile and shining those big brown eyes on me and brushing back her long brown hair with one graceful hand and carrying on a cheerful conversation as if she had known me for a long time and not just for fifteen minutes, and it was my guess that she *did* know me, or knew about the power she had, anyway, though she may not have known that I would flirt with somebody like her but I would never endanger my career or even my reputation in the department—or at least I would never endanger those things until the remarkable Kayla Blaze came along, and now they were all shot to hell and didn't matter anymore. I even contemplated an invitation to the young woman, a cautious invitation just to see if she was as interested as she acted and looked, nothing serious, just the chance to see her again in some other context, realizing as I now did that I was an extraordinary lover, the Cassanova of my age, the department Lothario if you prefer, and capable of successfully wooing even the most attractive of young women. I contemplated it, and what stopped me from pursuing it was not moral reservation or respect for my lover, Kayla Blaze, or even the fear that I would somehow get myself in trouble with my employer. It was a lack of courage, plain and simple. I didn't want the complication in my life if I were successful, and I didn't want the rejection if I weren't. I gave her the advice she asked for and sent her away, realizing as she made her slow way out the door that the attraction lingered, and that I probably had a shot with her. But of course I had Kayla.

Juliet Stinson came by around eleven-thirty and was there for half an hour. I'd had her in American lit., twice, the before-1860 course and the after-1860. She was a delightful young woman with a large intellect whose views on everything social and political were antithetical to mine and whom I'd enjoyed teasing mercilessly in both classes. She gave it back as well as she took it, and so she was one of those people who made the profession so damn interesting and at times rewarding almost beyond comprehension (it was hard to comprehend how a person could get paid for doing something so damn pleasurable). She was pushing thirty and had followed a circuitous path to matriculation, and her matriculation itself had been disturbed and disrupted by various divergent wanderings into drugs and alcohol and messy relationships and bizarre employment, perhaps the one constant being that she loved reading in general and loved reading fiction in particular. Her experience of the world had infected her rabid idealism with a tinge of realism that made it palatable and even at times refreshing. Certainly it was much easier to take coming from Juliet, who had lived, than from some twenty-year-old who had enjoyed a pampered existence and was in a position to criticize almost nothing about it as far as I was concerned. She was working as a server in a restaurant but I had encouraged her to think about the professoriate because she knew a great deal and had things she could teach people. Moreover, I thought she might find contentment there. She had come by to leave me a list of books she recommended, and we chatted about one thing and another, mostly books and literature, and promised to keep in touch, and then she was on her way.

In the early afternoon, around one-thirty, it was Paul Amundsen who dropped by. I hadn't seen him in a year and was surprised to see him that afternoon. Paul had been in my American-lit-before-1860 class but not the same semester as Juliet, and although he was bright he was not a particularly good student. In fact he missed class a lot and made a lot of excuses about personal crises in his life. He was a huge fan of Emerson, claiming the horse-faced old Unitarian had been the principal inspiration in his life—had inspired him to do great things himself—and assuring me that in another year, with his first degree securely under his belt, he planned to leap immediately into the doing of those great things. Well, after he got married to his fiancé, a pre-med student, brilliant herself by his own certification and a perfect match for him, a fellow world beater who planned to devote her internship and her first few years as a practicing physician to some free clinic in some ghetto (or maybe she'd practice in some underdeveloped country), and after that she'd become a researcher, perhaps a lecturer, and raise a family. (She was no fool who would raise her kids in some squalid foreign country; they would enjoy the finest private education available in the States.) In the meantime her husband would support her through medical school, working as a history teacher in a junior high or high school, and pursue the first of his advanced degrees, and then when the appropriate time came—when she could give more of herself to the children, that is—he would launch his career in politics and begin to "make a difference." We would see some real changes, substantive changes, in our misguided and misdirected nation once Paul got behind the wheel and redirected us. He sounded much like Emerson all right, only a lot less articulate and with an even more inflated sense of his own intellectual capacity and importance. He stayed for over an hour despite repeated polite hints from me to get the hell out, and finally, after promising to get out of my hair, he pontificated for only another fifteen minutes before at last fulfilling his promise.

Seeing him off, I amused myself with the image of him as our president one day. We'll probably deserve him.

Not fifteen minutes after Paul left, right around three o'clock, I received my last visitor of the day, a young man named Shawn Owens who had taken both halves of the American lit. sequence with me the year before and who, like Juliet, had been an earnest, diligent, enthusiastic student who read all the material and actually thought deeply about it. Also like Juliet, he enjoyed talking about the material as much as he enjoyed reading it, and the depth of his observations in class sometimes intimidated students who were less engaged or in many cases just not as bright. But again like Juliet, and like at least one somebody probably every semester I was at the college, Shawn and those of his ilk were precisely the people who made my job not merely pleasant but downright thrilling, something to look forward to with pleasure if not quite with zeal. He had been in the evening section of the lit. class both semesters, and at that time, with no Kayla Blaze to go home to, I had developed the habit of staying long after class with him and one or two other enthusiasts to hash and rehash the evening's material and myriad incidentals that cropped up between the end of class and the passing of the security guards to lock up the classrooms, which was usually our signal to call it a night. Shawn had worked in a bank for ten years, since he graduated from high school, and though he had risen and was rising still he was not satisfied and wanted to change the direction of his life before he completely lost the blush of youth. He loved reading and he loved literature, especially the kind you spell with a capital L, and after his second class with me he professed that I had inspired him to enter my own profession. After I apologized for that, not entirely in jest, I began advising him on the path to take. He'd heard the stories about the displacement of literary studies by the study of obtuse, exhaustingly pedantic theories of literature and culture, especially at the universities—stories whose veracity I had reluctantly confirmed—but neither the stories nor my confirmation of them had sufficed to dissuade him (such was his love of literature, I guess); and now, a year later, he had returned to visit me and sadly confide that the literature landscape at the local university was at least as bleak as I had painted it. He had just finished up a class in Native American literature taught by a visiting lecturer who was alleged to be widely known, and who, he said, was poorly organized sometimes to the point of being incomprehensible. "I got an A," he said. "I felt like all I had to do was repeat the same mantra about how the white man committed near genocide on the Native Americans and robbed them of their culture, and I was home free. It was like painting by the numbers." He had come to me for solace, perhaps a pep talk to bolster his flagging spirits. I joked with him. I told him he suffered from two of the handicaps of a potential applicant for employment in modern higher education: He was both white and male. But he had a trump card: He was gay. So he could do as the Romans did and devote himself to queer theory, so-called, where he might find a niche and hence employment trading on his assets. He was unappeased though. He had complained even when he was in my class—the second of the two, about midway through which he had confided in me alone after class one night that he was gay—that he didn't want to be pigeonholed, and he would hide in the closet if necessary to keep from being characterized as "the gay guy in the seminar." "I don't want to be defined by my sexuality," he had said to me at the time. "There's more to me than that." And now, seeing him disconsolate, and on the verge myself of disengaging from that strange place and its strange, repressive culture, I had nothing but a snide remark and a snicker or two to give him. When he left my office, I think I felt as bad as he did.

But that was also why I went back to my email with a sort of vindictive relish, a virtual eagerness to offend. One thing I had made time for early that morning was a quick email to the president of the watchdog organization that had made me aware of Warren Kefauver's predicament. I did not know anybody else in the organization to contact, and so I wrote to him though I didn't figure I had much of a chance at a response. Surely the president of an organization with such an important agenda and so many similar situations to look into across the country, so many cases to investigate and intercede in—surely the president of such an organization would have little time for email requests from English teachers in the hinterlands, at least when those English teachers were at most peripherally involved in one of the organization's cases. So I wrote the president of the organization, whom I knew to be an attorney, an expert in constitutional law, but I did not expect to hear back from him. I wrote to inform him briefly who I was, to tell him that Kefauver's situation was being hush-hushed by the district, and to thank him for his intercession. Without his organization's help, I said, it appeared entirely likely that Warren Kefauver would be permanently ushered out of the math department and into the unemployment line without a peep from anybody, which was exactly what our district's administration wanted anyway. That way it would satisfy the interests of a powerful and vocal special-interest group and thus maintain that group's support, and it would do so without a peep from the general public because the general public would be unaware of what was happening. Perhaps the newspapers were even unprepared to bring the issue to light and provoke the ire of the local powerbrokers. That might be why we hadn't heard word one from the local press. I emphasized the fact that Kefauver's ostensible allies, his colleagues in the faculty association, were providing him only with the quietest of assistance if they were assisting him at all. I asked him, in closing, if Kefauver would benefit or suffer from my attempting to bring his situation to the public's attention—through whatever means I might devise.

The unexpected reply I received from him was short and sweet. He said that I could only benefit Warren Kefauver by putting his situation in the public's view. (To his credit, I thought, he avoided the worn platitude that sunlight is the best disinfectant.) His organization was attempting to do the same thing but from nearly an entire nation away. It did not have the resources to assault the local media en force, and so whatever help it could get from me or anybody else was welcome. Publicize away, he said.

In so advising me, he inadvertently decided the entire course of my life. I should qualify that dramatic pronouncement by suggesting that sooner or later something would have had to give anyway—but I'm not so sure. Had it not been for the district's bald-faced maneuver to appease a political juggernaut, to preserve whatever was left of its own reputation as a good corporate citizen, to avoid gross embarrassment, and to silence a meddlesome dissenting voice all in one fell swoop, I might have contented myself to rest on my tenure and ride my comfortable position all the way to a comfortable retirement—perhaps even with Kayla Blaze along for the ride to ensure many happy endings in the course of my journey. Warren Kefauver the man meant essentially nothing to me. The circumstance in which he unjustly found himself, and the reason for his being in that circumstance, meant vastly more than I had expected it would. I had dim recollections of other platitudes, suddenly no less significant for being platitudes, and the echoes of them banged around in my head with the force of aftershocks from an earthquake, those aftershocks that had been disrupting my peaceful and secure life ever since the news of Warren Kefauver's innocuous gesture of dissent and its consequences had entered my consciousness. They reminded me, in essence, that moral and ethical decisions are easy when the consequences are slight to negligible—when the stakes are low in other words. When the stakes are high they become the moments that define our true character. It was rank egotism that convinced me to define myself in a particular way no matter how unpopular it was bound to make me.

Yet I did not welcome the ostracism that I knew awaited me—that's not me, looking to martyr myself by thumbing my nose at the mainstream. I know people who thrive on that kind of self-aggrandizement, the sado-masochistic thrill of drawing attention to themselves by endlessly criticizing others, usually those in power, but doing it in such a way that they cannot be punished for it usually because their criticisms are so vague that they can't be construed as slander or libel against a particular person; they can only be taken as broad swipes at a particular entity in general. "The administration of this college is fat and lazy." Or, "Most of the faculty members at this college are only interested in maintaining the status quo." Or, "The atmosphere at this college is one of stagnation and hanging onto the past, not of looking to the future and moving forward to embrace it." We had a guy like that at the college, in the business department, a guy who clearly devoted more time to composing long, critical messages than to doing research or revising his classes or advising his students. At least once a week he assaulted every employee of the district (not just those at our college, and not just faculty, but every IT nerd and maintenance man who might check his email as well) with a seething new missive in the name of what he called "constructive criticism." Not infrequently the messages mentioned other employees by name—his department chair for instance—but the "constructive criticism" he offered was so vague as to be completely useless. "You have valuable industry experience and great leadership abilities, but you don't apply them in ways that will make our department more viable and more vital in the 21st century." That was about as specific as he got. By offering such gems he could revel in his role as the district's "rebel" (colleagues naturally referred to him as a "loose cannon"), appeal to a cult following of malcontents who praised him for his insight and his courage, and risk absolutely nothing in the way of retribution. His academic freedom protected him, and because his insults were never politically incorrect—he scrupulously avoided targeting any person by race, sex, place of origin, religious creed, age, or any other personal characteristic that might cross wires with the district's public agenda—the district and the college felt insecure about trying to stifle him. One could hardly be "offended" by the generic criticism of being "afraid of change" (one of our loose cannon's favorites) especially when the criticism was being directed at the entire administration not at a particular person, and any attempt to muzzle such criticisms could very easily have been made to look like harassment. After Kayla Blaze proclaimed herself a "rebel" that night at my house, I almost slipped and compared her to our loose cannon, whom she knew from his emails just as all the other district employees knew him, even those who couldn't have identified his face if he'd been standing next to them. I *almost* slipped and connected her with him, two "rebels" whose "rebellions" were nothing but temper tantrums, aimless protests against "the bullshit." But I knew such an observation would draw more wrath from Kayla than I wanted to face and would change absolutely nothing besides, and so I kept my opinion to myself.

Not so in the case of Warren Kefauver, though, whose tiny rebellion had substance and who had in staging it put his career on the line. I had no desire to draw attention to myself; I wanted to draw attention to him. In fact, if I could have kept my mouth shut and accomplished the same objective, I'd gladly have done so. But an anonymous message to the district masses was technically impossible for one thing. It was cowardly for another. It would have been roughly equivalent to hiding behind him to avoid being hit while he fired at the enemy—perhaps loading his weapon for him but not putting myself in any danger. To be meaningful, the gesture I made, whatever effect it might have, had to be identifiable with a person and a personality.

Late that Tuesday afternoon I sat at my computer and composed the first of several messages on the same topic that I would compose in the next two days, all of those messages aimed at making Kefauver's plight as public as I could help to make it. This first message was addressed to the thousands of my fellow district employees, and I gave it the subject heading "Warren Kefauver's suspension is a crime against us all."

The memo itself began with a casual but caustic remark on the irony of my learning about Kefauver's suspension and impending dismissal from Philadelphia and not from my own city where the suspension had taken place. It did not sit well with me that a colleague was targeted for expulsion from the faculty ranks and that not a word about the incident reached my ears or my eyes from my own faculty leadership. Typically, if a faculty member was beset by the administration, or if any syllable of criticism was uttered about our faculty in whole or in part, by any fellow employee or any outsider, a maelstrom of rebuke for the critic ensued. What demon from hell had the unmitigated gall to accuse any of us— with a few noteworthy exceptions (but every basket of apples contains a few rotten ones)—of being anything less than dedicated professionals who policed ourselves to ensure that what we delivered was nothing less than a quality education? When the public had the temerity to take one or all of us to task, our inboxes shortly filled up with responses from our colleagues, it never mattered much what the alleged offense was. Our inboxes quickly filled with bristling responses, our fuming colleagues reacting with righteous indignation and furious accusations that the yellow press was out to smear us for devious motives of its own. (One could only guess what those motives might be. Sometimes there was speculation, and sometimes that speculation was nearly as entertaining as the articles in newsstand tabloids.) But Kefauver was one of those rotten apples in the basket who had estranged himself by not parroting the company line (or by not simply keeping his mouth shut if he didn't wholeheartedly embrace the company line—if you can't say something nice, don't say anything at all!). One could not bristle with righteous indignation for somebody who had the nerve to express an opinion that ran contrary to the prevailing current. One had to let that somebody pay the price of speaking up, and the less said about it the better. But I was not so explicit in my memo to the masses. I simply pointed out the curious irony that I hadn't heard a word about the suspension from anybody in the district; I had to hear about it from outsiders—not merely outside the district but outside the city and even the whole state—outsiders whom I identified by name in addition to identifying the organization's interest in the matter. It was this very type of tactic that our district administration was using, this clandestine bullying of students and employees by college and university administrations across the country, that had prompted me to subscribe to the organization's listserv in the first place. That's what I wrote. But even at the time I subscribed, and even as I was reading press release after press release from the organization—the infractions I read about, the badgering and occasional dismissal of employees, the disbanding of student organizations that were not PC, the suppression of views that did not jibe with the PC status quo—had all seemed like distant abstractions, the stuff of fiction, perhaps of Hollywood. McCarthyism lives! I could intone to myself, and there was a certain mockery in it along with indignation. Was all this stuff really serious? But now that the impingement had hit so close to home in the case of Warren Kefauver, the mockery was gone. Kefauver wasn't somebody I knew personally, but he was certainly somebody real. I knew about him by reputation. I knew where he worked. I knew one of the people in his department personally. And Gillian had confirmed his existence for me. He was no figment of my imagination.

I read over what I'd written so far and recognized it as deliciously melodramatic. *This* was juicy stuff—too juicy maybe. You didn't need a fancy education to recognize that I was hyping the incident for all it was worth. Even the uninitiated could probably hear the jackboots stomping between the lines. It was too much. People wouldn't take me seriously. They'd accuse me of blowing the whole business out of proportion.

Then I went over it again and realized I didn't care about the melodrama. I wasn't lying after all. Any employee who questioned my message could easily verify it. When I thought about it long enough, I recognized that the melodrama actually served a very important rhetorical purpose. It would get my fellow employees' attention. It would also get them talking. Some of them, at least, would want to know the truth. I left my opening the way it was.

Then I went on to explain, briefly, the details of Kefauver's dismissal, his violation of the recently enacted administrative regulation. He was being evicted from the premises, I snidely observed, for violating a rule that could be very selectively enforced. I cited several previous instances of announcements being made that would almost certainly be construed as "offensive" by somebody in our district's employ. Handily, I was even able to remind them all of an incident that had occurred just a few weeks before. Somebody in the district had circus tickets to give away, and the announcement to fellow employees touched off a lively email discussion in which one side expressed its dismay and anger that anybody in our district would support the inhumane practice of treating animals in such a way—and the equally inhumane nonchalance of paying money to view this "spectacle"—while the other side generally questioned what all the fuss was about, suggesting that "abuse" of the animals was exaggerated, etc., etc. I did not take a side in the discussion; my point was that nobody had been fired over the incident. So why was Warren Kefauver being fired for "offending" fellow employees? "In a free society," I wrote, "we are all bound to be offended. There is no protection from it; nor should there be. In a free society people will express different opinions, and some of those opinions are bound to offend, sometimes even when no offense is intended by them."

I alluded then to Kefauver's track record with the district and implied that his historical "offenses" were the root of his current problems. It wasn't so much that his opinions offended; it was that they offended the wrong people, a powerful group capable of exerting fierce political pressure on our leadership. Kefauver knew that. And he deliberately flouted it. He stuck his neck out against a powerful political foe knowing that recrimination would probably follow—and in doing so, I glibly pointed out, he followed the tradition of the man he used to incite the ire of certain colleagues in the district, our first president, a man who, as I put it, "knew something about the perils of dissent himself." I didn't know Kefauver from George Washington, but I knew one thing: He alone in this ugly mess had behaved heroically.

I concluded my little diatribe with a call for the math teacher's reinstatement—and compensation for his losses. More pointedly, though, I left my fellow employees with a caveat: "If the District ships Warren Kefauver off to the gulag for being a bad little comrade," I said, "it will be setting an ugly and dangerous precedent, a precedent of which we all have good cause to be wary."

I went back over the whole message and deleted a word here and added one there. What I discovered, though, was that I was very pleased with the substance and most of the style in the hastily written exposé. On a second, a third, and a fourth reading it was continually better than on the first. The substance of the message was concisely worded and perfectly arranged. The tone was vaguely sarcastic, vaguely humorous, cautionary but not alarmist. I came across not as a crackpot but as a somewhat cynical and yet very concerned observer not shrieking that the sky was falling but not at all happy either that the district could be so flippant about putting one over on us all. That the administration felt the need to use the tactic it had chosen—running Kefauver out of town on a rail at the very end of the semester and with as little publicity as possible—was telling in itself. I had no qualms about the accusation implicit in my message. I was saying nothing I would ever feel compelled to retract or apologize for.

I hit the send key, shut down my email program, stood up, grabbed my coffee cup, and left my office for home.

TWENTY-ONE

What about *My* Feelings?

Kayla Blaze was lying on the couch in my TV room when I got home. She wore thong underwear and my dress shirt, and she was lying on her stomach in such a way that the part of her anatomy the thong made a minute pretense of concealing was largely unconcealed and staring me right in the face. I was being taunted; dense as I am, I could figure that much out. Kayla was tormenting me in the best way she knew how, the way she so frequently liked to employ. She was tormenting me, but of course she was making a pretense of *not* tormenting me, pretending as she was wont to do to be innocently absorbed in a TV program of vast importance, such importance that she could not pull her attention away from it for fear of missing something of great significance to her personally and perhaps to the world at large. When I started to speak she raised a finger in my direction without turning her head and shushed me. "Just a minute."

The program on TV was the "real life" show that was familiar to me through my students and of course Kayla, the very same program to which she had subjected me—an entire episode's worth no less—the week before. It followed the stagy interactions of a group of teenagers or young adults who had ostensibly been "thrust together" as roommates and who clearly loved playing to the camera. Though I had never personally seen the show until Kayla subjected me to it, I had known about it before by its reputation. Sometimes we mocked it in my classes. My students mocked it too. But somebody was watching it because it had been on for years. Nonetheless, it was a show you could not admit to liking if you valued your self-respect. You had to pretend in public that the show was despicably trite and shallow, unworthy of a moment of your attention even in passing, and then when nobody was looking you could give yourself license to get completely engrossed in it. But Kayla made no pretense of not liking the show. She was good at making me suffer by making a pretense of not taunting me with her body, but she didn't even bother to make a pretense of not liking the show. She didn't care. People could say anything they wanted about her. She found the show fascinating and made no bones about it.

I, of course, failed to see the attraction.

In the show that early evening a young man named Mario, perhaps in his early twenties, of apparently mixed racial heritage—by which I mean there was some light in him and some dark in him—was having it out with a girl named Monica in the very finely appointed kitchen of a house that I hoped neither of them could afford (because people so young should not be able to afford such luxury). I was vaguely acquainted with Mario and Monica from my previous encounter and of course from Kayla's briefings. She sometimes talked about the people on the show as if she knew them personally, and she clearly cared about the intimate details of their lives as if those lives were actually, genuinely somehow intertwined with her own. But I paid little attention when she talked about the show or the people in it, thinking perhaps about sex with her as she was spewing the incredibly uninteresting details of their incredibly uninteresting lives. And so I was very remotely acquainted with Mario, meaning essentially that I recognized his name and face. What I also recognized was that he was a young Lothario—a play-uh in the vernacular of the times and the cultural subgroup—something I recognized simply from watching him interact with young Monica and other young women on the TV. He had longish hair by today's standards, far from collar length but equally far from close cropped, curly and black, carefully styled so as to look completely natural and disheveled; narrow cheekbones; thick, full lips; dark eyes that were not quite effeminate but certainly "sensitive." He was thin and appeared fairly tall, at least average height for a man, hardly strapping but lean and muscular, and when I had been coerced by Kayla to watch the show I had noticed that he seemed to favor apparel that flattered his wiry physique. In other words, like the girls on the show who wore tight tops and short shorts to get the audience's attention, Mario did his best to draw attention to his own looks while trying to appear to do no such thing. It didn't work; or at least it didn't work with me. The boy wanted us to notice what a handsome specimen he was and how little that meant to him.

In fact Monica, a buxom blond with golden ringlets, eyes that seemed to be perpetually adorned with dark liner, and lips that had to be (probably like those breasts) surgically enhanced, seemed less intent than her vain companion on making sure the audience noticed how good looking she was (maybe "cute" would describe her better). She was more aware of the camera, you could tell, but for a different reason. Monica seemed to feel a sort of girlish enthusiasm for acting "normal" on national television not so much because she wanted the audience to notice how attractive she was but because she simply couldn't act "normal" when she knew everybody was watching. It was a game they were playing, and we were all watching, and Monica seemed incapable of putting that reality out of her mind, and she always had a kind of silly grin on her face as if she found it impossible to take herself any more seriously than I did. Indeed, it is quite likely that many people in the audience took her more seriously than she took herself.

It seemed quite likely as well that the producers of the show, or perhaps the director, had told the participants to play up any bit of drama they could seize on for the benefit of its entertainment value. For it is impossible that real people—even real adolescents or young adults—could have as much drama in their lives as these kids did. I had noticed that, of course, and Kayla had noticed it too, of course, the difference being that in my case the awareness prompted condescending smirks and in hers it engendered intense concentration as if she were watching something as monumental as Neil Armstrong landing on the moon or the towers of the World Trade Center collapsing.

In this episode Monica was apparently confronting Mario about his womanizing. It was clear that she was not morally repulsed or peeved that he was violating one of the program's ostensible primary rules: no romantic relationships between regulars on the show. What bothered her was that she had a crush on him, and in her seemingly vapid mind she had deduced, as any person of modest intelligence would have deduced after watching Mario in action on the show, that he would never take more than a superficial interest in her. Her feelings were hurt.

"That's not it," he was saying in his own defense.

"It is. That's exactly it."

They were sitting at a lavish dinette table that appeared to be positioned in some sort of alcove or bay with long plates of glass abutting each other to form a semi-circular wall around them. The camera naturally looked out from the kitchen, so that the backdrop would not be appliances (however pricey they might be) and perhaps dirty dishes but the skyline of a smogbound city—probably L. A. The vantage point was up high on the side of some indubitably pricey hill, so that the camera as it captured the tense encounter between two of the Beautiful People—or at least two who aspired to be Beautiful People—also dazzled the viewer with a spectacular background that the show exploited whenever possible. You could as a viewer be enraptured by the Beautiful People or by the beautiful scenery or perhaps both. You had your choice.

Monica had her long legs folded beneath her, the same way Kayla often sat in a chair, especially a straight chair, and the fingers of one hand traced the rim of a huge coffee mug while the index finger of the other hand kept wandering up to squeeze her lower lip, a nervous habit that the show's producers, or perhaps its director, had surely begged her to avoid exhibiting on camera not because it made her look unattractive (it didn't) but because the audience would want to see the whole of her pretty face. Mario sat across from her in a sleeveless t-shirt, elbows on the table, a hand on his coffee cup. His cup was smaller than hers. His face was lightly stubbled—without question for effect. His hair, as I mentioned, looked tousled. Everything about him said he was a young man who didn't care about his looks. He could do it all—whatever "it all" might be—with personality. That, I suppose, and sincere good intentions. He was a good boy, a nice boy—but clearly misunderstood.

"It's not," he insisted. "You don't understand."

"Not much I don't."

"You're not even listening," he said. "You don't wanna hear."

"He's right; I don't," I said.

"Shh!" Kayla said. Still, her head didn't turn.

"First it was Daphne. Now it's Susan. What don't I understand?"

"Don't forget Tom and Dick and Harry," I said.

"Shh!" Kayla said.

"What about Susan?"

"You slept with her!" Monica said bitterly. "You think I don't understand *that*?"

"He slept with *Susan*?" Kayla Blaze gasped.

"Who hasn't?" I said.

"Shh!" Kayla said.

"You're so disrespectful," Monica said. "You don't respect anybody."

"I can't believe he slept with Susan," Kayla said. She said it to the TV, though, or to herself, not to me.

"I can't believe *anybody* would sleep with Susan," I said.

"You would," Kayla said. "Why do you say that?"

"You've got a dick between your legs."

"My head is just a little messed up right now," Mario was saying. Jesus, I winced. Did people really *fall* for this shit?

"Mine is too," I said.

"Shh!" Kayla said.

"You're so full of it," Monica said. Her eyes welled with tears and she did not smile anymore, even with just the corners of her lovely mouth. It appeared she had momentarily forgotten about the camera.

"I think I took the first step toward quitting my job today," I said.

"You're so full of it," Kayla said. At last she turned to look at me.

"I need a beer." I went into the kitchen and got myself a beer. Then I just stayed in there and drank it, sitting at my own dinette table, which was not nearly as lavish or as strikingly situated as the one in the TV show.

"'Zat why you didn' answer your phone today?" she said. She was standing in the doorway in all her loveliness, leaning into the jamb on one side, her arms across her chest, her legs crossed at the ankles, the hem of my shirt hanging provocatively around her thighs. "You knew I called. You were in your office."

"Leave a message," I said. "I was busy."

I told her about my email message to the world—or at least my little sector of it—and she just shook her head. "Are you crazy? You'll end up just like that guy."

"What? Fired? I guess I don't need to worry about that if I quit anyway."

"Jesus," she said. "You kill me. You're so ... boring!" She had her head lowered so that her hair covered most of her face, and she was swiping at the tile floor with the toes of one pretty foot. "An' you go an' tryda play James Dean or something."

It occurred to me that she had lowered her head because she was crying and didn't want me to see. "You're so ..."

But she didn't finish. She turned and went back the other way. I thought at first that she was just going back in to watch the show. That would have been all right. But she didn't return. Finally I took my beer and followed her, and when I found her she was in the bedroom. She had even turned off the TV on her way through that room. She was in the bedroom sprawled out face down on the bed.

"They can't fire me for having an opinion," I said. It may have been the first time in our relationship that I felt a powerful interest in appeasing Kayla Blaze.

"No kiddin'? I thought we had this conversation. Like a week ago?"

"What the hell can they do?"

"He musta said the same thing." She kept talking into her pillow—and it was "her" pillow—so that everything she said sounded muffled. I could tell she was still bawling, and her bawling was a lot like Gillian Greenback's bawling when I confronted her about Warren Kefauver and apparently reduced her to tears. It was suppressed bawling in other words. It was bawling she didn't want to do and didn't want anybody to see. I wouldn't have bet on Gillian, but I would have bet a healthy amount that all the bawling Kayla Blaze had ever done in her life had been this type of bawling: self-conscious, resistant, even angry.

"I just called their hand," I said. Then, "It doesn't matter anyway."

"Not if you're quitting. You sonofabitch."

She rolled over suddenly and got up and pounded past me into the bathroom, hiding her face from me en route. She closed the door and was in the bathroom for at least a minute. I heard her blow her nose. I heard water running. I heard her blow her nose again.

The door swung open and she stood in the doorway, much as she had stood in the kitchen doorway before, stork-like with her weight on one foot, her arms across her chest. Her eyes were extremely swollen (it seemed to me) for no longer than she'd been crying. "You're such a genius," she said. "Do you know how hard it is to get a job like that?"

"I have some idea," I said.

"You're such a damn genius," she repeated. "Thanks, Professor."

"You're welcome," I said dryly.

"God *damn* you," she said. "Why the hell would you quit a job like that? Nobody ever quits there. They make jokes about it. People just die an' they bury 'em right on the campus."

"I don't know," I shrugged. "I guess I'm just rebelling against all the bullshit."

To which she replied by stepping back inside the bathroom and slamming the door in my face.

TWENTY-TWO

The Day of Reckoning—or, The Totalitarians in Our Midst

Wednesday brought, first of all, a news story on Warren Kefauver in one of the local dailies. It wasn't much of a news story. It told of his suspension and pending dismissal, of the Thanksgiving Day proclamation, of Kefauver's violating the email policy the administration had established—in writing—nearly a year before, of his having "offended" fellow employees in our district, and of his contacting the advocacy group in Philadelphia. There was a quote from the president of that organization, who said the case would be laughable were it not for the predicament Warren Kefauver faced, having been deprived of pay or benefits for nearly two months and now confronted with imminent unemployment. The story did not disclose who had been offended by Kefauver's dastardly affront or why Kefauver had deigned to put his job on the line by deliberately violating a policy he was fully aware of. It did not explain that the violation was a form of political statement and of dissent.

I had pulled the news story up on my home computer while performing my daily Internet search for news of the Kefauver incident. I was gratified to discover that stories were appearing all over the country from New York to Seattle. That fact implies that the stories were numerous, though, and they were not. There was a handful of them so far, maybe ten, but at least they were appearing in disparate venues far and wide across the country. So the exposure was "broad" at least in the geographic sense. The watchdog organization in Philadelphia's website also informed readers that Kefauver's story had been told by the other media. Notably, he had been interviewed on a local radio talk show in San Francisco or San Diego (I can't remember which). I still wondered how big the total audience was so far—how many people nationwide had actually heard about the whole affair from one media outlet or another and how many of them took more than casual interest in it. I even wondered, in a mildly paranoid way, if the majority of those who did hear the story, even if they didn't get intensely worked up about it, at least sympathized with the ousted math instructor. It would be a sad commentary on the state of support for individual freedoms and personal rights in America in the early twenty-first century, I worried, if this guy's treatment didn't at least provoke the ire of a majority of his compatriots who heard about it. Like the president of the watchdog group, I was counting on the curative power of public exposure to set things right, hoping for an outburst of indignation to back the district down and restore Kefauver to his position. It would be a sad state of affairs if an individual's subjection to tyranny were to meet with stony indifference.

The story I saw that morning was the first I'd seen in a local paper. Of the nine people who eventually posted responses to it, eight believed that Kefauver was the victim of an injustice. The dissenter was somebody by the email handle peace2u who lamented that an instructor had to pay for his action with dismissal but reminded us all that Kefauver was aware of the policy he was violating when he violated it. It was incumbent on organizations to protect the few from the many, the writer said, and while regrettably individuals such as Dr. Kefauver might have to suffer harmful consequences for voicing their unpopular views or for criticizing organizational policies, the overall effect of such policies would be to protect the "marginalized" from the "mainstream." In case we needed a reminder, some populations in the United States had historically been marginalized and therefore required such protection. In his position, Dr. Kefauver should have recognized that better than most Americans. peace2u didn't explain why Kefauver was in such an exceptional position to recognize marginalization when he saw it, but I'm guessing it was because he was in the field of education where marginalization is such a precious commodity.

The most strident response on Kefauver's behalf was a diatribe by one freeforever that called peace2u a "liberal PC wacko" and suggested that he or she remove him- or herself to a country that was more amenable to policies like the one by which the math teacher had been stricken. Cuba was suggested as a possibility. China's name was also thrown in. freeforever commenced not only to blast away at the institution that would enforce such a ridiculous, ill-conceived, and oppressive policy but at the government that would permit such an institution to exist. In a country that ostensibly proclaimed freedom for all and trumpeted the rights of the individual, freedomforever shrilled, it was a travesty that so little value was placed on personal freedom and free expression by its own institutions of "higher learning" (freedomforever placed that phrase in quotes). He or she went on to lament in an eloquent if irrelevant non-sequitur that we would be overrun with Mexicans soon and they were destroying our economy and we should all learn Spanish, posthaste, or else we'd find ourselves unable to survive in the new America.

The other posters were less passionate if perhaps even more resigned. One said that Kefauver should have realized what he was getting himself into no matter how ridiculous the policy was. Several blasted political correctness as one of numerous tokens of America's declining power and inevitable fading glory in the new millennium. We were now, that is to say, beginning to experience the signs of an empire that had passed through its maturity and was entering its gradual deterioration as a world power. More than one of these several questioned why any of us should be surprised that our powerful country was following the natural course followed by all powerful countries historically.

And one poster said simply, "It's too bad. He's a good teacher."

The newspaper article, and the responses to it, merely whetted my appetite for a day of such gaiety as I anticipated the responses to my own commentary from employees district wide. To put it bluntly, and for the most part accurately, I felt myself inadequate to face a day of recrimination or at least accusation from colleagues who would in one way or other respond to my call for Kefauver's immediate reinstatement.

But that wasn't the whole reason I stayed home from work that day without even calling in. It was part of the reason but not the whole reason. The rest of the reason lay in the fact that I had made a decision concerning my life and posterity, a momentous decision at that, and I was now already entering a transitional phase. Thus I had no real inclination to face anybody at the college for any reason—not merely because I had publicly taken up for Warren Kefauver but because I had started looking past the institution and on down the road into my own future. There was a giddy sense of liberation in the state of my mind that morning, a sense of having set myself free; but at the same time there was an ominous sense of uncertainty, the realization that I had taken my momentous step with little forethought and with absolutely no plan for proceeding to the step beyond it. I felt, in other words, free and constricted at the same time, an appropriate frame of mind, it seemed to me, for the circumstance in which I found myself (in which, metaphorically, we all find ourselves perhaps every conscious minute of our lives).

I sat in baggy shorts and t-shirt in front of my computer and contemplated my next move, which, I had already decided, would be to check my email at work to see if the missiles had already been launched and if so, how great was their number, how wide their range, and how potent their effect.

The attack had begun. Before I could evaluate it, though, I had to field a call from Kayla Blaze, the soft, sensuous, and beautifully scented creature who had left my house less than two hours before. She had taken an early smoke break and was calling me on her cell phone.

"Ju oversleep?" she said.

"Sorta. I guess you could say that."

"Your name is on everybody's tongue around here."

"Izzat so?"

"Yeah, only they won't say anything in front o' *me*. To my face. Bastards. They're talkin' about it, though. You did yourself proud." I heard her take a drag on her cigarette and then exhale.

"Well," I said. "It had to be done."

"Did it?"

"I thought so. Yes."

"Are you comin' in t'day? Or will you be lookin' for another job?"

I laughed. "Comeda think of it, I might do that."

"It might be a good idea. Einstein."

"Prob'ly I'll just sit around in my underwear all day."

"Want me t'come and join ya?"

"It's a beautiful thought," I said. "But maybe you'd better stay there. You might have to support me."

"On what I make? Good luck, Professor."

There was silence for a moment after that—a sort of loaded silence, it seemed to me—and then I said, "Well, I better go."

"You want meda have Ellen put you down for a sick day?"

I chuckled. "I guess you can if you want."

"You're not comin' back, are ya?"

"I don't think so."

After we got off the phone I went back to my computer to check the damage. The missiles were streaming in all directions, from every quarter of our district except the District Office itself, conspicuous, I thought, by its silence. Happily, I suppose, several of my colleagues had publicly taken up my defense against an attack they knew was forthcoming, applauding me for my courage in pointing out the district's cowardly subterfuge not to mention its repressive action to squelch dissent. Two of them admitted that they'd been aware of Kefauver's plight, apparently through some collegial underground, but had been afraid to speak up about it for fear of reprisal. They attributed to me their will to speak out and be heard, to voice their own dissent. After years in the classroom during which it was often difficult to gauge my effect on anybody, I could finally confidently claim to have inspired somebody. I wasn't sure how I felt about that.

Many of the votes of confidence came from non-faculty employees, people who had genuine reason to fear reprisal since they didn't have the faculty's prestige or power base to protect them (for all the good it seemed to be doing Warren Kefauver—but remember, the assault against him came from his own, his fellow faculty members, which made his case "difficult" as Gillian had put it), people who could not have spoken out the way I had done because they *knew* they would pay for it—somehow they would pay for it—and who, like my own parents, went about their business day by day seething at their own powerlessness but afraid to try to do anything about it for they lacked the resources to do better for themselves than they were already doing—or else, simply put, they lacked the guts to risk what they claimed to cherish so little in the first place. All these responses to my message, and there were about a dozen of them in all, were sent as private emails, immune to detection by the administration unless some nosy IT snoop happened to be watching or—and this was the possibility the emailers probably hadn't reckoned on—unless the administration's snoops were looking in on employees' private but district-sponsored, district-maintained accounts. To me it was a matter of not much consequence since I was divorcing myself from them all anyway, and though I was tempted to acknowledge their adulation if for no other reason than to voice solidarity, I refrained from doing so. I didn't have the heart for it—at least not yet.

I was saving my own enthusiasm for my antagonists, the raft of educated educators who would chide me for my indiscretion, ridicule me for my ignorance or lack of sensitivity, and try to correct the misapprehension of Kefauver's case that I had fostered. They came at me in droves, bees assailing the hive as if to ward off an intruder and protect the queen. The majority expressed some kind of sympathy for my intention but took me to task for my poor sense of timing. Did I not know that making Kefauver's situation public could only incite more bad press, more public scrutiny and reprobation? Had the good people of our district not suffered enough? This lament returned inevitably to a pity party for the sad treatment we had received from a malicious and vindictive yellow press, a press eager to sensationalize and equally eager to tarnish the reputation of a fine educational institution, an institution that had done much for its community that apparently went unnoticed and unappreciated. Had I half a brain, I'd understand that the Kefauver affair was one of those matters best handled internally within our own "family."

Before the day was over I would draw a public reprimand from the faculty association president, who said I had dramatically misrepresented Kefauver's case and thus risked inadvertently drawing precisely the wrong kind of attention to his cause. My woeful misunderstanding of the issue demonstrated the same kind of limited grasp of a delicate situation that made a free but ignorant (not to mention attention-seeking) press a menace to our unfairly maligned professional ranks. In trying to expose an injustice I had exposed only my own shortsightedness and poor judgment along with my lack of professionalism. Our faculty leader was himself Hispanic and proud of his heritage, yet in mediating the Kefauver affair he had sought only an amicable settlement for all parties. For two months now he had been working diligently behind closed doors with the administration's lawyers, an independent counsel retained by the faculty association—and paid for by faculty-association dues, he reminded us all—on behalf of Warren Kefauver, with the fellow district employees Kefauver had so egregiously offended, and with the community association to whom the offended employees had turned to assist them in attaining a remedy. An agreement had been within reach, he felt, an agreement that would have placated the offended and satisfied perhaps even the grandstanding offender, who—the association president reminded us all—had willfully defied an administrative regulation to create the disharmony in the first place. Now, though, who could say what might come of the whole mess? With a hostile press in search of blood and discord threatening our great organization's stability from within, he could no longer confidently conjecture that the accord eventually reached would be mutually acceptable to all parties. It could be, the president concluded, that in arrogantly asserting myself—without the authorization of the organization that represented my interests (he meant the faculty association not the district administration), I had done irreparable harm to the cause I lobbied for. If that turned out to be the case, I had only myself to blame.

A more vociferous condemnation came from a sociology instructor at one of the other colleges with whom I'd worked on a special project once and whose contributions turned up frequently on the faculty listserv whenever there was controversy. Judging by the substance, tenor, and general illogic of many of his contributions, I'd had a feeling right from the start that he was one of the employees "offended" by Kefauver who had clamored for his dismissal. His tirade that day did nothing to dispel that suspicion. He got straight to the point, accusing me of ignorance and then, naturally, of racism. How my defending free expression in principle or in practice made me a racist he did not bother to explain, but I would have expected as much (or as little) from him. He had a penchant for wild accusations, inflammatory rhetoric, and emotional appeals, so he was merely using the strategy that seemed to come naturally to him. He implied that I was guilty by association, that only a racist would come to the aid of a racist, and that those who defended Kefauver were as odious—and as threatening—as the instigator himself. Mine was one of the more insidious forms of racist attack because it pretended to derive from a desire to protect constitutional freedoms. But we all knew the history of race relations in this country, the persecution suffered by those previously marginalized by the white mainstream majority. What I was manifesting, he said, was simply latent resentment and anger toward people of color— and women, of course. My "kind," as he put it, saw our power base threatened by his kind and by the new prevailing sentiment for justice and recompense for past wrongs. Kefauver, he said, was getting precisely what he deserved for his transgression (I do not believe he was actually referring to the transgression of the administrative reg.; I think he had some kind of broader, more abstract transgression in mind, i.e., the oppression of people of color that Kefauver doubtless secretly championed). Moreover, perhaps others in district employ who shared Kefauver's prejudices should take heed of his example.

There was another, similarly incisive, similarly brilliant condemnatory gesture from a fellow English instructor at one of the colleges whose name I didn't recognize. But she identified herself as an "expert" in the canon of American literature and regarded herself— perhaps immodestly, she admitted—as something of an authority on American literary and cultural traditions. She reminded me that America's earliest favored literature had been that of a group of persecuted adherents to a religious faith who, having escaped religious persecution themselves, promptly began to inflict it on others in addition to visiting genocide on the prior inhabitants of their "New England Canaan." "Those you call your forbears," she wrote, "were indeed infamous for their own treatment of dissenters. They brooked no challenge to their religious authority and hounded from their midst any questioners of their own faith or powerful status in the sociopolitical hierarchy. It would behoove the white male, in this epoch when his domination of the oppressed and underrepresented is weakening, to remember the example of those who preceded him in trying to exercise that dominion. Their venture ultimately disintegrated into paranoia and accusation culminating in that horrific episode in American history now known as the Salem witch trials, during which a small number of brave dissenters, mostly women, faced persecution and even death themselves in order to challenge the status quo. Professor Kefauver is but a symbol of what can happen when those in power presume themselves too mighty."

I couldn't resist a reply to that attack, and so I shot a "reply-all" to everybody on the listserv, my first of but two public acknowledgments that day that I was alive and listening in on the discussion.

> Dear Patrice [I wrote],
>
> Although my own "forbears" did not arrive on this side of the Atlantic until well after the Puritan experiment had ended, I will not object to your referring to the Puritans as though they were my direct antecedents. It seems reasonable to me to suggest that they are indeed all our "forbears," in a manner of speaking, even of those people of color they slighted. Thank you also for pointing out the grave danger to which utopian fantasies subject us all the moment anybody takes them too seriously. A person or group can wreak a whole lot of havoc and devastation with sufficient righteous indignation and religious zeal. The Kefauver incident does indeed illustrate that. Allow me, though, to correct one significant inaccuracy in your assessment of the current situation and its analog in American history. In your analogy, it should be the district administration, with support from religious zealots like yourself, whom you characterize as the guardians of religious faith. It's Warren Kefauver who is the dissenter—a sort of modern-day Anne Hutchinson if you will. He is indeed the victim of a witch hunt, however, and I applaud you for pointing out the similarities—not so tenuous as one might imagine—between his predicament and that of the Salem antinomians. It intrigues

me that you respond to the suppression of dissent in your own "culture"' (if I may presume to call our district family your "culture") by criticizing the suppression of dissent in an antecedent culture of which you obviously strongly disapprove. I frankly cannot imagine why you believe your commentary would advance your cause with those of us who are less enlightened than you are, and I can only conclude that you must have been suffering from premenstrual symptoms when you wrote your message and thus weren't thinking clearly or rationally. Or perhaps you are simply another among the legion of modern academics who believe that clear and rational thought are dispensable vanities of a bygone intellectual tradition. In any event, I thank you for your constructive comments, however ill conceived. You have certainly helped to reinforce my faith in my own convictions.

My favorite hectoring of all, though, and the most eloquent, came from my gently condescending colleague Linda Ham, who lectured me politely all the way from Canada where she was on a sabbatical doing "peace studies." Apparently her preoccupation with peace was not so consuming that it kept her from her employee email; nor did it preclude her participation in discussions she considered worth her while, and late in the afternoon her lengthy response to my plea for Kefauver's reinstatement arrived in tidy, thoughtful, orderly paragraphs, so well conceived and written that they might lead one to believe she was working with Aristotle himself as her editor. I was often impressed by the substance and arrangement of ideas in Linda's long memos, and this one was no exception. It appeared she had not given peace much of a chance that day, or else her clement reprimand was some kind of exercise in "peace" itself. I didn't bother to ask for I didn't really care.

Her message began with a sweet reminder that we were in the era of "Bush the Second" and that the "neo-cons" (Linda liked that word a lot, using it in most of her instructive emails to our department, the college at large, and the district) had used a reactionary manipulation of recent catastrophic events to "engender paranoia" by convincing the masses that the Islamic world was a threat to us all, that our very "freedom" and "way of life" were in jeopardy, and that the threat was grave enough to justify subtle but sinister infringements of the constitutional rights of certain individuals, some of them American citizens, in the interest of "protecting" the mainstream citizenry. The neo-cons (those filthy swine) were concerned that their power base was eroding, that "liberals" were gaining momentum in Congress and on the Supreme Court and might soon become the dominant political party and perhaps even capture the next presidential election—so presumably she was referring to the Democrats—and that the evil capitalist enterprise that supported the nasty neo-cons might eventually come crashing down around their ears. Their strategy now was to create a panic that would keep the mindless masses preoccupied, stricken with fear that our next-door neighbor might be preparing a bomb in his basement, investing our tax money and our attention in an absurd imperialist siege of a faraway country toward which most Americans (in our ignorance) were unfavorably disposed anyway. So far the strategy had been marginally successful, but it was losing strength. People were tired of the war. They were tired of the Republican rhetoric. They were tired of the rich getting richer while the rest of us only got further in debt. A sea change was coming. If I listened closely, I could hear it on the wind.

Warren Kefauver was himself a neo-con, less insidious than those with direct political power but insidious nonetheless, for he bore an implicit power that was not officially sanctioned by the State any more than it was sanctioned by his employer, but it existed by virtue of his stature as a public employee in a position of prestige and respect. People listened to him, and they believed him. "Picture your own students," Linda bade me. "They're young, they're impressionable, they're subservient to your authority. It's not the authority of the tyrant with the fisted glove; it's the velvet authority of those whose power rests in the very gentleness of their demeanor, in the influence they have on the young people whose minds they shape." She cited a scholar who claimed that among those who have amorous affairs with people in positions of power, the highest percentage of those affairs by far is with teachers. (I don't think she knew about Kayla and me.) She cited another scholar on the "implicit power" of the teacher. Warren Kefauver had the power to influence people, and he knew it. And he was willfully abusing that power.

It was an unfortunate circumstance, Linda conceded, that a member of the professoriate should lose his job over his unpopular opinions. It was also an understandable impulse to claim his constitutional rights had been violated as I had done. "But the issue of 'free speech' has been complicated by recent developments on the intellectual frontier," she wrote. Free speech did not mean absolute license as I had implied that it did. As educators, we had a professional obligation to "public civility," and that was an obligation that both Warren Kefauver and I seemed to have forgotten. She cited two more scholars on "the limits of freedom in public discourse," one of whom proclaimed that "conservatives are fond of trumpeting the virtues of 'free expression' when it's their own expression that's being threatened. They're less virtuous when the expression is that of, say, an Islamic Fundamentalist." Linda herself used the example of the college classroom in which free expression was illusory. "Imagine one of your students screaming racial epithets at another," she urged. "Would you condone it? Could you allow such uncivil behavior in your classroom?" The questions were rhetorical. Patiently, indulgently, Linda made her point that the "free speech" we Americans claimed to cherish was largely a fiction, yet another tool of oppression invented for the purpose of giving the masses the feeling but not the substance of participation in society. It was the powermongers in our capitalist society who controlled expression—told us what could be said and what couldn't, what must be emphasized and what shouldn't. The mass media, the advertising moguls, the lobbyists for powerful corporations—*they* were the ones who controlled both the substance and the tenor of communication in our (corrupt) society. Hence the dismissal of Walter Kefauver might be regrettable in one sense—the sense that it was too bad he didn't know when to quit—but it was entirely praiseworthy in a more important sense, the sense that (as I interpreted it) the savvy few among us (the "enlightened," or perhaps the "evolved" would be a better way of putting it) had to serve as the corrective to the massively powerful and perhaps inexpugnable toxins of mainstream society. His termination was therefore a necessary sacrifice in a just cause. She only hoped, as a colleague who had never before felt compelled not to trust me, that I could be amicably dissuaded from further rousing of the local rabble. She implied (though she did not explicitly state) that I had redeeming qualities that disinclined her from pursuing my own expulsion from our worthy ranks. "There are many among our colleagues whom I would gladly see coaxed, cajoled, or even cast from our midst," she ended. "You're not one of them. Please don't make me revise my opinion."

Almost gleefully I had read through Linda's memo, enjoying her eloquence, chuckling at her humor, taking a certain satisfaction in being, for the first time in our acquaintance, the target of one of her saccharine invectives. It was flattering really. Linda was a woman with a large brain to match her (extremely) large girth. To be singled out for her excoriation was something of an honor. And I could not help feeling that she had put even more thought into her response to me than she put into most of her responses, at least, to Jared Willow (neo-con wretch), her favorite intradepartmental target and intellectual equal. I felt, abruptly, that I had achieved a certain stature among my colleagues. Too bad I was leaving them.

Before I did, though, I had to reply publicly to my favorite critic, Linda Ham. I clicked on the "reply-all" tab again and started typing:

Dear Linda,

Thank you so much for your collegial words of wisdom. I'm not sure my own words will be adequate to convey my feelings at being patronized by a colleague—however impressive her educational pedigree or her eloquence. I'm not an eighteen-year-old looking for the shortest, least-obstructed path to a degree—and a better life. More's the pity, I suppose. All that eloquence wasted.

I too am mortified by ideologues who would foist their ideas and their will on the unsuspecting masses. In fact, wasn't it one of your own "authorities" who said that liars in power often conflate their own interests with the public interest? I'd have to look it up. By your reckoning, you and I have power. The difference between you and me appears to be that I'm leery of all liars in power not just those damned neo-cons. The quickest way to tyranny is to convince yourself that your own ends justify any means. Those who attempt to impose peace and harmony on the world inevitably do so through the use of force. Ironic, don't you think? Theories about the subtle influence of this group or that group on the minds of the masses may appeal to you and Karl Marx, but I have more faith in the masses. Perhaps the only ideological principle I adhere to is that no power is trustworthy or desirable that stifles opinions no matter where or from whom those opinions come. With all due respect to you and your authorities, I'll put my money on the ignorant masses whence I proceeded.

If I might offer a piece of advice myself: Perhaps you should consider losing a hundred pounds or so. The evil capitalism you detest has made you fat as a whale, and I have read somewhere that obesity contributes to poor health. Maybe it was just another lie from the lips of the neo-con powermongers. But who knows for sure?

I hit the send key, and then I typed another message, this one to Roly McDowell:

Dear Roly,

It is gratifying to submit my letter of resignation to you and not to your successor. I say that not because of any feelings of ill will toward your successor but because I've always thought that you and I enjoyed a mutually respectful (and for me a very satisfying) professional relationship, and I feel it's somehow fitting and proper that you be the recipient of this message. I have carefully avoided cultivating a personal relationship with you, as I have with everybody else in the department, the better to maintain the integrity and the trust of our professional interaction. As a department chair, you have served me well. I think you should know that before I take my leave. My resignation is effective immediately, but don't worry, I promise to turn my final grades in tomorrow before I go. Let's end this thing on the up and up, so to speak.

Thank you again for your service as chair and to me as a colleague. The experience has certainly been educational.

TWENTY-THREE

Only You Know and I Know

Kayla came to my house as soon as she got off work. She was wearing a sort of frumpy silk blouse and a blue business skirt that flattered her figure less than her other skirts and dresses did—which is to say she still looked stunning; she just looked a little less overtly sexual. There was no hiding Kayla's charms; nor did she try to hide them. Now and again, though, she might disguise them just enough to fool the ignorant appraiser into thinking perhaps that she was not a young woman with an extraordinary lust for sex and that perhaps she wasn't even aware of how attractive she was.

She wore lower heels that day, too, than the standard attention-grabbing Fuck-me-pumps, and she slipped them off as soon as she hit my front door. I happened to be in the kitchen rinsing off some dishes when she walked in, and she had the shoes draped up over her right shoulder by the straps, which as always made her look more petite than statuesque and somehow younger and more innocent. She was by no means innocent, but then in my world nobody is.

"Practicing for your future?" She stood in the doorway to the kitchen again, leaning against the jamb.

"As a dishwasher?"

"Well, maybe. I was thinking more like a bum."

"Should my ears be burning?" I loaded two saucers into the dishwasher.

"I don' know. I stopped paying attention. Bastards wouldn' say anything in fronna me."

"An' you didn' eavesdrop?"

"After a while I didn' care. I wouldn' be too sure about who your friends are around there though."

"I guess it doesn't matter anymore."

"I guess not." She looked off away as if she were examining the ceiling for blemishes.

"Wanna beer?"

She shook her head, still not looking at me.

"You sure? I been drinkin' all afternoon. It feels pretty good, to tell ya the truth. I'm even ready t'go out t'night. How 'bout some place just a little rowdy?"

She shook her head again. It finally dawned on my impervious ass that she was starting to cry. Again. I saw the tears glistening in her eyes and figured out, mildly inebriated dummy that I was, that she did not want to look me in the eye. It was like the night before all over again but different too because this time she soon gave up the pretense of nonchalance and brought the shoes back over in front of her and took an indelicate swipe at her nose with the back of her shoes-holding hand. She was not quite looking at me yet, but her glistening eyes were at least aimed in my general direction.

"I should take that as a no?" I quipped brilliantly. Humor, they say, is a great weapon against tension. And clearly the air in my house hummed with tension.

But I guess I wasn't funny because she ignored my clever quip. "Now it'll be my turn," she said.

"I don't follow."

"Like hell you don't." She was looking at the floor or else at the shoes that were now dangling by her side. Finally, perhaps as a last resort, she screwed up her courage and looked me squarely in the eye with that withering look she used when she wanted you to think she was a real tough guy and did not care about you or anybody else.

"Awright. I do. Sit down."

She shook her head. She had that hard look in her eyes despite the tears, and she bulged her cheek out with her tongue to contribute to the look of insolence and indifference.

Probably, it was also a way of holding back the sobs. I had seen the hard look before—minus the tears and the bulging cheek—but I had not seen it directed at me.

I was through with the dishes. I went to the fridge and grabbed a beer and held it up to her from across the room. "Sure you don't want one?"

She shook her head again. I heard one shoe clack to the floor and then the other one, and I saw her looking down at them as she made herself taller again by stepping into them. Still looking at her feet, or just at the floor, she folded her arms across her chest. Was it possible for her to adopt a more defensive posture? I don't really think so.

"So where did you see this going, Kayla?" I twisted off the beer cap and tossed it on the counter.

Apparently she was unprepared for the question because it seemed to "knock the sass right out of her" as my parents might have said. Abruptly, she sagged again and looked more morose than defiant.

"Marriage?" I said. "Children? Happily ever after?"

"I don't know." She had fluid burbling into her mouth from somewhere—wherever fluid burbles in from when a person is overcome with such emotion—and speech was on the point of becoming difficult for her. Tears streamed down her cheeks, and her nose was running, but she did not want to swipe at it again.

"Did you think we'd be together from here on out? Till death do us part?"

"I don't know what I thought." She was battling to sound tough and defiant again, but she only managed to sound like a teenager whose feelings were hurt. "I don't think about that stuff."

I took a long pull on my beer again. It seemed to me a fortunate thing that I was already somewhat numb. "So it's no big deal then? We can just throw it away. You didn't think anything about it anyway."

"I didn' say that."

"You just did. You just now said it."

"Don't put words in my mouth. That's not what I meant." She put her hand up to form a tent over her eyes so that I couldn't see them. I'm not sure what she was looking at then.

"Awright. So what *did* you mean?"

"I don't know what I thought. I guess I thought I just didn't want you to kick me to the curb."

"I'm not."

"Whatdayou call it then?" She took her hands away from her eyes when she asked the question. Her face was a mess. For somebody who tried so hard to conceal her emotions she certainly did a poor job of it—or was doing a poor job of it at the moment anyway. But she tried to laugh, too, as if she were amused or as if she wanted to be sarcastic, and all that came out was a sort of gurgle. "You're not kickin' me to the curb?"

"I don't know."

There came that laugh again, that was not a laugh but a bubbling sound. "Now who's indecisive?"

"You're so *young*, Kayla."

"But I wasn't young before?"

"Yes. Of course you were."

"But you didn't mind *fuckin'* me." She placed very heavy emphasis on the word "fuckin'."

"I got news for you, girlie. I don't mind fuckin' you *now*. In fact, I love it. You can keep showing up every night if it makes you happy."

"But that's all it'll ever be." Her cheeks were very red and her eyes were swollen. It was *amazing* what a mess she looked.

"What has it been up to now, Kayla?"

This time when she laughed she managed to make it sound as though she was scoffing at me not just gurgling at me. She was manipulating me into saying she had never meant anything to me except an easy piece of ass, so that when I "kicked her to the curb" she'd feel justified in hating me.

"Do you want to keep seeing me?" I asked her. "Is that what you want? You want me to say I'm tired of you? Don't come back? Izzat what you want?"

She said nothing, and I had to keep pressing. "Help me out here, Kayla. Just for a minute. You want me to tell you to keep showing up every night?"

"No. Not if that's all it is."

"I don't know *what* it is. But I do know you're less than half my age. I know sometimes I wonder what keeps you coming back. You wanna be out with your friends; you've said that. I'm old. I'm weird. I'm a geek. I'm everything you say you don't like or respect or want to be yourself. And here you are."

"Here I am."

"I hold you back," I said. "That's what you say. And when you don't say it you imply it. You wanna be out here; you wanna be out there. And I don't. I just don't. It's that simple, Kayla. I enjoy having you around. I really do. Even when we're not in the sack I enjoy your company. I know I said I didn't, or I implied I didn't, but I do. But I don't wanna go out all the time and you do. I'm not a teenager and you are. It's that simple. You had this image in your head. This guy you saw on TV."

"No!" she said fiercely. "That's not it." It was the first thing she'd said since the tears started flowing that did not sound forced or gurgling. She must have realized it, too, for she repeated, still fiercely, "That's not it."

She had made me watch *Revolver* so that I could see what a handsome man I was, or looked like. The character was actually funny—not smug or cocky or macho but a sort of clever, affable type who seemed to fall into his successes—and I did not so much mind being "Revolver" once I had seen him on TV. Hell, it was better than being "Hitler." As far as I was concerned it was better than being "Kennedy" or "Redford" or even "Pitt"—or for that matter anybody the world considers handsome because I get no kicks from being told I look like somebody else no matter who that somebody else is. Kayla had me watch this guy on TV so I could see how good looking I was, and I suppose I was flattered but not very much. She was not the first person to tell me I was good looking, and I suppose I would certainly rather be good looking than ugly—surely it had been an advantage in many aspects of my life—but after a while it was like having somebody tell you, "You're black" or, as in the case of Shawn Owens, "You're gay." It is part of what you are for better or for worse, but it does not define you. It only defines you in part. And you are acutely aware of it and don't need to keep hearing it. And sometimes it doesn't mean anything at all as when you are compared to a TV character, and even though you find the character likable he is still nobody to you.

"You're not Revolver anymore," Kayla said stubbornly. "You're the Professor." And she seemed very passionate about the distinction as though it really mattered to her, as though she had given it enormous quantities of thought.

"Fine. I'm the Professor. The dull Professor."

"Who's kicking me to the curb." She put just one hand up to shield her eyes this time because she was disintegrating into tears again. Her body slumped against the door jamb and she did not even look sexy. She just looked broken up.

"I did not say that."

"Not in so many words."

I took a very long swig of beer this time because I was frustrated. "Okay, Kayla," I said. "Let's get married. Fuck it all. Fuck them all."

"Oh, that's priceless." She was trying to smile again, sarcastically, and not doing a very good job of it. There was too much gurgling going on again. "I love your sincerity, Professor. I just love ..." and then her voice dropped away. This time she covered her face completely and sobbed. Then she turned away from me, and then she walked away, padding along slap-slap-slap on bare feet. It was precious, to tell the truth. It broke my heart. I mean it.

She had gone to the bathroom, and she was gone for a very long time, almost an entire beer. When she came back she had made great strides toward self-composure, and yet her face was still swollen up like a bloated sponge—like one of those little gizmos you buy and then soak it in water and it turns into a dragon or a snake or something. But she had made a grand attempt.

"Stay with me," I said. "Don't leave."

She shook her head. She already had her shoes on to add to her air of composure, and now she draped her purse over one forearm as if she were off to the ball. She was just the image of propriety with her clothes all arranged and her purse neatly over her forearm. But her face was bloated as if she'd submerged it in the pool for an hour.

"Stay with me, Kayla. We'll talk this over. We'll give it some time."

She shook her head again. Then she gave the speech that she had prepared while she was away and composed herself to deliver. It was a very somber speech. "Just remember that this is all on you," she said. "You quit your job, and you quit me. This is not my doing. It's not what I want."

She left me then, a composed and dignified young woman (albeit with a face like a Puffer fish's) marching somberly out of my house, and it was the first night in more than two months that I had spent without her. I could not have felt more alone.

TWENTY-FOUR

American Dreams and American Dreamers—or, Man's Search for Closure—or, Castles in the Sky?—or, Idea for a Bumper Sticker: "Reality Is a Vast Right-Wing Conspiracy to Undermine Postmodern Thought"

It was almost four o'clock the following afternoon when I showed up to drop off my grades. Roly was there but I would not talk to him then. I came in the back way and tip-toed into my office at the end of the hall and quietly closed the door. I pulled out my grade rosters and went over them officiously, decorously, as if they really mattered to me, as if it were a matter of national security to fill them in accurately. I laugh about this when I think about it. How many times had I made jokes about grades? How many times had I joked with my students that their grades meant nothing to them or anybody else? They didn't believe me. But I was serious. "For Pete's sake," I would tell them. "Stop worrying about your grades and just get this over with. Get that piece of paper and move on with something else in your life, something important." They thought I was mocking them. In a way I suppose I was. But I was serious about the advice I gave. That was not mockery. Some of them got it but most didn't. Most seemed to believe their grades were truly important. "If you're trying to get into Harvard Law School," I said. "And if it's that important to you, what are you doing here anyway?" And now here I was going over my grades for the last time as if lives depended on them. I'd heard stories about people who left our jolly profession, and when they left they simply gave all their students A's as a send-off, a parting gift. The institutions they worked for hated them for it, but the institutions had no power over them anymore. I should do that. I should give my students a parting gift. But I went over the rosters meticulously as if they meant everything to me.

I was just getting ready to drop the completed grade rosters at the records office when a knock came at my door. I should not answer it, I thought. I should sit here quietly and pretend not to be home. Whoever it is will never know the difference. And I won't care. I won't be seeing any of these people ever again in my life.

But I didn't listen to the wise voice that told me not to open the door. I listened to some other voice. When I opened the door Gillian was standing there. She wore an expression neither of amusement nor of anger. It didn't say much of anything really. There was nothing in her eyes and nothing in the corners of her mouth—nothing twinkling at me but nothing scowling at me either.

"Got a minute?"

"Come on in," I said. I sat down again behind my desk—the desk that had been mine but was no longer mine, would no longer be mine after I turned in those grades. I felt a touch nostalgic.

"Can I sit down?"

"Be my guest."

She did, in a flurry of expensive fabric and chic jewelry and stylishly coiffed sandy blond hair, bringing with her into the room the pleasant scent of some subtle and doubtlessly pricey perfume. As she was sitting down she said, "Roly would like to talk to you."

"I'll talk to him one o' these days."

"He won't try to talk you into staying; don't worry."

"I'm not. I'm not worried."

"I'm not sure that would even be possible. To stay, I mean. Especially after the crack at Linda. That was sexual harassment."

"Sexual harassment? Good Lord. There wasn't a damn thing sexual about it."

"Well, it was some kind of harassment. Workplace intimidation or something; I don't know."

I said nothing, and after a short pause she followed up with, "He'd like to see you though. Maybe he just wants closure."

I still said nothing and so she had to come up with something else: "He's always thought so much of you, y'know."

"No, I didn't."

"If it hadn't been for Roly you probably wouldn't have been hired. That, and we needed a white male. And you were cute."

"It's nice to know one is appreciated," I said. "Isn't *that* sexual harassment?"

"So sue us," she shrugged. "Sue me. I was on your hiring committee. Remember?"

"Are we flirting, Gillian? Is that what this is?" This was not the first time in the years I'd known her that Gillian Greenback had given me the impression she wanted to be two things at once: the arch feminist on the prowl for minute signs of sexism and the coy if well-traveled schoolgirl testing the waters to see if she still had sufficient allure to make the boys' dicks hard.

She gave a breathless little laugh. It was one of those wholly insincere, nervous laughs offered up by somebody who is used to laughing artificially. "I wanted to see you before you left. I just wanted to say good-bye."

"That's thoughtful of you," I said. "No, I mean it."

"I'm the only one who knows. I promise. I'm the only one Roly's told. The others will find out later. When things die down. He'll make some quiet reference to it—not even a public announcement. He'll just let it be known and that'll be the end of it. Except that he might field questions about it privately. Gracefully. You know."

"Yeah, I know. Except he won't be chair anymore in a month and a half. So maybe DeCrisco'll make the announcement."

Of a sudden she had this stricken look on her face at being reminded of Roly's tragic fall. It was priceless. But she pretended not to be ruffled at all, composing herself quickly and smiling that artificial smile again. I remember being in the pet store one time years ago, and there was this advertising poster of a little girl embracing her beloved doggie, arms latched around the doggie's neck as she beamed at the camera. Only you could tell she was terrified of the animal because the smile frozen on her cute little countenance could not begin to mitigate the fear in her big brown eyes. I got the sense that she was holding on for dear life only on the promise of payment for the ad or because she was just so desperate to be a cute little child model—or even perhaps because the threat from her parents if she didn't do as she was directed to do was more fearsome than the panting savage beast she was required to hug. The look on Gillian's face reminded me of the look on that little model's face except that it wasn't fear she was disguising; it was something more like contempt or maybe just puzzlement. I believe she had decided, after our tense encounters over first Kayla Blaze and then the Kefauver Affair, that I was an odd duck whom she had summed up years before but now, abruptly and unexpectedly, had to sum up once again, and the sum she was achieving now did not measure up to the previous sum. It was a look, in fact, a good deal like the look Kayla was always showing the faculty out of sheer bewilderment.

But she spoke ever so casually, of course, intimate friend of mine that she pretended to be. "So what's next, Marty?"

"I haven't figured that out yet."

She shook her head. "I could never do what you're doing. Just quit a job without even having another one to go to. How do you do it?"

"Spur o' the moment," I said, feigning enthusiasm as I said it. "Ask Kayla. She'll tell you I'm Mr. Spontaneity."

"I suppose we'll still have *her* around," she said, her tone and her expression amply demonstrating her distaste.

"I couldn't say. We're parting ways."

"Well. That's good, at least."

"I suppose."

"It is. Come on, Marty, you recognize that. Tell me you do. I don't know how you could ever—well, I suppose I do. But that's not a basis for a relationship."

"It isn't? What is then? Money?"

"Don't be crass, Marty. I wanted to part with you on decent terms. I've never had a colleague leave this way. Under such circumstances. It's hard to accept."

"Well," I said, "for what it's worth, I consider us to be on decent terms. I have no plans to storm the hill and bomb the mansion."

"Comforting."

"It's not such a bad thing, Gillian. In fact, it's a little bit of a relief."

"I'm not sure how to take that."

I knew what she meant, and I smiled at her. The fact that she felt uncomfortable meant that she understood what I was implying. What I was implying was that I was relieved to be putting *them* and *that place* behind me. "It's awright," I said. "Consider us on good terms."

"I will. But I still don't see how you can give this up. I would never *wanna* give this up. But even if I wanted to I don't think I could."

I shrugged. In saner, more practical moments, moments that would come to me soon enough, once the exhilaration, the visceral stimulation of the incisive moment of rebellion was behind me, I would come to feel the anxious chill implied in her words, the chill of knowing you have thrown aside the comfort and the safety and the certainty of a stable government appointment; you have, in other words, leapt from the sluggish, inept, insulated cradle of the State into the maelstrom of the private world with its pressure to produce *actual* results and its vilifying consequences if you don't. I would wonder, too, if Warren Kefauver had felt that same anxious chill as he was contemplating his innocuous little gesture of defiance. Clearly, if he *did* feel it, he did not let it deter him.

I did not myself feel it yet, though, sitting in my office on that last day that it was my office, entertaining a colleague who had thought she knew me well enough to measure me up and dismiss me, count me into the fold as both harmless and trustworthy; but who having been forced to reassess me could not content herself to let me escape until she had achieved another type of mastery called "closure." What I felt then was not anxiety or caution but that same reckless impulse that had goaded me into issuing personal insults—quite public personal insults—to two of my esteemed colleagues, now erstwhile colleagues, the previous afternoon. In the wake of those two outbursts of heartfelt contempt I had felt a sense of liberation that bordered on euphoria. Free! I was free! Free to unleash the kinds of thought that had previously been imprisoned inside my head, denied utterance but never eradicated, and perhaps laced with malice precisely because they had been stifled. But it wasn't just that they had been stifled; it was the reason they'd been stifled. I'd have stifled them myself out of a sense of common decency, a desire not to offend; but stifling them out of fear of reprisal at upsetting the PC beast had turned them gangrenous, so that now when they were evacuated they left a feeling of healthy exuberance in the void their departure created. Freedom! It was like Arthur Dimmesdale's giddy recklessness on deciding to leave Salem and his guilt behind him. Mine too was a sin of omission, Arthur! I had kept my mouth shut when I needed to speak up! And now the sin of omission had been obviated, expunged. It had been redeemed by a public expression not radically dissimilar from the one Dimmesdale found himself compelled to make. The sin of omission was no more. Dimmesdale, though, couldn't live with his freedom, constrained as he was by a sense of moral purpose, of righteousness, and of a higher calling. Not so Marty Frey. That beast, unleashed, was free to advocate for the devil. He could speak out against oppression, however modestly, but he could also do more. He could give voice to the insults that he had previously restrained behind the guise of an affable—an inoffensive—countenance. You ain't gotta be black to play the signifyin' monkey. You just gotta have a malice to conceal and a motive to conceal it.

My motive now abandoned, voluntarily relinquished, I felt Dimmesdale's giddy compulsion to offend to excess. But I felt simultaneously an impulse to reign in the beast, to take my quiet leave of that place and those people and put the whole business behind me, having said my piece quite publicly as it needed to be said, and done all the damage I needed to do. I had this sense that I had said exactly the right things and to the right people, and if I said more I might spoil the perfect impression of me that I had left them with and somehow taint my departure. But there sat Gillian Greenback with that phony smile of hers, wanting to circumscribe me again, to rewrite me in her own mind so that she could again dismiss me, fold me back into her own tidy explanation of the world (hell, we all do it), and again be satisfied with what she understood. Closure.

Caught between these conflicting extremes, I said only, "I guess I've lost sight of the objective here."

"The objective?" She was, in all her phony friendliness, her wealthy, well-bred, magnificently groomed and dressed and manicured collegiality, suspicious of such a vague response; the sudden arch in her eyebrow told me that. But then she quickly resolved her suspicion into her own smug certainty. "The objective is education," she said. "Or were you just talking about the English department? Or maybe just this conversation?"

"No, you understood me correctly."

"I'm glad. It's so nice that we understand each other."

"To what end?"

"To what end? To what end what? To what end do we try to educate the people who come to us? Who pay money to sit in our classrooms? Is that the question? I believe it is.

"To the end of creating an informed citizenry, Marty. You know the mantra we chant. You know the role we perceive ... all this"—she gestured broadly around her, even turning her torso slightly in the gesture to apprehend the whole of the department, the college, hell, the whole of the entire enterprise of higher education—"to play. Don't play dumb with me, Marty. It doesn't become you. Dumb is one thing you're not. Crazy, maybe, but not dumb. I let you mock me once, but that was once. I liked you then. I might even like you still. But your charm only goes so far.

"Awright, we're idealists. I suppose you don't choose this life unless you're an idealist. Guilty as charged. I admit it. And you've lost your idealism. I feel bad for you. That's a terrible thing to lose. I think the world would be a better place if we'd all retain a little more of our idealism."

From where I sat, we were having fun. The quest for closure is a journey of introspection, utterance, response, further introspection, further utterance, further response—an endlessly unfolding human text. Just another great mind tease in other words, to set the world down properly in our minds, each to his own perceptions—or hers, of course. Let nobody be excluded.

"I think we understand each other," I said to Gillian Greenback.

"That's what I'm afraid of."

"I don't see why you need to get so defensive."

"And I don't see why you need to be so cynical. I'm not dumb either, Marty. You were gonna take me right back down the path of that bastard Kefauver. How can we say we're creating informed citizens when we stifle public opinion? Izzat it?"

"Yes, that's pretty much it. To use your own words, 'Dumb is one thing you're not. Crazy, maybe, but not dumb.'"

"*Dammit*, Marty, I wish you could just let it go. I came here to shake hands and part as friends. I don't know why we can't just let it go at that."

She was lying, of course. Perhaps she was lying even to herself, but she was most definitely lying to me. She had come to my office so that she could realign me in her mind, get me set down straight there, so that the chapter on Marty Frey in the Book of Gillian would have its proper ending—but even *more* important, much more important, she had come to make sure I left that institution with the proper impression of *her* in my *own* mind. In other words, it was not the Book of Gillian she was interested in correcting; it was the Book of Marty. The beauty of arguing the world with anybody who has an ego as big as Gillian's is that you can go right on arguing forever, and you will never lose though you will never win either unless you change your own mind, for she is so convinced of her own supremacy and her own righteousness that she will never be satisfied until you have conceded that she is right. And at that point there is no argument anymore. Until you agree with her completely and absolutely, the argument continues. In this case, that meant admitting that she and her faculty cohorts were justified in having spurned the spurious Warren Kefauver, bastard traitor to his profession, misfit, rogue, malicious miscreant, and boat rocker to boot.

But I would admit no such thing, and so the Book of Marty, Gillian Greenback's draft of it, could not yet be revised and sent off to whatever destination it might find its way to next.

All I did was extend my hand across the desk toward her.

But she did not take it, for if she took it that might mean she'd have to leave the Book of Marty unrevised, and I would go away from her forever not comprehending how good and right and wholly justified she was in everything she was and everything she stood for in her life. "Y'know, I feel sorry for you, Marty," she said. "I really do."

"Does that mean you won't shake my hand?"

"I feel sorry for you because you're cynical and bitter and jaded, and you're giving up a very good job and a very worthwhile mission ... to do what? What will you do now, Marty? Sell aluminum siding?"

"Is there a market for aluminum siding out here? I thought everything was stucco." I finally withdrew the proffered hand and put it back on my desk.

"Bastard. You might not be so smug when you find out what it's like out there."

"I already know what it's like out there."

"It's not like you have some great skill you can offer the corporate world. The demand for English teachers is pretty limited outside the Academy."

"I'm well aware of my limitations, Gillian. But thanks for pointing them out to me just the same."

"This is a noble calling, Marty. What you're leaving behind is a noble calling. It has purpose. It has meaning."

"Not for me it doesn't. Not anymore. I guess it did at one time. It must have. I don't even remember."

She shook her head at me, and I remember just then feeling that first twinge of fear at entering the unknown world outside the shelter of that public institution—and entering it so abruptly even of my own volition. Maybe the intoxication of self-righteousness was wearing off already. Maybe Gillian was scaring it right out of me like an exorcist chasing demons away. Christ! What the hell was I going to *do* with myself? I had a mortgage to pay! I had a mouth to feed!

She was shaking her head at me. Sadly. Patronizingly.

And that smug self-certainty of hers, that look of gloating superiority and resolution promptly resurrected the demon in me and banished—if only temporarily—the wheedling realist who would let fear of the real world and its wicked ways cow him into meek abeyance. I said, abruptly, "Do you know who Ramón Garza is?"

The patronizing sadness—pity—quickly fled her eyes, displaced again by vague suspicion. "Awright, Marty, I'll bite. The name sounds familiar, but I don't know who he is. Who is Ramón Garza? Enlighten me."

"He's the groundskeeper who takes care of this part of the campus. Everything from the old library north is his. And from the administration building west. All the way to the corner out here." I gestured in the direction of the intersection at the northwest corner of our campus. "He gives me landscaping tips. Tells me when to plant. How to water. Very useful stuff."

She seemed wholly untaken with that digressive tidbit of information. "You learn something every day. So what about the janitor's name, Marty? The custodian?"

"Angelo. It used to be Mike. The skinny kid. He was a heroin addict. I think he lost his job over it. Missed too much work."

"I'm sorry to hear that." But she was not sorry to hear it. She felt absolutely nothing about it except that I was using it to set some kind of trap for her. I could see the clouds of suspicion gathering in her well-heeled eyes. The goddamn Book of Marty just continued to resist her velvet editorial touch.

"He was a reader, Mike was," I said. "Religion and philosophy. Religious kid. We talked about it a few times. Nice kid. Called himself an Anarchist."

"I'm sorry he lost his job, Marty. Izzat what you want me to say?"

"I don't care what you say, Gillian. It's not your fault he lost his job. Your fault or mine."

"So why, then, are we talking about janitors and groundskeepers all of a sudden?"

"My old man was one of those guys," I said. "Member of the faceless herd. The ignorant masses.

"He worked in a vacuum cleaner plant." I said the name of the company because I knew she would recognize it. "Ran a punch-press. Made that steel plate that covers the roller brush and the belt on the bottom of the machine." I gestured with my hand as if to fashion a shiny steel plate for her in the air, but I have a sneaking suspicion she'd never seen the bottom of a vacuum cleaner much less used one.

"Union shop," I said. "So many parts per hour, and not one more or less than the prescribed quota. Each to his own capacity to meet the quota as Marx might say. But everybody must be able to *meet* the quota. So you set your standards low, make damn sure all you achieve is mediocrity no matter who's doing the job. If you made your quota in fifteen minutes, you occupied yourself for the next forty-five until it was time to make your next hour's quota. Go to the break room or something. Read a book. Take a dump. Whatever. That was my old man's world.

"He used to come home smelling like machine oil," I said. "That's what I remember. Machine oil and sweat. They used machine oil to lubricate the steel, so it wouldn't fracture when they punched it. Get a nice clean, smooth bend."

"My father was an attorney," she offered. "I'm sure he used to sweat though. He used to do a lot of 'manly' things. Work outside in the yard. Go hunting with his cronies and slaughter poor little animals. 'Manly' things. I don't remember the smell of his sweat though. What I remember is his cologne. A kind of musky smell. Very 'manly.'"

"Here's my point," I said. "My old man worked in the shop, and upstairs, on the second floor, were all the offices. That's where all the clean-smelling office types worked. The secretaries and clerks but also the salespeople and the engineers and the purchasing agents and the managers. The college-graduate types. My old man hated those people. Said they seemed so young, most of 'em, and so smug. Like they had to be superior or nobody would take them seriously. Then they'd lose their nice cushy jobs and have to get real jobs. That's what my old man would say. He hated 'em. Said they sat up there and made decisions that affected his life—what to produce and how, policies and procedures, when to lay people off. Did not give a rat's ass about anybody down in the shop. Not as a person. They were all just part o' the big machine that kept the suits' jobs secure."

"But your father had the union to protect him."

"Yeah, and he hated them too. He said once you got to be a big shot in the union all you did was work with the suits upstairs. Everybody washing everybody else's back. But nobody washing the old man's back, not as far as he could tell. That was his version of the story. He put in his time and kept his nose clean and minded his own business and got thirty years outa the place."

"So that's your point, Marty? Your father worked for thirty years at menial labor and hated every minute of it?" She told me a story then, as if to get even, of her father-in-law, Burt's father, a bent-backed bricklayer and abusive alcoholic from whom Burt had escaped at the tender age of fifteen to begin the life that would lead to his staggering success as a minor corporate empire builder. "Do I get some credibility now, Marty?" she said when she had finished the story. "Do I get some measure of respect from you now? Is that what it takes? Tell a sad story?"

"I've always respected you, Gillian," I lied to her. And I think she knew I was lying but decided not to call me out for it.

"I hated school with a passion," I said. "But it meant so much to my old man. My mom too. They sacrificed for me. They put money away whenever they could so I could go to college. I worked too, but they worked harder. And they rammed school down my throat like you wouldn't believe. Like the parents who force their kid into gymnastics when she's three so she can be in the Olympics. Like that."

"They wanted you to have a better life than they did."

"Ah, yes, of course they did. Education was a means to an end. They could see that. You're goddamn right they could; they were smart people. Get an education and you could move upstairs. Be one o' the educated pricks up on the second floor." "And there was something wrong about them wanting that for you?"

"Of course not. Not at all. They could see education was a way up in the world. And it is."

Gillian's patronizing eyes glittered at me. She really had very pretty eyes, eyes like emeralds, not a solid green but variegated, with bits of flash and dazzle in them. And when she was worked up, as she was now, the flash and dazzle seemed more pronounced, like tiny flashbulbs popping within the iris itself. The eyes could hardly have been fabricated to be more striking. "Now you're making perfect sense," she said. "Perfect sense. Education is a way up in the world, so you don't want any part of it. Brilliant, Marty. I understand your thinking perfectly now."

"I believe in education every bit as much as you do, Gillian. I might even see it as more than just a way up in the world. But it's still just education."

"What the hell is *that* supposed to mean?"

"You say this is a 'noble calling.' What's so goddamn noble about it?"

"You just explained yourself what's noble about it. It gives people a way up in the world."

"But it doesn't make you any smarter or any better than anybody else. Not any groundskeeper or janitor or punch-press operator in a goddamn vacuum cleaner plant. Or any bricklayer either, for that matter."

"I never said it does."

"No, but you were thinking it."

"I wasn't. But all right, if it'll make you happy, I *do* think education is more than just a way up in the world. Much more. I'd like to think it helps people to understand themselves better. Understand each other better. Understand their world better."

"Lovely. Lovely thoughts. Y'know what I think? I think you believe that if we all get properly 'educated' the whole world will just be a better place."

It's true, too. To this day I have the powerful impression that Gillian, hippie chick from the sixties grown middle aged and exceedingly comfortable, not to mention legions of others of like mind, wanted and continue to want all of us in the world to have "closure," to sit around and have good feelings for each other and live in peace and harmony and perfect cooperation. It's a Marxian wet dream, a dream that everybody will get "educated" and come to understand each other, the faceless masses in their teeming daily struggle finally understanding what Gillian high up in her mansion on the mountain already knew, and what she was trying in her "noble calling" to impart to them, to put an end to prejudice and hatred and bigotry of every kind, to dissolve nations and obliterate borders and end poverty and starvation and all manner of suffering and deprivation imposed on divided humanity by the historically determined conditions of their miserable lives. Marx's dream lives! But wait, there was more to it than that, as Freud plainly recognized. There had to be an end, too, to every petty human frailty, to every sickness of the body and the soul, every wayward human emotion—pride, jealousy, greed, envy, anger, insecurity, fear, lust, personal ambition—every potential source of conflict between or among human beings vanquished or permanently subdued so that all of us, every teacher and student and groundskeeper and cop and construction worker and housekeeper and rocket scientist and bank president and politician and journalist, every warmonger and powermonger and suicidal manic-depressive and heroin addict and pedophile and rapist, the bright and the beautiful, the fat and the thin, the ugly and the infirm, the tall and the short, the bookish nerds and the muscle-bound jocks, the loquacious and the reserved—all of us could put aside our differences and live like Gillian Greenback in an ecstasy of perfect understanding and communal good will. Gillian, and the other little übermensches who shared her grand ambition for us all, were Freud's disciples and they didn't even know it! All hail the power of "education"! And all we had to lose was ourselves! All we had to do was submit our collective will to the wise counsel of the "educators" among us. Never mind that they squabbled among themselves like two-year-olds fighting over a piece of candy. Where *our* best interests were concerned, they were united. As long as there was an "other" who needed "education," they had a purpose, indeed a mission in life. If we could all just *know* what they *knew,* the world could finally be perfected after all. It dawned on me that I felt more contempt for Gillian and her fellow dreamers than for the evangelist preacher who pockets his adoring followers' rent money and then sits back in his limo to enjoy the ride home to his palatial abode. The preacher's only offering the shiftless herd an entrée into heaven. Gillian's offering them heaven on Earth!

    I had reached the core of her illusion, the fantasy that sustained her. With that fantasy to empower her, she could stand on her magnificent perch above our valley, smile benignly on the dense spray of lights below, and enjoy the extraordinary material comforts of her existence knowing in her heart of hearts that she was pure and good. She could wear the fancy clothes and eat the fancy meals and take the fancy vacations and hobnob with the Beautiful People and remember all the while that she was making the world a better place with her fantasy about the transformative power of formal education. The future world she imagined would look back on her and smile, as she smiled now on herself, and extol her virtues as one of the good ones, the virtuous ones who had made utopia possible. Closure.

I had reached the core of the illusion and not only mocked it but sneered at it in contempt. And that really pissed her off.

"You're goddamn right it'll be a better place!" she snapped suddenly. And the pretty eyes flashed brilliantly. "You got a problem with that? I let you patronize me once before, Marty, but I told you, I'm not doing it this time. I came here to make peace. But I can make war, too, if that's what you want."

"Should I call Security?"

"Fuck you, Marty. To use your own words. Your mind is poisoned, and you want out. So be it. You're out. But don't denigrate the rest of us for having more faith than you do."

"Izzat what you call it, 'faith'? Faith in what? In your glorious vision of a better world? Is that what makes this a noble calling? Now at least I know what Kefauver's problem is: The man lack's 'faith.' I guess he doesn't understand what you mean by 'informed citizenry.' He doesn't realize it only means you should be 'informed' in a certain way. So let's send the bastard packing—the heretic."

"Oh, Christ. Here we go again. You take something complex and turn it into something so simple. So black and white. I tol' you, we're on both sides on his case. I tol' you, we're paying the sonofabitch's legal bills. I tol' you, we will give him his legal due."

"That's why he's being quietly shown the door. It's being done quietly—but it's still being done."

"I give up on you, Marty." And then she said it again as if she hadn't quite believed it herself the first time. She stood up, and the flash of anger in her eyes had dissipated entirely and been supplanted by a look of consternation mingled with pain. Not a look of defeat by any means but only of resignation. It was a setback on the journey to utopia but only a temporary setback, I'm sure. "Goodbye," she said. And she turned to the door.

"You wanna make a better world, Gillian? You won't do it by shutting up the people who disagree with you. That's been tried. It doesn't work. Not in my book it doesn't anyway."

But she was out the door and down the hall already. The Book of Marty remained stubbornly unabridged.

"It's America, Gillian," I said to myself. "We're required to tolerate each other. We're not required to respect each other. Or love each other either."

She was long gone. Sometime later, though, when I went back for the rest of my stuff, there was a note from her shoved under my office door wishing me luck and offering me assistance if ever assistance, even financial assistance, was required.

TWENTY-FIVE

Let Freedom Ring!—or, Lookin' at the World through a Windshield—or, Pour Me Another Cup of Coffee, for It Is the Best in the Land

As it turned out, Gillian was right when she insisted that Warren Kefauver would get the protection he deserved no matter how personally distasteful she found that prospect. To this day I have not met Kefauver; nor have I seen his picture. I wouldn't recognize him if I stood next to him on the street corner. And he probably wouldn't recognize me either. I don't care.

Gillian was only partially right, though, and she was not right in the way she would have you think she was right—if she were here to tell you this story herself. She would tell you that the diligence of the faculty association won Warren Kefauver a pardon. A faculty committee decided his fate, and the committee decided to retain him as an instructor. He was reinstated to his position, though the precise terms of his reinstatement remain a mystery to me. I read about it not in the local press, where it was nowhere to be seen, but on the website of the advocacy organization that lobbied on his behalf. The article said that part of his settlement agreement with the community-college district was a pledge not to reveal the circumstances of his return to employment by the district. What it *could* reveal was that the terms were amenable to all parties. Later on I discovered that among those terms was another pledge by the mathematician, a pledge to keep his poisonous political opinions to himself, a pledge he has to my knowledge honored faithfully to the letter. I guess the math whiz ran the numbers and decided his own interests were best served by promising to behave himself if the district would agree to continue buttering his bread. Such is the dispensation of justice in our perfect world, I suppose: I'll scratch your back if you'll scratch mine. You can decide for yourself if any cause other than the cause of protecting hides was served.

But at the time I knew only that a settlement had been achieved and that it included retaining Warren Kefauver in the district's employ. The Philadelphia watchdog organization considered Kefauver's reinstatement a complete triumph for his cause and the cause of freedom in America. Having made the triumphant announcement it went on to name two more threats to freedom looming imminent on the horizon. The Kefauver battle was won but the war continues.

Gillian would probably remind you that it was a faculty committee that voted to reinstate Kefauver, but only in a strictly technical sense would she be right. In reality, as the article on the watchdog organization's website pointed out, it was the barrage of letters, emails, phone calls, and nasty press across the country that forced the committee's hand. The people spoke, and the district was forced to listen. Had it not been for the voice of the people, and of course the advocacy organization who enlisted the people's aid in the first place, Warren Kefauver could have been safely shunted off to the unemployment line and few of his fellow citizens would have been the wiser. The insidious powers that be would have pulled a fast one on Kefauver and felt little if any the worse for it. What after all is one stubborn dissenter in the face of a righteous cause? Stalin himself noted that personal sacrifices, sometimes grave personal sacrifices, must be made for the cause of correctness, of subverting the will of the people presumably for their own good. And Stalin was a guy who knew something both about correctness and about subverting the will of the people. But in this case, at least, the people's will could not be subverted, and the people, once they were made aware of an injustice, voiced their will and reversed the injustice, thus nimbly demonstrating where true political power resides. I resist the urge to wax effusive like Tom Joad, for though I share his faith in the people,

I do not share his apparent naïve faith in the goodness of the people. Me, I've got a little more of the Marxist cynic in me. It's not goodness that motivates us. We the people do it for ourselves, and I do not need a lecture from Linda Ham to convince me of the potential tyranny of popular opinion. You will never hear me argue against the proposition that it is a reasonably broad and yet perilous path we perpetually walk between oppression by the many and oppression by the few, and the need for vigilance is endless. Still, give me the will of the people over the will of the ideologues who despise the people—and who are sure they know better than the people—any day of the week, or almost any day of the week, and give me the freedom of self-expression, the freedom to offend and to be offended, *every* day of the week. For I refuse to accept the proposition that people like my hardworking parents, or the students who sat in my classrooms, are less qualified or less trustworthy to decide the fate of humanity than the educated class whose honesty, integrity, and sincerity I found occasionally suspect.

So I would be loath to give either Gillian or her colleagues too much credit for "doing the right thing," and yet if I ran into her again I'd probably congratulate her, and through her them, just the same. I don't know that I could resist the fiendish urge. I'd acknowledge that when push came to shove, the faculty having been pushed decided to shove as the situation required. Hollow praise, as the shrewd Gillian would promptly recognize in my reminder that it was only the push that brought the association to the shove. In other words, it was a sense of principle and a strength of conviction born of self-protection, an instinct to avoid the withering reproach of the community. So much for inherent righteousness. But maybe I wouldn't bother to congratulate Gillian, for now, I think, knowing me as she came to know me in those brief last days of our professional relationship, she might very well be undaunted by my cynicism or my sarcasm.

She might even, in fact, return them with cynicism and sarcasm of her own, reminding me once again that Kefauver's had been a "sensitive" case, a case of "us against us," and perhaps further reminding me that she had been on the other side of the case from me, unkindly disposed toward Kefauver and perfectly willing to see him sacrificed to political correctness and the tyranny of the few. She might very well, in other words, be perfectly willing to reestablish the line between us in the sand and then to glower defiantly at me from her side of the line. And after that she'd return to her classroom, light some incense and put on some Native music, and try to instill in her captive audience a sense of divine harmony and oneness with each other and with their surroundings. I have to admit I would take perverse satisfaction in that.

I did want to see Roly, I truly did, but then I lost my motivation and did not visit or call him after all. I took care of my business at the District Office and turned my keys in to Ellen in a letter envelope, and that was the end of it. Ellen left a message on my home phone about some business I was supposed to take care of in the department office, but I replied by voicemail that it was already taken care of. Like a thief in the night I had ransacked my own office and, as far as I was concerned, my connection with the place was finally and terminally ruptured. I had none of the institution's possessions left to my name, and none of the other tiny formalities Ellen reminded me of mattered to me. She could worry about them if she chose, but I wouldn't.

The district was to keep its place in the local news for a good two more years with news stories breaking about every month or so on some newly discovered impropriety or indiscretion. An instructor was terminated for inappropriate use of college funds, then countered with a publicity campaign of her own to justify her use of the funds, all of which (allegedly), in addition to funds of her own, were spent in her students' (and therefore the public's) interest. A group of visiting faculty was terminated for being unqualified, and the dismissed faculty members countered with a discrimination suit of their own. A program funded by "soft money," grant money from a federal agency, was exposed as fraudulent in the ongoing sheriff's investigation to uncover corruption in the district and in particular at my old college. The program had been continued by the college because it was intended to benefit the Hispanic community, and its Hispanic director, who was himself taking in a salary higher than our salary scale permitted for his level of training and experience, had threatened continually to sue the college and the district—and of course to go to the press—if his program were discontinued. To avoid the bad press the college naturally had relented, and his program had been continued for a number of years despite serving few people in the community besides the college's own employees, who made their living from it. The program's director was known for his leverage, gained primarily through his love of litigation and threatened litigation; but this time the college and the district had to risk the bad publicity of another discrimination lawsuit and turn him loose.

And so on. The public humiliation lasted several years, the colleges' faculty carping all the while that they were being singled out for public degradation by an "anti-education" element in the public and the press—always as if the mission they performed were beyond moral and ethical question and as if it were the cretinous public's fault that they were suffering such embarrassment. The unsophisticated public was incapable of understanding the higher intellectual functioning of the educated class. The public did not understand why abuses of public funds were justified on some higher moral plane. Then again, neither did I. Nor, I'm sure, would my dead parents have understood, who put higher education on some higher plateau of attainment not because it made the educated better people but because it provided them a better quality of life. If you wanted higher moral ground you could look at my parents themselves ... but I start to sound like Tom Joad again and know better. My parents needed their religion to keep them in line (or to keep them believing there was a legitimate reason to stay in line). No, that's not exactly it either. Simply recognizing that we have no better alternative is enough to keep us in line. They needed their religion, I suppose, for precisely the reason Marx suggested they needed it: to provide the promise of a brighter, a more just, humane, and equitable future beyond the grave. Or maybe it was just to assuage their feelings of insecurity and guilt that they could not number themselves among the powerful and secure. They could not achieve that sense of comfort and certainty and fulfillment, of absolute contentment with their lives that they must have believed somebody, somewhere *had* achieved. They were not morally superior; they were jealous—jealous and protective of their own. They were, in a word, human.

The embarrassing exposure continued for several years, and then the public lost interest and the press lost steam, and almost as quickly as it had become the brunt of criticism the district returned to being just another large, wasteful bureaucratic public entity. It was a useful entity after all, the savvy, cynical public surmised (and surmises), and it was for all its faults valuable to the community and probably not more corrupt than other public entities. As one of my wiser colleagues at the college had conjectured during the developing controversy, "We'll suffer for a few years, and then this'll all blow over." What he worried about was the ways in which we, collectively, as employees of a public institution under severe public scrutiny, might suffer in the meantime, and his anxiety was justified. The district's knee-jerk reaction was to proclaim publicly and loudly that it was cleaning up its act and then privately to institute reactionary controls over its employees and internal processes. Hegel's great organic collective exercised its "will." Suddenly threatened by the autonomy of its own constituents, the minute and insignificant cells that comprise and sustain it, the district took strict authoritarian measures to constrain those constituents and ensure their proper functioning—to ensure, that is, that they were serving the right master, the body politic. The organic state would, as Marx of course informed us all, protect itself. It would divest itself of any cells that had turned cancerous, carve them out and dispose of them to rid the hideous political beast of the sickness they are causing. It would take appropriate measures, even drastic measures, to ensure its own health and safety.

But let's dispense with the Hegelian metaphor for it is a sham and a counterfeit, and let's dispense with Marx for Marx was a fraud. The state possesses no "will" of its own; what it possesses is hordes of self-interested individuals who will protect *their* interests, and to hell with the interests of other individuals who stand in their way. Those diseased cells are not cells at all; they're people. They're flesh-and-blood people with hopes and dreams and desires and interests entirely their own. In the district's case the "will" that was exercised was that of its powerbrokers, who moved swiftly to protect themselves and theirs by restoring some measure of trust among their most important constituents, their ultimate food source and indispensable provider, the taxpaying public. The shrewdest of the bureaucrats are always mindful of who supplies their sustenance for they are political creatures, else they would not have attained the bureaucratic heights they have attained. That they are parasites goes without saying; that they are so adept at it speaks to the acuity of their survival instincts. The most successful bureaucrats are the most adroit bloodsuckers. Evolution has favored them.

The powerbrokers quite predictably wielded an iron fist for a while just as my colleague had said they would. Working in the district became a tad less relaxed and a tad less pleasant. Suddenly it became necessary, I heard through the grapevine, to "sign a loyalty oath just to go to the bathroom." The reputation the district had earned for "innovation," not to mention for being a stimulating environment in which to work, suffered mightily. The same shrewd colleague who had predicted the controversy's gradual passing, its fade into oblivion, had predicted also that the district would not only have greater difficulty attracting "quality faculty"; it would also have greater difficulty retaining the employees it already had. He was right on both counts.

I kept in touch with him, still do, but in the meantime I needed work and so I went in search of it. A good year before I left the district's employ, when I was mulling over my life and surmising that I was not happy with it, not content, I had heard an ad on the radio about long-haul truckers. The ad said there was a huge demand for them and that the demand would continue to grow. Naturally, the ad made the industry and the job sound like a panacea; that's what ads do. If the ad were to be believed, I (or somebody like me) could enter the trucking industry confident that plenty of work awaited me, that the work was both "challenging and rewarding," and most important, that it was lucrative. Trucking companies wanted people in or approaching middle age just like me, and they wanted married couples to push those big rigs over our nation's highways in tandem. Hubby could nap while his wife covered that stretch between Joplin and OK City, and then he could take the wheel and push the rig on into Amarillo. They'd be together, they'd be complementing each other, and they'd be making money! Can a marriage get any better?

I did not have a spouse, but I had driven trucks before and had some idea what I was in for. I went and got the appropriate license and got my first job in time to hang on to my house, though not my savings. For a while money was tight, but I was not bothered anyway because the little rebel in my head, the one that had goaded me into turning my scandalous voice loose on the entire district in defense of Warren Kefauver and his minute mutiny, kept entertaining thoughts of relocating to rural Oregon or Washington or Idaho or Montana where the anti-government nut-jobs are said to live, with their weapons and their reclusive ways and their willingness to turn their tempers and their weapons on any fascist busybody who might come prying or just spying. I did not know exactly where the nut-jobs lived, but I knew they were up there somewhere in the Northwest as well as in the Plains states, where I had never been but where I now had the impulse to go just to get away from the escalating madness of the Southwest, which was turning into a brown version of the East with its strictures, or perhaps the West Coast with its hedonism, or perhaps some strange synthesis of the two. In the end, though, I did not go—or perhaps I should say I have not gone yet. Sometimes I still think about it, think about a property in rural Anystate where the backwoods culture suits my backwoods sensibilities, and I can stretch out my limbs and survey the world from my front porch and feel that I have some small chunk of it to myself. It's a pipe dream, of course, but don't we all have our pipe dreams? And anyway, our time is short among the living on this planet, and there is only so much damage we can do or that can be done to us in the short time we have.

But I have not gone yet, and here I am in the same place Kayla Blaze left me. For two years I drove other people's trucks, and then I financed my own, a 1995 Peterbilt tractor that I bought used for $52,000 and will drive, I have decided, until the expensive wheels roll off or disintegrate. I bought a $20,000 dump trailer to pull behind the tractor, and now I cover the U.S. from southwestern Louisiana to northern California, mostly carrying grain from the elevator to several large dairy operations that use it as livestock feed. The two primary runs I do now are nearly fifteen-hundred miles apiece, one way, each twice a month, one to the east and one to the north and west, running my tractor and trailer at the highest speeds and for the longest stretches that prudence and relative safety will permit. The runs are grueling; they eat up huge chunks of my time; they keep me on the road more than I'm at home. They wear me down both physically and mentally.

I worry at times that the road ahead of me will blur into a dissembling mirage, an apparition of comfort and safety, a world secure and peaceful and inviting, beckoning me like a warm bath; and then of a sudden I'll crash into something oncoming with the force of several hundred horses hell-bent-for-leather, and my life will end in a flash of fathomless pain and an instant of bewildered questioning. And yet I feel for all the dizzying, mind-numbing grind of the road that this new life suits me in a way, for I am a single man who was lonely before and who can manage loneliness on the road as well as he could manage it at home. Moreover, I have the feeling of doing something substantial, something with a definite purpose whose outcome is clearly understood by all constituent parties, the transportation of commodity A from point B to point C in such and such time and for such and such money. It is an important job, albeit one that is taken largely for granted by the great American buying public that expects its food in the supermarket and its clothes in the department store and its electronics stores stocked from the floor to the rafters and all with little regard for how these commodities came to be in these places at precisely the time the consumer sought them out. Working hard—which is to say running six days a week as many as twelve hours a day as I do now—I can easily net more money than I did in the classroom on a work schedule that was considerably more relaxed. And that's even after the enormous expenses of maintenance, insurance, and of course fuel.

I take my books on the road, and my laptop, and life is not so different—the means of earning money aside—from the way it was several years ago. I have much time to myself—much time for contemplation and much time to listen in on the sounds of the world. What's more, I have not lost my ardor for certain principles that have meaning for me, my own rebellious little übermensch still asserting itself inside my head, unwilling to be silenced or forgotten. It makes itself heard publicly in the flier that I carry with me everywhere I go, a flier that I composed several years ago for the express purpose of leaving it in truck stops and diners and gas stations wherever I roam. It is my statement to the world, and I photocopy it and photocopy it again for distribution. I photocopy it with a sense of purpose and post it with a sense of mission and simultaneously of satisfaction, pinning it to some bulletin board amid the clutter of announcements: tractors and trailers for sale, or sometimes homes for sale, or other vehicles for sale, or tools for sale, help wanted, jobs wanted, business opportunities for those with initiative, pets lost, pets found, training available for those who seek a new career, new careers available for those who are willing to train, services available at reasonable rates, rides wanted, travel partners wanted, the Word of God available to those who are properly disposed to hear it, church services on Sunday, singles seeking partners, clubs seeking new members, estate sale on Saturday, concert on Saturday night, new store opening, old store closing, tutors available in various subjects, dance lessons available and it doesn't matter if you have two left feet. I join my voice to the great cacophony and from doing so derive a tiny measure of fulfillment and even of pride. The rebellious little übermensch inside me is pleased if never satisfied.

Every now and again a witness catches me in the act of exercising my freedom in my own unobtrusive way. Some Texan in a cowboy hat, some Californian in Birkenstocks, some New Yawkuh in a backwards ball cap sidles up alongside me and looks over my shoulder or maybe just looks the whole board over and then zeroes in on my flier and reads it word for word whether out of genuine interest or out of deference to me—having stuck their nose in they do not want to appear rude by removing it before paying the full measure of polite attention even though I am on my way before they finish reading. But I look back. I see the reaction. Not always but most often, though it is not approval that I seek, it is approval that I see. The jaw sets, the head nods. We are in agreement.

Here is what we are agreeing on:

Let Freedom Ring!

People of the world, or at least this part of the world: Like it or not, for better or for worse, we are the heirs of a tradition of individual autonomy that is still unknown in many other parts of the world and perhaps unappreciated in this one.

Even the commonest among us has a right to a say-so. So the tradition holds. It is not a religious tradition as some of you would have it, though it is certainly in large part informed by a religious tradition. In the main, though, it is a philosophical tradition in which we ourselves and not our gods are held central.

We claim to embrace the tradition. We extol it, we pay homage to it, we serve up laudatory banalities to those who have sacrificed to preserve it.

But we do not always appreciate the tradition, and we do not always afford it the sanctity we pretend it deserves. Often when our rights are threatened for the "common good," for an ounce of safety or security or maybe just to take some of the pressure off ourselves, we consider it acceptable and even desirable to trample on the rights of another or of others. We will sell our own freedom for a little comfort, and we will certainly trade the rights of others to breathe a little easier.

But every such bargain with the devil diminishes us all. I beg you to resist the urge. As the old saying goes, "With freedom comes responsibility." The freedom to choose for ourselves brings with it an inherent responsibility to choose as intelligently as we know how.

So be aware as you're enjoying your freedom that interests domestic and foreign continually seek to deprive you of it, to talk you out of it if that's possible, to take it from you by force of law or force of arms if it's not. Not infrequently these interests will claim to have your own welfare at heart, to want to do what is "best" for you from the arrogant perspective that they know more about what is good for you than you do. Indeed, their intentions may not be malign, but we all know that the road to hell is paved with such ostensibly beneficent intentions.

Cleave to your freedom then, for freedom, though easily lost, is hard won. Closely examine the claims of those who would pretend to understand the true nature of things and who would, in so pretending, attempt to deprive you of the opportunity to judge the world for yourselves. The road we travel is lined on both our Left and our Right with those who covet our support whether it is won by dint of friendly persuasion or coerced by government strong arm. There are but two ways to organize a government: with freedom for those governed or without it. And the freedom of those governed is frequently a threat to those who govern. They will sell you the promise of a peaceful and secure life, but be careful! Complacency can have the subtle allure of a mood-enhancing drug, but the price of protection is high. Think long and hard before you agree to pay it!

Do this for me as a fellow denizen of the world and a fellow sinner. I promise to return the favor. And if not for me, do it for yourselves! Yours could be the next voice deemed dangerous or even just offensive, and as such it could be the next voice deemed worthy of suppression. Speak up now, while you can!

I see them nod their agreement and am amazed. It amazes me that such near-consensus exists in principle, that such broad and wholehearted acceptance abounds of the credo of individual autonomy, the right to self-government, the passionate embrace of self-determination. In the minds of the people it exists with a passionate certainty, even with self-righteousness. In principle people embrace what they do not always embrace in practice. They will indeed forswear the rights of another to protect their own interests; they will even forswear their own freedom to preserve their own comfort. Linda Ham was not wrong about that. But in principle—in principle they'll ride the high horse of freedom to the four corners of the Earth and beyond; they'll swear by freedom on penalty of torture or death, sometimes merely imagined but in rare cases all too real. I am amazed at the unfaltering, unquestioning, unmitigated embrace of freedom in principle as it shows on so many of their affirming faces.

In the back of my mind the minute fear sometimes installs itself that one of them, some innocuous traveler in sheep's clothing, has been assigned by the powers that be to watch me, to observe and document my rank and persistent acts of subversion. Maybe someday they'll come riding up on me, Big Brother's (or Big Sister's so as not to be sexist because we all know from our reeducation classes that sexism is bad) zealous enforcers, they'll ride up on me with tanks as they rode up on David Karesh and turn my humble "compound" into a pile of rubble while I'm out back trimming my roses or skimming my pool. But I doubt it. Conspiracy theories tend to be the province of those who can't find a better way to explain the vast inequities of life satisfactorily to themselves, and I'm not one of those. As I have said before, I can handle the truth, and I am neither a prophet of salvation nor a prophet of doom. I regard myself, rather, more as a quiet but not irrelevant voice in the human chorus, unremarkable perhaps but not inaudible. Like Parson Weems, itinerant bookseller, who rambled the Eastern Seaboard in the early days of the young republic, I am both a recorder of my impressions and a purveyor of my own ideas, and I don't mind acknowledging that those ideas might be regarded as dangerous or that I might be considered subversive. I can handle the truth.

TWENTY-SIX

Born Romantics—or, Dreamin' Just Comes Natural

In the years since I parted company with Kayla Blaze I have not changed my residence. I am still in the same house, and with most of the same furniture and décor, in which my lovely Kayla used to lounge in her underwear, provoking me to new heights of sexual fantasy and then often fulfilling those fantasies with a sort of ravenous cupidity I have not encountered in any other woman I've been with before or since. She fulfilled them, in other words, as if she were on some kind of mission or quest. Did she consider me a conquest or a co-conspirator of some kind? And if we were co-conspirators, what were we conspiring to achieve—besides the most obvious and elemental? Or is the obvious and elemental all that *can* be achieved? Hell, I don't know. What I do know is that there was a kind of fluidity about it, a naturalness, as if during that period of sexual engagement the universe seemed perfectly aligned and nothing else mattered. I imagine Eve with her Adam in the mythic Garden. Misgivings are only entertained when the mind drifts off to the things that will occupy it once consummation is achieved. Until that moment arrives, yin and yang are in perfect balance, nirvana is the dwelling place.

After Kayla left me that last night of my employment at the college, she returned only once, about a month later. In the interim, we had phone contact several times, but we did not see each other, at least not face to face. The phone contact we had was not particularly pleasing. We talked about things that did not interest either of us very much—by which I mean that my things didn't interest her and hers didn't interest me. It was important to her that she get the upper hand in the dissolution of our relationship; she made that clear. It seemed to please her that I was not seeing anybody else—and I would not see anybody else for quite some time—and it seemed to please her even more to report that she had started dating again. Already. It seemed important to demonstrate to me that she was a young woman who could at the literal snap of her fingers command the fawning attention of men. Not only that, she could with haughty self-assurance pick and choose the men whose attention would be returned, in what measure it would be returned, and with what type of attitude. But nobody had to tell me how easy it was for Kayla Blaze to get the attention of my sex or what it was about her that drew their attention. Nobody had to tell me that Kayla could afford the luxury of being choosy. I knew those things as well as Kayla knew them herself, and perhaps better, since I had once been smitten by her myself and knew firsthand, and acutely, how it felt to long for her from a distance. So I let Kayla tell me what she needed to tell me to make herself feel better by making me feel worse, and I did not really feel worse; I merely felt that our conversations were pointless and we were wasting each other's time. There was an emptiness in our interaction that always seems to accompany the breakup of a romance. Our time is over; let's move on. And yet the impulse for contact remains, like a habit long ago acquired and now better abandoned. I did not enjoy hearing from Kayla, and she did not seem to enjoy contacting me. And yet she did contact me.

Once, and only once, I caught her fleeing my neighborhood like a child caught in the act of committing some domestic transgression: crossing the busy street to play in the park where she wasn't permitted to play alone, for example. She was walking along a side street perpendicular to my own along about dusk. She wore sandals and a smock of some kind—one I'd never seen before—that fell to mid-thigh, and perhaps nothing else. Maybe there was clothing beneath the smock, but it wasn't visible to me, and I have a sneaking suspicion that at most there was a thong. I do not know what her plan of action was; nor will I ever know because I talked to her only twice and saw her only once after that, and I did not confront her about the incident (for surely she would have regarded it as "confrontation"). At any rate, I happened along in my car at an inopportune moment, coming down the street from a different direction than usual because of road construction on the main drag, and when she spotted me—more important, when she recognized that I had spotted her—she looked positively stricken, as if she'd just been told she had a terminal disease. The panic shortly fled her face, though, giving way to a studied composure, a look deliberately contrived to convey either indifference or contempt. So what if I had caught her stalking me? It meant nothing. She did not care about me, or if she did care what she felt was cold hostility. I know she saw me, but her eyes wouldn't meet mine. Instead she kept them fixed on some point out in front of her, some object apparently requiring her intense concentration and perhaps her spite as well. She moved urgently along the sidewalk as if her destination, wherever it was, could barely wait for her. For my part, I stared wide eyed, slowing down the car and gaping at her dumbfounded and uncomprehending. The impulse yanked hard at me to stop the car and question her, invite her in, hold her hand, perhaps sit and gaze into her eyes. But I resisted. A few minutes later I was back at home sitting blankly in front of the TV to distract my thoughts from her and not being distracted. Cold ran through me, my breathing was constricted. It took me an hour or more to relax.

Perhaps two weeks after that I got my last call from her and then my last visit. She came to my house again, but it was as if she were there for the first time. She had called ahead and arranged the visit on the pretense that she had a few things still to pick up, things that in the preceding months apparently had gone unmissed but that suddenly were remembered and required. We spent a few awkward minutes in conversation and then moved awkwardly to the bedroom where we had awkward, unemotional sex, like the actors in some hardcore porno flick hammering away at each other for the camera, working mechanically toward consummation as if they are shingling a roof or framing a wall. Bang! Bang! Bang! Hand me another box of nails. When it was over she dressed quickly despite my invitation to stay longer, perhaps spend the night, and then she left me and did not return. She said something about her "boyfriend" on the way out, implying I suppose that she did not want to risk his discovering the infidelity, and as she was leaving I realized that the visit for her had served a very important purpose; it had put a final punctuation mark—an end-punctuation mark, if you will—on the episode in her life that involved Marty Frey (or perhaps Dirk Revolver—or both). Breakup sex. Her sensibilities had required it to provide closure. She could not enjoy it, mind you—at least she could not feel it meant anything. When it was done, she was done, and she left my house with a stiff "Goodbye" and hasn't called me or stopped by (to my knowledge) in the years since.

For a while after that, perhaps a week or so, I thought about her often, my feelings hurt at the final gesture she had made—a gesture of defiance, it seemed to me, more than anything else—but after that week or so I started to smile again, thinking about her less and less and finally not at all. It took a year or more, though, to get to the point where she didn't flit into my mind at least once a day. It took significantly longer to arrive at the place where I think of any one person more than I think of her. And even now, as I go along my lonely way, a single man untrammeled by fantasies of love and companionship, unencumbered by the burden of caring deeply for another or others, she'll steal into my thoughts every great now and again, perhaps once a month, perhaps less often than that. I don't really calculate how often she visits me for it is pointless to think about. Odds are that by now the lovely Kayla Blaze has lost some of the bloom of youth. It would surprise me if she isn't married, or at least if she doesn't have a child, perhaps more than just one child—for Kayla loved children.

When I do think of her, though, the memories are not erotic. I never remember her with her legs spread waiting to receive me, beckoning me to come and satisfy my lustful interests, to indulge the stifled primal drive of a man in need of consummation and release. Instead I tend to remember her, oddly, as I saw her that day in my neighborhood, caught in the act of spying on me and mortified at being caught in the act, probably—no, certainly—more aggrieved at that disgrace than at the rupture of our love affair in the first place, humiliated and showing it, her face stiffening with revulsion, her back stiffening too as her long legs carry her away from me and whatever it is I represent to her, eyes frozen dead ahead, the breeze generated by her fierce gait delicately lifting her long blond hair.

APPENDIX

A Few Words about the Quotes Used in This Story, Mostly in the Chapter Titles—or, Giving Credit Where Credit Is Due

- The first epigraph, "So that one class *par excellence* may appear as the class of liberation, another class must inversely be the manifest class of oppression," is from the bearded old man himself. It's from the enchanting introduction to Marx's critique of Hegel. You can find it on page seventy-nine of the David McLellan translation, first published by the Oxford University Press in 1977.
- The second epigraph, "'[I]n the view of Infinite Purity, we are sinners all alike," is from the final chapter of one of America's greatest novels, Nathaniel Hawthorne's *The Scarlet Letter*. You'll find the quote on page 271 of the Penguin Books edition published in 1983. The novel was first published by Ticknor and Reed in 1850.
- Epigraphs three and four are both from Alexis de Tocqueville's multifariously insightful and frequently prescient *Democracy in America*, first published in 1835. I use the Henry Reeve translation printed by Bantam Dell in 2002. Read the book if you get the chance. It's pretty amazing what that dude both saw and foresaw.
- "A Confederacy of Dung Beetles" is a play on the title of John Kennedy Toole's 1980 novel *A Confederacy of Dunces*, published by the Louisiana State University Press, and the Jonathan Swift

epigram from which it was adapted. No dung beetles were harmed in the writing of this story.
- The quote from Christopher Lasch is from his *The Culture of Narcissism,* first published by Lasch in 1979. The quote is taken from the chapter entitled "Schooling and the New Illiteracy," page 150 of the W. W. Norton & Company paperback edition, published in 1991.
- "There Were Ghosts in the Eyes of All the Boys You Sent Away" is a line from Bruce Springsteen's "Thunder Road," first recorded on the *Born to Run* album, produced by Springsteen, Jon Landau, and Mike Appel for Columbia Records in 1975. Great song.
- "An Affair to Remember" is the title of a 1957 film starring Cary Grant and Deborah Kerr, directed by Leo McCarey, produced by Leo McCarey and Jerry Wald and distributed by 20th Century Fox.
- "Nothin' but Mammals" is from Bloodhound Gang's "The Bad Touch," from the album *Hooray for Boobies,* produced by Jimmy Pop for Jimmy Franks Recording Company and released by Interscope Records in 2000.
- "The Call of the Wild" is the title of the 1903 novella by Jack London, published by Macmillan.
- "I Only Have Eyes for You" is the title of a 1934 song by Harry Warren and Al Dubin, perhaps most famously covered by The Flamingos in 1959.
- "This Magic Moment" is a song written by Doc Pomus and Mort Shuman, first recorded by the Drifters and released in 1960 by Atlantic, covered by Jay and the Americans and climbing high on the pop music charts in 1968.
- "Just One Look" is a song written by Gregory Carroll and Doris Payne, recorded by Doris Troy and released by Atlantic in 1963. It has since been covered by a number of other recording artists.
- "A Girl Just Like the Girl" is from William Dillon and Harry Von Tilzer's "I Want a Girl (Just Like the Girl That Married Dear Old Dad)," copyrighted by Harry Von Tilzer Music in 1911.
- "I Got Those Roadhouse Blues" refers to "Roadhouse Blues," by John Paul Densmore, Robert A. Krieger, Raymond D. Manzarek,

and Jim Morrison, produced by Paul A. Rothchild for Elektra Records and released on the *Morrison Hotel* album in 1970.
- "We Are Family" is the title of a song written by Bernard Edwards and Nile Rodgers and performed by Sister Sledge, among others. It was produced by Rodgers and Edwards for Cotillion Records and released on the album *We Are Family* in 1979.
- "The Devil Wears Pravda" is a play on the title of Lauren Weisberger's novel *The Devil Wears Prada*, published by Broadway Books in 2003.
- "Tropic of Cancer" is the title of the Henry Miller novel first published by Obelisk Press in Paris in 1934. Copyright 1961 by Grove Press, Inc. Used by permission of Grove/Atlantic, Inc.
- "Wild Nights!—Wild Nights!" is from a poem by the great Emily Dickinson.
- "Girls Just Wanna Have Fun" is adapted from "Girls Just Want to Have Fun," the Robert Hazard song most famously adapted and performed by Cyndi Lauper on the *She's So Unusual* album, produced by Rick Chertoff and William Wittman and released by Epic Records in 1983.
- "Rebel from the Waist Downwards" is a quote from George Orwell's *1984*, first published by Harcourt in 1949. The quote is addressed to Julia, the female protagonist, by Winston Smith, the male protagonist.
- "It Takes a Village: And Other Lessons Children Teach Us" is the title of a book by Hillary Rodham Clinton, published by Simon and Schuster in 1996.
- "A Man for All Seasons" is the title of Robert Bolt's play about the life of Sir Thomas More. The play in its final form was first performed in London in 1960.
- "The Crucible" is Arthur Miller's 1953 play, first performed in 1953 at the Martin Beck Theater in New York.
- "You Take the Low Road" is a play on the line "You take the high road," from the old Scottish folk song "Bonnie Banks O' Loch Lomond."
- "The Totalitarians in Our Midst" is a chapter title in F. A. Hayek's 1944 classic *The Road to Serfdom*, published by the University of Chicago Press.

- "Lookin' at the World through a Windshield" is the title of a 1968 song written by Jerry Chesnut and Mike Hoyer, performed by Del Reeves and a number of other folks, among them Ferlin Husky and Commander Cody and His Lost Planet Airmen.
- "Dreamin' Just Comes Natural" is from the chorus of John Prine's "Donald & Lydia," written and performed by Prine and released by Atlantic Records in 1971 on Prine's self-titled debut album.

Oblique references are made to other public figures and their public comments, and to other works of literature and popular culture, as well as to mere cultural phenomena. I gratefully acknowledge all these gracious if inadvertent contributions. What would life be without them?

www.ingramcontent.com/pod-product-compliance
Lightning Source LLC
LaVergne TN
LVHW041920070526
838199LV00051BA/2683